EXODUS

(1st Edition)

by Jasper T. Scott

JasperTscott.com

@JasperTscott

Illustration © Tom Edwards

TomEdwardsDesign.com

TABLE OF CONTENTS

Acknowledgments 5

PART 1 - CONTACT 7

Prologue 8

CHAPTER 1 14

CHAPTER 2 25

CHAPTER 3 35

CHAPTER 4 43

CHAPTER 5 54

CHAPTER 6 64

CHAPTER 7 74

PART 2 - CONTAGION 84

CHAPTER 8 85

CHAPTER 9 92

CHAPTER 10 102

CHAPTER 11 120

CHAPTER 12 132

CHAPTER 13 147

CHAPTER 14 159

CHAPTER 15 165

CHAPTER 16 173

CHAPTER 17 181

PART 3 - ARRIVAL 185

CHAPTER 18 186

CHAPTER 19 191

CHAPTER 20 198

CHAPTER 21 204

CHAPTER 22 215

CHAPTER 23 225

CHAPTER 24 236

CHAPTER 25 242

CHAPTER 26 251

CHAPTER 27 256

CHAPTER 28 266

CHAPTER 29 270

CHAPTER 30 273

CHAPTER 31 280

CHAPTER 32 285

PART 4 - FOUNDATION 290

CHAPTER 33 291

CHAPTER 34 296

CHAPTER 35 301

CHAPTER 36 306

CHAPTER 37 312

CHAPTER 38 327

CHAPTER 39 333

CHAPTER 40 342

CHAPTER 41 346

CHAPTER 42 349

CHAPTER 43 352

CHAPTER 44 355

GET JASPER'S NEXT BOOK FOR FREE* 362

KEEP IN TOUCH 362

OTHER BOOKS 364

ABOUT THE AUTHOR 365

ACKNOWLEDGMENTS

This book comes to you thanks in large part to my wife, whose tireless support allows me to focus on my writing. I'd also like to thank my editor, Aaron Sikes, and my volunteer editor Dave Cantrell for their help in tracking down problems with the early draft of the book. Finally, a big thanks goes out to my advance copy readers: Bruce Thobois, Daniel Eloff, Dave Topan, Davis Shellabarger, Duncan Mcleod, Earl Hall, Gary Matthews, Gaylon Overton, George P. Dixon, Henry Clerval, Ian F. Jedlica, Ian Seccombe, Jim Meinen, LeRoy Vermillion, Mary Kastle, Michael N. Madsen, Raymond Burt, Rob Dobozy, and Wade Whitaker. Thank you all for your help in making this book the best that it could be!

To those who dare,
And to those who dream.
To everyone who's stronger than they seem.

*"Believe in me / I know you've waited for so long / Believe in me /
Sometimes the weak become the strong."*
—STAIND, Believe

PART 1 - CONTACT

"If aliens ever visit us, I think the outcome would be much as when Christopher Columbus first landed in America, which didn't turn out very well for the American Indians."

—Stephen Hawking

PROLOGUE

"Lieutenant Commander... Remo Taggart?" Doctor Procyon looked up from his holo screen with a tight smile as Remo walked in.

Remo nodded. "That's me," he said, taking a seat in one of the chairs in front of the doctor's desk. He folded his hands in his lap, trying not to look as nervous as he felt while Doctor Procyon sat back and read the results of his latest scans.

Remo still remembered the diagnosis back on Mars: *"I'm afraid there's nothing we can do for you at this stage, but make you comfortable. If we had caught the tumor earlier, maybe we could have operated... but..."*

In other words, you're screwed, Remo thought. He'd been diagnosed with stage IV GBM—Glioblastoma Multiforme—an aggressive brain tumor, the kind that his medical implant was supposed to have detected in its early stages. One in ten thousand tumors went undetected, either due to an implant malfunction or just plain old bad luck. In a way, he'd won the lottery—1st prize: death.

At a time in human history when people were all genetically engineered from birth to be immortal, the only thing that could kill someone was a fatal accident or a rare disease. Remo had been unfortunate enough to see what was lurking behind door number two.

But that hadn't been the end of it. He had refused to accept the inevitability of his death. He'd spent day and night obsessively pouring over the net, looking at experimental treatment programs for all kinds of deadly diseases.

Eventually his search had led him here—Nano Nova, an Earth-based company run by androids. Remo's lip curled at the thought of it. He was no fan of androids—a firm believer that they would eventually turn on their human creators, but what choice did he have? It wasn't as though he had a lot to lose.

Now, after three months of treatments that his Solarian Navy insurance refused to cover, he still wasn't sure if it had been worth it. He'd maxed out all his credit cards and sold his habitat back on Mars to pay for everything, leaving him destitute and sleeping on his brother's couch, but then again—if he didn't live, what would any of that matter?

"So?" Remo prompted, watching the doctor's face for any hint of a reaction. He should have known better. Androids were banned from poker tournaments for a reason.

After a moment, Doctor Procyon looked up from his holo screen, bushy black eyebrows raised. "Your scans are clear," he said in a bland monotone, as if reading the weather report.

Remo blinked and shook his head. "What do you mean they're clear?"

A hint of a smile lifted the corners of the android's mouth. "You are cured."

Remo sat very still, and said, "I don't think I heard you right. Could you say that again, please?"

"You're cured."

Remo's heart pounded in his chest. Hope soared, making his head feel light. This had to be a dream. "One more time," he insisted.

"The tumor is gone, Mr. Taggart, and there are no signs of the usual markers in your blood."

Remo could have jumped up from his chair and danced on the doctor's desk. He could have kissed the man on his icy bot lips.

But he didn't do any of that. Instead, he remained frozen, his eyes wide and blinking. "Now what?" he asked.

"Now, you get on with your life."

Remo nodded. His life. He had one again. He watched the doctor push a folder toward him. "What's that?"

"Sure Life insurance."

"Life insurance?" he echoed. "I thought you said I was cured? What do I need life insurance for?"

"So that you won't have to pay for future treatments with us."

"I don't understand."

"This life insurance policy isn't a payout when you die. It's a guarantee of our work. We take a map of your brain and a scan of your body. It's to ensure that you'll never have to worry about death again. We don't just treat cancer here, but a wide range of terminal problems. Our nanites will sit dormant in your blood and report back to us when there's even a hint of something dangerous going on. They're much more accurate than the typical Meditect implant. The insurance is included free with your treatments."

Remo took the folder and scanned through the legalese. It appeared to be everything Doctor Procyon had said. He grabbed a pen, his hand shaking with pent-up elation, and signed the policy.

"Good deal," Remo said, passing the folder back across the desk.

Doctor Procyon nodded. "Yes." He thrust out his hand and stood up from his desk. "Congratulations, Mr. Taggart."

Remo took the doctor's hand and shook it, enduring the android's icy grip with a smile. "Thank you."

"Don't thank me, thank Benevolence. Nano Nova is his company."

Remo's smile faded to a frown, and he withdrew his hand from Doctor Procyon's grip as a shiver slithered down his spine. "Benevolence owns this company?" The android ruler of Earth had created a company dedicated to saving *humans* from terminal maladies. What was his angle? Remo didn't buy the benevolent dictator act.

Doctor Procyon nodded. "Is that a problem?"

Remo flashed a tight smile. "No problem. Thanks again, Doc. I better be going." He turned and walked out the door, breezing past dozens of patients in the waiting room.

He stepped outside into the heart of the City of the Minds, the capital of Earth. A gust of wind sent dead, dried-up leaves skittering down the sidewalk. He looked up to the sky—pure blue, not red, like the Martian sky. He scanned the park in front of Nano Nova's treatment center. Half naked trees rained multi-colored leaves, their branches shivering in the wind. Children played in a playground, laughing and screaming as they ran around, kicking sand into the grass—*skrish, skrish, skrish...*

He took a deep breath and opened his arms, palms up to the sky, feeling the sun beat down on his face. Even now in autumn, the sun was much brighter and warmer than it was on Mars. Earth was ten times—*a hundred times*—as habitable as Mars. It was humanity's birthright, and yet here it was, crawling with androids. Remo glanced down the street, toggling an infrared overlay on his Augmented Reality Contacts (ARCs) to scan the passersby.

Fully half of them were bots, but just like Doctor Procyon, they didn't look like bots. They looked human. Remo shook his head. *Do they imitate us out of envy or respect?* He strongly suspected the former.

A stiff breeze blew down the street and inflated his jacket with air, whipping the fabric around his torso and fluttering it like a flag.

There's a storm coming, he thought. All Martians knew it. They'd known it since before he'd even been born. It was just a matter of time before envy and imitation turned to hate and resentment. A month ago Remo didn't think he'd be alive to see a war between humans and androids, but now he had to take the threat seriously. As a pilot with the Solarian Navy, he'd be on the front lines, among the first to die when war broke out.

He'd just been given a new lease on life and now he had to live with this dark cloud hovering over his head. Remo thrust his hands into his pockets and started down the street, going for a walk to clear his head. The breeze blew. Leaves skittered. Pedestrians smiled and nodded as he passed by. Remo smiled thinly back, wondering if androids ever grew tired of being so cloyingly friendly. *How can anyone possibly smile and nod to thousands of people every day?* Instead of making him feel welcome on Earth, it made him feel uneasy, like they all knew something that he didn't. Leaves rained over Remo's head, a few getting stuck in his hair. He reached up and brushed them away.

A storm is coming, he thought again, nodding to himself.

He reached Center Square and stopped to study the holo

screens blazing from the sides of the skyscrapers. One of them in particular caught his eye.

Travel to the stars aboard the Avilon*! Join Earth's best and brightest on a mission to Wolf 1061! Apply now!* A geometric code of black squares on a white background flashed up on the screen, and Remo studied it with his ARCs. An error flashed before his eyes: *Code Invalid.* Then Remo noticed the fine print. *Applicants must all be androids, model C or newer.*

Remo smirked. *Figures.* But the Solarian Republic was also sending out a colony ship—the *Liberty*—and theirs was going to Proxima Centauri, much closer than Wolf 1061. Like the *Avilon,* the *Liberty* also restricted its applicants—*human only.* And they weren't just accepting the best and brightest; they were also charging for passage. Five million Sols per ticket.

Not a chance he could afford it.

But a ship like that is going to need pilots. Cooks. Waiters. Remo nodded slowly to himself. If he was lucky, he'd be accepted to fill one of the joe jobs. Then he'd be able to leave the Sol system and all of its looming wars behind for good.

Remo grinned at the prospect: a new world, a new frontier, heading out to explore the unknown... and best of all, no androids. It sounded like paradise. All he had to do was pass their entrance exams.

Here goes...

CHAPTER 1

The Year 104 AB "Anno Benevolentiae"

Alexander leaned over his wife's seat to gaze through the holographic "side" window of the shuttle. That window was configured to show a view from the shuttle's bow cameras so he and Catalina could watch their approach. They were headed for a glowing white square of light in the outer hull of the *Liberty*. From a distance that square looked no bigger than the window he was looking through, but as they drew near, he saw that it was a yawning hangar big enough to swallow their shuttle whole. The number 72 was stenciled in bold white numerals to either side of the opening. Alexander recalled reading that the *Liberty* had seventy-two shuttle bays for each of its ten sections, one for every five degrees of their circumference.

Their shuttle glided inside the hangar and set down in the middle of a vast chamber. Thunking sounds echoed through the hull as magnetic docking clamps secured them to the landing pad. A moment later, the entire landing pad rotated with a mechanical rumble. When it stopped, the view from the bow cameras showed outer space and the distant red orb that was Mars. This new space-facing position would enable the shuttle to launch at just a moment's notice in the event of an emergency. The giant hangar doors began sliding shut, and Alexander's view of Mars and the black void that embraced it quickly narrowed from a square to a rectangle, then to a bar and finally to a pencil-thin slice.

One of the shuttle's flight attendants, Ana Urikov, came back on the comms indicating that they should remain seated until Section 7 finished spinning up the ring decks to simulate artificial gravity. Alexander waited, breathless with excitement, eager to get out of the shuttle and start touring his new home. Beside him, Catalina was notably less enthusiastic, wide-eyed and gripping the armrests of her chair in bloodless fists.

"Take it easy, darling," he said, placing a hand over hers. They felt a jolt of movement as their seats rotated one-hundred and eighty degrees. Now they faced the back of the shuttle, but it was impossible to tell because they couldn't see over the tops of other passengers' chairs. The shuttle was divided into twenty-five matching compartments, each with four passengers, and a tram car running between sections.

Captain Lieberman's voice crackled over the intercom: "Ring decks spinning up, please stand by."

Alexander felt himself growing gradually heavier, the rings' rotation pulling him back against his chair and telling him what was "down" and what was "up."

Ana Urikov spoke through the overhead speakers once more: "We are currently simulating Martian standard gravity—0.38 Terran Gs. You may now unbuckle and gather your belongings. We will begin debarking with compartments one and two. Please make sure you board the tram car as soon as it arrives at your compartment. Thank you."

Alexander unbuckled and crawled out of his seat into the aisle. Since gravity was pulling him toward the bow, he found himself standing on what had been the wall of the compartment when he'd first boarded the shuttle on Mars. What used to be the overhead luggage compartment had now become a footlocker.

Catalina peered up at him from her chair, making no move to unbuckle.

"We made it," he said, grinning at her as he bent down to pop open the luggage compartment and retrieve their bags.

Catalina nodded slowly and unbuckled. She had to crawl across his seat to get out. He held out a hand to help her up, and she stood, swaying on her feet. Alexander steadied her with a hand around her waist.

"Are you okay?"

"Yes... just disoriented."

"That's normal. Going from zero-G to artificial gravity is hard even for experienced spacers. I'm surprised you didn't need to use your barf bag."

Catalina winced and clutched her stomach. "Don't... let's talk about something else."

Alexander chuckled and grinned. "All right." He turned and nodded to the tramway between them and the other side of the shuttle. "We're up next." Theirs was compartment number four, near the front of the shuttle. Alexander watched the glowing green number above the doors drop down to *1*, pause, and then climb to *4*. The doors parted with a *swish*, letting in a gust of cool air. Directly opposite them stood another pair of passengers with their bags—a man and a woman, holding hands, each dragging a bag on wheels behind them. Another married couple no doubt. Alexander nodded to them as he slung his carry-on over one shoulder and handed Catalina hers. The bags were easy enough to carry. With just 0.38 *Gs* their twenty-five-pound bags weighed less than ten.

Once they were standing inside the tram, the doors swished shut on both sides and it dropped down to compartment three. *Swish.* Another four passengers stepped in—a woman and a young boy on the left, and two more women on the right. Each of those women looked to be in their early twenties, but looks were deceiving. Technically both he and Catalina were almost one hundred and sixty years old, but neither of them looked a day over thirty.

Alexander considered the two on the right, wondering where their partners were. The *Liberty* was a colony ship first and foremost, but in an age of immortal, genetically-engineered *geners*, artificial insemination was child's play, so he supposed that the colonists didn't necessarily have to be coupled up.

"Hi, I'm Benjamin," a small voice said.

"Nice to meet you, Benjamin. I'm Catalina."

Alexander turned to see the young boy who'd entered on the left shaking hands with his wife. That boy couldn't have been more than ten years old.

Benjamin glanced at him. "Who's your friend?"

"That's my husband, Alex," Catalina replied.

"Hi, Alex," Benjamin said thrusting out his hand once more.

Alexander smiled and shook hands with the boy. His mother looked on with amusement.

"He thinks he's going to get to know everyone on board," she explained.

"I have to. We're all family now, and family should know each other. At least their names," Benjamin explained.

Alexander nodded. "It's a big ship. You're going to have

your work cut out for you."

"I know. Ten sections with 7,344 people each. That's 73,440 colonists."

The tram stopped and the doors swished open, but this time only on one side. "You're very good at math," Alexander said, waiting for Benajmin's mother to leave the tram first. Benjamin craned his neck to continue the conversation as she pulled him along by his hand. "Want to know what else I'm good at?"

"What's that?" he asked as he and Catalina followed them out. They walked by one of the flight attendants at the shuttle exit. She smiled and nodded to them as they left the shuttle and started down a long, cylindrical boarding tunnel.

"Recognizing faces," Benjamin said. "I never forget a face. Yours looks familiar."

"Not likely. I'm from Earth, and I've been out of touch for a while. Maybe you met my clone."

"You have a clone?"

Alexander's lips twitched into a mischievous grin. "No, I was being facetious."

"Oh. So was I."

Catalina shot him a broody smile when Benjamin looked away. This was why they'd joined the *Liberty*—to have children of their own. Earth's population controls made that prohibitively difficult. You had to win the monthly lottery to have kids, or wait your turn, which could be centuries. Not to mention any children they did have would have to compete with all the emancipated androids running around doing every job humans could do, but better and faster than humans could do it.

They could have settled on Mars or one of the other

Solarian colonies, but with an AI ruling Earth, and humans still firmly in command of the rest of the solar system, all-out war was just a matter of time. This was the only way to escape it all. Board the *Liberty* on a one way trip to Proxima Centauri with its human-only crew.

They came to the end of the boarding tunnel and another pair of flight attendants greeted them there. "Please wait at the gate until all passengers and crew have finished debarking," one of them said in a familiar voice. Alexander noted that her name badge read, *Ana Urikov*.

The waiting area on the other side of the gate reminded him of the analogous version in an airport back on Earth. A wall of windows looked out into the hangar, and rows of seating furnished the room. Alexander took Catalina's hand and walked up to the nearest window. Maintenance drones rolled to and from their shuttle using both the walls and floor with equal ease. Their shuttle was clamped to the wall to their right, hovering impossibly above the deck. Higher up, Alexander saw a second tunnel extending to offload their checked bags.

"Feeling better now?" he asked Catalina.

She nodded. "A bit, yeah."

Out of the corner of his eye Alexander saw another group of passengers spill out into the waiting area. He and Catalina turned from the windows and sat down along the nearest bank of seats to wait while the rest of the passengers filed out. Alexander spied Benjamin and his mother sitting along the row of seats opposite theirs. Benjamin spotted him and grinned; then his grin faded dramatically and his eyes went wide, as if he'd suddenly remembered something.

"I know where I saw you!" Benjamin blurted out. "I read

about you in history! You're Captain Alexander de Leon, *the Lion of Liberty*. You made everyone stop fighting after The Last War."

Catalina turned to Alexander with eyebrows raised. "They put you in the history books?"

"News to me."

"Are you the Lion of *this* Liberty?" Benjamin asked, looking awestruck.

"No, I'm just along for the ride," Alexander said, shaking his head.

"Why do they call you a lion?"

"Benjamin..." his mother said.

"But Mom!"

"That's enough. Leave the poor man alone."

"Okay... sorry, Alex."

"That's all right," he said, smiling. "They called me that because my last name is *de Leon*. *Leon* means lion where I'm from."

"Oh. So you were born a lion."

"Something like that."

"That's so *crimson!*"

"I'm sorry?"

"You know, like *spectral,* or *ace...* or *facetious!*"

Alexander smiled. "You might want to look up that last one."

"I can't. Mom made me disable my ARC lenses AND my comm band when we boarded the shuttle."

"I think we can activate them al—" Alexander caught an urgent look from Benjamin's mother. She placed a finger to her lips and shook her head. "—pretty soon," he finished.

"Hope so!" Benjamin said, looking away to watch as

another group of passengers joined them in the gate room.

Soon the waiting area was crowded with more than a hundred passengers and crew. Alexander looked out the windows into the hangar to watch as the boarding tunnel detached from their shuttle and folded away. Then a commanding voice echoed through the room, drawing his attention away from the windows.

"Welcome aboard the *Liberty*. My name is Ling Chong, and I am the governor of the *Liberty*." The governor wore a spotless white uniform with glowing white piping. Short, jet black hair contrasted sharply with both her uniform and her pale, porcelain skin. Her amber eyes roved through the room while she waited for everyone's attention.

She went on, "Whoever you are, wherever you came from, know this: the *Liberty* is an entity unto itself, a new territory with its own people, and its own culture. Yes, we answer to the authority of the Solarian Republic, but we are passengers and crew of the *Liberty* first and foremost, so leave all of your prejudices behind. From this moment on, it doesn't matter whether you think of yourself as a Terran or a Solarian. What matters is where you are headed, and we are all headed in the same direction."

The governor turned to a man standing just behind her and to her right. He wore a deep maroon uniform with glowing red piping, gold buttons, and black epaulets with golden tassels. A single gold star glittered on each of his epaulets, marking him as an Admiral in the Solarian Navy. "This is Admiral Urikov," Governor Chong said.

Same name as that flight attendant on the shuttle, Alexander thought, wondering if they were related.

The admiral stepped forward, and the governor

continued: "Admiral, would you care to explain your role aboard this ship?"

Admiral Urikov nodded. "Of course. The Navy is in charge of the external defense of the *Liberty*. In the unlikely event that we need to defend ourselves from an external threat, we have ten squadrons of manned fighters and thirty squadrons of drones. That's one and three squadrons respectively for each section. Due to the fact that there are very few clear lines of sight between the ship's stationary core and its rotating rings, nearly all of the *Liberty's* defenses are deployable rather than attached to fixed hard-points, but we do have a significant forward-facing arsenal, and our sensors are state-of-the-art, so we should have plenty of time to deploy fighters and drones if need be. That being said, we don't expect to run into any external threats.

"For internal threats to security, we have the Marines. They will act as law enforcement aboard the *Liberty*. Rest assured, however, they will only carry non-lethal weapons while performing their police duties."

Alexander saw Catalina turn to him, her brown eyes wide. "The Marines are going to be our police force?" she whispered.

"I guess they wouldn't have much to do otherwise," he whispered back.

"Marines are trained to *kill* people, not arrest them."

"You heard the admiral—they won't be carrying lethal weapons."

"There's plenty of ways to kill someone without using a weapon."

Alexander frowned and looked away from his wife.

The admiral finished speaking, and Alexander wondered

what he'd missed.

The governor addressed them once more: "Each of the *Liberty's* ten sections is identical, except for Section One, which is where myself and Admiral Urikov reside along with the rest of the ship's command staff and the majority of her crew. The other nine sections are primarily made up of colonists like you, and each section will have a councilor whom you will elect at the end of your initial six months training. That councilor will report directly to me. Until then, your acting councilor will be in charge. Likewise, there is a naval commander in each section that reports directly to Admiral Urikov. You can think of each of the ship's sections like a city, with Section One as the capital."

Alexander nodded. They could easily carry that command structure forward with them into the new world.

"I will now hand you over to your section leaders for a brief explanation of this ship's facilities. We wish you all a pleasant and comfortable stay aboard the *Liberty*." The governor cracked a tight smile and nodded to them. "May the Universal Architect be with us all." With that, both she and Admiral Urikov vanished into thin air.

Alexander blinked in shock. *Holograms,* he realized, now noticing the projection plates where they'd been standing. The speeches must have been pre-recorded. That made sense. With seven hundred and twenty shuttles on board, they couldn't possibly be expected to welcome each group of colonists personally.

The projection plates rolled away to their charging stations along the wall. Moments later a set of doors *swished* open in that wall, and in walked another man and a woman. Their uniforms were the same colors as their Section One counterparts—white with glowing white piping for government, and maroon with bright red piping for the Navy. This time their roles and genders were reversed—a female naval commander and a male councilor.

"Hello, I am Mikail Markov acting councilor for Section Seven, and this is Commander Audrey Johnson. You're lucky. Your shuttle is the last to arrive for this section, so you get to move around under a full Martian *G* rather than using magnetic boots."

The councilor was clearly of Russian descent, but Commander Johnson might have originally hailed from the Americas. Alexander caught himself there, the governor's words echoing through his head, chiding him: *leave all of your prejudices behind.*

Old wars and old enemies no longer mattered.

"Please follow me," Councilor Markov said.

The flight attendants from the shuttle helped usher everyone out of their seats. Ana Urikov clapped her hands for attention and spoke in an amplified voice. "Let's go. Everyone up! Baggage drones will take your checked bags to your quarters for you."

Alexander stood up and slung his carry-on over his shoulder once more. Turning to Catalina, he found her doing the same.

"Ready?" he asked.

She nodded and grabbed his hand in an anxious grip. "Let's go."

CHAPTER 2

On their way to the elevators, Councilor Markov painted a broad picture of the *Liberty's* layout for them. The ship was divided into ten sections, each with two types of living areas—the stationary core for extended periods of acceleration and deceleration, and the rotating outer rings, where gravity could be simulated while cruising through interstellar space. The rings were relatively thin, putting vertical space at a premium, with just ten decks for each section, but each deck was massive, with a circumference of about 3700 meters by three hundred and twenty meters in width. The opposite was true for the stationary core where those three hundred and twenty meters became over sixty floors of vertical space.

In both the core and the ring decks, the use of the space was the same: crew quarters, mess and recreation, agriculture, training, maintenance and manufacturing, command and administration, services, storage, medical and research, and of course, the all-important hangar bays. In the core, many of those decks were duplicated, while there was just one deck dedicated to each purpose in the rings.

Alexander wondered what they'd use the core for after the initial six months of acceleration were over and they transferred everyone to the rings for the next eight years. Would all those duplicate decks and equipment just sit there collecting dust? For now they would stay aboard the rings, until all of the shuttles had arrived for the remaining sections.

They reached the nearest bank of elevators—ten in a row. Alexander and Catalina ended up sharing an elevator with Councilor Markov and about twenty others. The councilor selected a button marked *5-DORM* from the control panel. Ten decks, ten buttons.

"Councilor, I have a question," Alexander said.

The man turned to him with his bushy black eyebrows raised as the elevator shot up to deck five. His expression never seemed to vary from a grumpy, no-nonsense frown. "Did you have to pay for passage aboard the *Liberty*?"

"No, I was selected for my experience. All the ship's crew and field specialists were. Otherwise you'd have a ship full of rich idiots living it up in anarchy with no idea of how to start an interstellar colony."

Alexander scowled at the indirect insult. The elevator arrived and the doors swished open on level five. The councilor's open disdain for all the "rich idiots" on board irked him. He and Catalina had each paid five million Sols to get aboard the *Liberty*, but they'd also passed their entrance exams—meeting or surpassing the minimum requirements for intelligence, education, adaptability, mental stability, conscientiousness, and so on. As for the money that had gotten them aboard—Sols meant nothing now. No doubt a new currency would soon be established, but in a place where all the accommodations were equal and luxuries probably few, money was unlikely to mean very much. Knowledge, talent, and skill would be what set the passengers apart for the duration of their voyage—a true meritocracy if ever there was one.

They filed out of the elevator and came face-to-face with a line of Marines wearing uniforms that were an even darker shade of crimson than the naval officers they'd met so far. Likewise, the piping on their jumpsuits glowed a dimmer shade of red than their Navy counterparts. A *Latina* woman with the three-stripe chevron of a sergeant stepped out of line and saluted Commander Johnson as she approached, whereupon the commander returned the salute and turned to face the colonists from the shuttle. "Sergeant Torres will give you your room assignments and shipboard uniforms, which you must wear from now on."

A few grumbles of discontent rose from the group, and Alexander smiled knowingly. He and Catalina hadn't bothered to bring clothes with them, but no doubt others hadn't read their orientation manuals as carefully.

The commander silenced those grumbles with a wave of her hand. "The reason you can't use regular clothing is that it cannot be pressurized with the simple addition of a helmet and gloves, and it won't keep you warm if the heating fails. For safety reasons, we're all restricted to the use of the ever-fashionable pressure-rated jumpsuits. They do come in different colors, but until you've finished training you'll all be using off-duty blacks. After that, you'll get a working uniform that's color-coded to your chosen profession.

"Now I'm afraid I must get back to *my* profession in the Command Information Center. If any of you have any security-related questions or concerns, please don't hesitate to speak with the nearest Marine. Are there any questions before I go?"

Alexander thrust up his hand. A few others raised theirs, too, but the commander pointed to him first. "Yes, de Leon?"

For a moment he was surprised that she knew his name, but then he remembered that their basic information was already registered and being automatically broadcast via their neural links. Everyone had to get a neural link before joining the mission so they could mentally interface with control systems on board the *Liberty*.

"You mentioned we could choose our professions," Alexander began. "Does that mean we can train for any job we like?"

"You'll go through various skill tests, aptitude tests, and a psych eval., all of which will be used to populate a list of possible professions. You'll be asked to select three, and based on those preferences the human resources department will determine where you are most suited and most needed. After that you'll go through six months training for your profession, and if need be, you'll apprentice under someone. Any other questions?"

Two more people had their hands raised, but one of them dropped his after hearing the answer to Alexander's question.

"Yes, Miss Adams?" the commander asked, pointing to the remaining person.

"Will we be allowed to get pregnant during the trip?"

"A very good question. I'm going to defer you to Acting Councilor Markov for the answer to that—councilor?"

He cleared his throat and stepped forward to address the group. "Birth control implants will remain activated for the duration of the journey, and any attempt to remove or tamper with those implants will result in strict sanctions."

Alexander wondered what those *sanctions* might be as the news drew noisy grumbles of discontent from the group.

The councilor had to raise his voice to be heard as he went

on, "BUT ONCE WE ARRIVE at Proxima B, those implants will be deactivated."

More hands shot up to ask follow-up questions. The councilor pointed to one of them. "Last question—Mr. Humphrey."

"Why aren't we traveling through the Looking Glass?"

Alexander recognized the name of the wormhole that had mysteriously appeared in the Sol system more than a century ago. That phenomenon had sparked the Last War and nearly wiped out the human race in a nasty nuclear war. He remembered his virtual trip through the wormhole to an earth-type planet, code-named *Wonderland*. The mission had been nothing but a clever ploy by the Alliance. Like that, they'd tricked the Confederacy into throwing away the bulk of their fleet in their rush to be the first to colonize Wonderland.

"The wormhole is not traversable," Councilor Markov explained. "So unless you have a death wish—"

"You're wrong," Mr. Humphrey interrupted.

"Excuse me?"

"The wormhole *is* traversable. Research has shown that with stronger hulls, better radiation shielding, and more precise nav calculations, a ship could theoretically make it through the eye of the wormhole."

"Even if that's true, you're talking to the wrong person—and you're about a decade too late to find the right one. I can guarantee you that the *Liberty* is not designed to those exacting standards."

"Well, it should have been. We need to find out where the wormhole came from, and who's waiting on the other side. *That* should be our priority."

"Again, wrong person, wrong timing." A few people waved their hands to get the councilor's attention, but he shook his head. "I'm sorry, I don't have time to answer any more questions. I need to get back to my duties on the command deck. You may direct any further inquiries to the ship's crew or prefects. Have a good night everyone."

Councilor Markov and Commander Johnson turned and headed back to the elevators together, while Sergeant Torres cleared her throat and asked them all to make ten lines according to their heights, from shortest to tallest. The Marines working with her helped to separate the group. Alexander ended up on the tall end and his wife on the short end. He waved to her, and she smiled back. Then Sergeant Torres and her Marines began distributing glossy black jumpsuits according to the heights of the people in each line.

As they distributed the uniforms, Torres said, "In your outer pockets you'll find physical keys for your assigned quarters. You can take them out now to check what room you're assigned to, but please keep them with you at all times. Those keys are for emergencies, in case of a power failure or a mechanical failure. Under any other circumstances, you can open doors with your ARCs—assuming you have the proper clearance, of course."

Alexander received his off-duty uniform and fished through the outer pockets to find his room key. It was an antiquated piece of metal, designed for use with a mechanical lock. A small rectangular key ring identified it as key number *7-5070J|15070.*

"The first number on your key ring refers to your section, in this case seven. The second number will be five thousand and something. That's your room number out here on the ring decks. There are 3510 rooms on this deck, with an identical number of rooms in the core's ten dormitory levels, which brings me to the third number on your key ring—fifteen thousand something. That's your room number in the core. Finding your rooms is easy. Just like an apartment building, the first one or two digits refer to the floor number, while subsequent digits refer to the room number on that floor.

"Here on the ring decks ten corridors from *A* to *J* run between rows of sleeping quarters, so that's what the letter after the number means. In the core, those corridors correspond to ten different levels from five to fifteen. There are three hundred and fifty-one rooms per corridor or level, at least ten of which are for the Marines and Navy, while room *one* is for your corridor prefect.

"Prefects are elected members of the government, and they report directly to the section councilor. They are responsible for the people living along each corridor and the corresponding dormitory level in the core. Your acting prefect is Ana Urikov—she was one of the flight attendants from your shuttle."

Ana raised her hand and waved to the group with a well-practiced smile.

Torres went on, "In case you haven't figured it out yet, this is a *big* ship. You can walk for a kilometer or more just to get from your room to one of the ten mess halls on this level, and you can walk for more than three and a half kilometers around each of the ring decks before you end up back where you started. The ship designers looked at a number of solutions to help make these distances shorter, but it was ultimately determined that the exercise would do us good.

"That being said, Naval personnel, Marines, prefects,

councilors, and various other types of crew have access to *Patrollers* to help us respond to emergencies more quickly." Torres pointed to a row of gleaming white, self-balancing, two-wheeled vehicles along the wall behind her and the other petty officers.

"To avoid accidents, please observe the yellow hazard lines running down the center of each corridor. Those lines denote emergency response lanes. Cross them with the same caution you'd use for a busy street. Walking in those lanes or otherwise obstructing them will result in immediate sanctions. Now, please follow us."

Alexander frowned, wondering once more what type of *sanctions* would be applied aboard the *Liberty*. He found Catalina through the crowd as the orderly lines of colonists flowed into a sea of bobbing heads. Sergeant Torres and the other Marines mounted their Patrollers and rolled off at a comfortable walking pace. Everyone in the group followed along, walking past corridors marked with glowing letters *F, G, H,* and *I.* When they reached *J* corridor, the Patrollers rolled into the right-hand side of the emergency response lane in perfect synchrony.

"You should be able to find your rooms from here," Torres announced from the front of the line of Patrollers. People were already taking her up on that and speeding down the corridor, eyes flicking between the glowing room numbers above each door. "Remember to activate your ARCs so that you can access the ship's personnel directory, itinerary, and deck plans.

"If you're hungry, dinner will be served in the mess areas in just under half an hour, but make sure you change out of your shuttle suits and into your off-duty uniforms first. Keep the shuttle suits in the back of your closets; you'll have to wear them again for landfall on Proxima B. On behalf of the *Liberty* and her crew, I hope you all have a good night. We'll be seeing you again soon."

"So?" Alexander asked, turning to Catalina with a grin. "How do you like our new neighborhood?"

She arched an eyebrow at him. "Well, it's a step down from our three floor lakeside mansion."

Alexander frowned.

Seeing the expression on his face, she hurried to add, "But we'll make it work. What's important is that we're together."

"Starting over is never easy, but we'll get back to where we were. Just remember why we're doing this. This is for our children, for their futures—and for ours. There's no androids to compete with on this ship, no benevolent AI to rule us, and no threat of war or impending doom—just an endless void full of possibilities."

Catalina arched an eyebrow at him. "A *void full?* Quite an oxymoron you have there. Let's find our quarters and get settled and then grab something to eat. Looks like the ten mess halls are each themed with different types of cuisine..." she said as brightly colored images flickered over her eyes. She was using her ARCs to check the ship's facilities. "Just like a cruise ship. How about we try Asian food tonight?"

Alexander smiled and leaned in for a kiss. "Sounds great."

Catalina nodded and matched his smile with a less enthusiastic version. They started down the corridor together and found their room on the left side of the corridor. The number 5070J glowed brightly above the door. Alexander highlighted it with his ARCs, and yellow brackets appeared around the door. He thought the word *open,* and heard a chime sound inside his head as those brackets turned green and the door slid open. Lights bloomed inside their quarters, revealing a simple kitchen, living room, dining room, breakfast bar, and even a small terrace with leafy green plants growing along the sides. A glass railing ran along the back of the terrace, and beyond that, a holographic sun peeked up at them from the hazy edge of a rippled gray ocean. Clouds like crimson tongues of flame drifted across an amethyst sky.

"A cruise ship complete with an ocean view balcony," Alexander said, nodding appreciatively as he walked up to the terrace doors and mentally opened them. A warm, tropical breeze blew into the living room as the glass doors parted for him.

As he watched, that ocean view transformed to a sandy beach with curling waves crashing and racing toward them.

"I'm afraid of heights," Catalina explained, walking up beside him.

Alexander grinned and wrapped an arm around her shoulders. He listened to the waves crashing on the shore and inhaled the fresh, salty air coming off the ocean. The illusion was convincing enough to make him forget that they were actually cooped up inside of a metal box. "Beach front property. Not such a step down after all."

"Maybe not," Catalina agreed.

CHAPTER 3

Sergeant Torres was right about the *Liberty* being a *big* ship. The walk from their quarters to the *Wok-King,* Section 7's Asian-themed mess hall, took twelve minutes, and according to Catalina's ARCs she and Alexander covered 1,220 meters to get there. Most of that was spent just walking past the rooms after theirs to reach the end of J Corridor. Catalina shuddered to think how long it would take to evacuate the dormitory level in an emergency.

The mess hall was well-decorated rather than utilitarian and cafeteria-style, adding to the cruise ship comparison she'd made earlier. A blocky metallic server bot greeted them at the door.

"Welcome to the Wok-King," it said with photoreceptors flashing bright green above its speaker grill mouth.

Catalina sensed Alexander stiffen at the sight of the bot.

It was the first one they'd seen, but a worrying sight nonetheless. The *Liberty* had promised *no androids* on board, but apparently that didn't extend to older generation *bots*. It was just a short leap from there to the mess Earth had landed itself in with a well-meaning AI taking over and elevating the working-class machines to sentient androids, indistinguishable from humans.

Alexander crossed his arms over his chest and jerked his chin to the bot. "What are you doing here?"

The bot's photoreceptors went from green to blue. "I am hosting guests at the Wok-King."

"I mean what are you doing on this ship," Alexander specified.

"My job is to make sure that unskilled labor positions are filled, thus ensuring that passengers and crew will be forced to seek employment in more fulfilling capacities."

"I thought there weren't supposed to be any bots on board," Catalina said.

"*Bot* is a colloquial term for an autonomous robot equipped with some degree of artificial intelligence. It is also a derogatory term for an android. I am neither, for I do not possess artificial intelligence, nor do I have a human appearance. I am colloquially known as a *drudge*."

"You must have some degree of AI or you wouldn't be able to answer our questions," Alexander said.

Catalina nodded along with that. She'd been about to point out the same thing.

"My speech routines are advanced, but my other functions are limited to host and waiter."

"What prevents you from being upgraded to serve a higher function?" Catalina asked.

"Upgrading my functions would be illegal and result in the immediate re-formatting of my core."

"Hmmm. I see," she said. "All right, then show us to our table."

The drudge's photoreceptors flashed bright green once more. "Of course! Right this way..." he replied, rolling away on two wheels.

They followed the drudge into the dining area, weaving a path between dozens of tables and hundreds of other guests.

The mess hall was massive. Catalina supposed that it would have to be with only ten such eating areas and over seven thousand people to feed in Section Seven. She guessed there had to be at least five hundred tables in the restaurant, but it was hard to tell with all the room-dividing furniture and Japanese folding screens to break up the space.

"Alexander the Lion!" a boyish voice called out.

Catalina glimpsed Benjamin waving to them from a table coming up on their right.

"Shhh! Don't yell, Benjamin," his mother chided before looking up with a smile. Benjamin and his mother were seated beside a holographic aquarium full of colorful orange and white Koi.

Catalina stopped beside their table. "It's a small ship after all," she said through a smile.

"Hah!" Benjamin's mother replied. "I think I burned more calories getting here than I'm going to get back." She held out her hand. "I forgot to introduce myself earlier. I'm Esther."

"Nice to meet you, Esther. I'm Catalina. I believe you already know my husband thanks to your son's fondness for history."

Esther smiled and nodded as she glanced his way. "Would you like to join us?" she asked.

"That would be lovely," Catalina replied. "Thank you, Esther."

Despite its inability to form an expression, Catalina thought their host looked flustered.

"Crimson!" Benjamin crowed. "You can sit here, Alex," he said, patting the chair beside his.

"Benjamin! That's Mr. de Leon to you!" Esther said.

Alexander smiled, and took his seat beside the boy.

Catalina sat between him and Esther.

"A waiter will come to take your orders soon," their host interrupted before rolling away.

"Can I call him Mr. Lion instead?" Benjamin asked, ignoring the bot. "It's easier to pronounce."

Esther looked puzzled, and a breathless silence blanketed the table as they waited for her reply.

Catalina cracked a smile and laughed. "Let's hear you roar, Mr. Lion," she said, grinning at his expense.

"Meow," he replied, and they all guffawed.

A server drudge identical to the host model showed up and took their orders. Their food arrived a few minutes later, whereupon hunger kept their mouths busy and conversations limited. Once they finished the main course and dessert arrived, they found more time for small talk.

"What was it like growing up on Mars?" Catalina asked Esther.

"Crimson. Totally crimson," Benjamin dead-panned before his mother could reply. "Red sand. Red sky. Red clothes. Red eyes. Red, red, red! At least you see green when you close your eyes."

"How's that?" Alexander asked.

"You see it in your dreams."

Esther chuckled. "He's lying. It was actually a lot like this—everything indoors, including *green* gardens and *blue* lakes for reservoirs," she added, glancing reprovingly at her son.

"But all under a red sky!" Benjamin insisted.

"Yes, under a red sky."

"Sounds like a dreary place," Catalina said. "I'm sorry— that was your home."

"Don't be. It *was* dreary. Why do you think we left?"

"Do you think Proxima B will be any better?" Catalina asked.

"I don't know. I hope so," Esther replied.

Catalina expected a barren wasteland like Mars with the possible addition of liquid water in the habitable band along the equator.

"I wonder what the Proxans are like?" Benjamin chimed in.

"The Proxans?" Catalina asked.

"You know, the aliens who live there."

Alexander intercepted a worried look from his wife, and he shook his head. "I don't think there are any *Proxans*."

"Why not?" Benjamin insisted. "Everyone keeps saying Proxima B is habitable, but if it's so habitable, wouldn't it already be habited?"

"*In*-habited," Esther corrected.

Alexander cracked a smile at the boy's logic. "Well, evolution isn't a sure thing. Even if you have a planet with all the right conditions for life as we know it, the odds of it evolving there are very slim. For all we know, we're the only intelligent species in this galaxy."

Esther shook her head. "We're not."

Catalina regarded her with eyebrows raised. "How can you be so sure?"

"Because I've met them."

"You met... *them?*" Alexander asked. Skepticism was written all over his face.

"Aliens," Esther replied, nodding. "I was abducted."

Catalina was about to say *I'm sorry*, but that didn't seem to fit. "What was it like?" she asked instead, wondering how much she should humor Esther's delusions before changing the topic.

"I was standing in Benjamin's room one night, seven months pregnant, looking up at Phobos and Deimos, and I saw a silver speck darting around in the sky. I wondered if it might be a drone. Then I saw a bright light, and suddenly I was falling into it. Something caught me and carried me into the light."

Esther shook her head and winced. "The next thing I knew, I woke up lying on a table, naked, with *them* all around me. It was so bright in the room—they were the only thing I could make out clearly. They were naked, too, but sexless, with wrinkly gray skin; giant, hairless heads; bulbous, slanting black eyes, and tiny noses and mouths. They were short, like children. Two arms and two legs like us, but only eight fingers." Esther grimaced and swallowed thickly, obviously struggling with the memory.

Catalina was having a hard time taking her seriously; she struggled not to smile. This had to be a joke.

"You're talking about the Grays," Alexander said.

Catalina turned to him with eyebrows raised. "The aliens she's describing," he explained. "There's thousands of abduction stories like hers—no real proof to back them up, but they all more or less agree on the general appearance of their abductors: gray skin, big heads, naked, hairless, and genderless."

Esther nodded along with that. "I didn't know anything about abduction stories before they took *me*, but that's what I found when I did my research after the fact. It was reassuring to know that I'm not the only one. Some of them were taken multiple times. Thank the Architect they didn't take me again.

That's one of the reasons I wanted to board the *Liberty*. Maybe they wouldn't know how to find me at Proxima."

"Hold on," Alexander held up a palm and smiled, unable to hold back his skepticism any longer. Catalina shot him a warning look, but he ignored it. "You believe in the Universal Architect, *and* aliens?"

"What's wrong with that?" Esther asked.

"Nothing if you don't mind logical inconsistencies. The Bible predicts that the end of humanity will coincide with the end of the universe, but if that's true, then it stands to reason we must be alone in the universe, because it's unlikely that a creator would end all of the alien civilizations out there just because humanity's time is up."

Esther didn't look happy with that logic. Images flickered across her eyes as she looked something up on her ARCs. *"The heavens will disappear with a great noise and the elements will melt in the heat*—you're suggesting that verses like that mean belief in a creator must go hand-in-hand with the belief that we're alone in the universe."

"I guess I am," Alexander said.

"The mind of the Architect is unknowable. His ways are not our ways, and his thoughts are not our thoughts. Maybe the predicted end of the heavens is a more local event. With so many translations between us and the original scrolls, it's hard to say exactly what the original meaning was."

Alexander inclined his head. "Touche, the ambiguous veil of faith wins."

Catalina shot him a dire look. "I'm sorry, Esther, I'm afraid my husband has forgotten the cardinal rule of polite dinner conversation—never discuss religion or politics."

Esther nodded her agreement, and the two women traded

awkward smiles across the table.

"Speaking of politics, any idea how we're going to choose electoral candidates for section councilors?" Alexander asked.

Catalina looked aghast, but Esther burst out laughing. Her laughter was contagious, and soon the rest of them were laughing along with her.

"Nice save, Mr. Lion," Benjamin whispered.

Alexander winked back at him. "Me-ow."

CHAPTER 4

Catalina woke up. Her skin felt warm, and she felt the bed shaking as if from an earthquake. For a moment she feared that was exactly what it was, but then she remembered she was aboard the *Liberty—there aren't earthquakes in space*, she chided herself. No, *she* was shaking, not the bed. The vibrations and warmth disappeared, and she lay there blinking up at the ceiling, wondering what had just happened.

Strange.

She was about to roll over and go back to sleep when she saw the shadow standing at the foot of her bed. She stared at it, frozen with horror. Big head, bulbous, slanting black eyes, small mouth and nose... it was exactly the way Esther had described it.

Catalina tried to scream, to turn to her husband and warn him... but she couldn't. She was paralyzed. Her heart pounded in her chest, and a cold sweat broke out over her entire body. The alien said something to her.

"*Nek wa-ra.*" That stuttering, warbling sound was like nothing she'd heard in her life. Utterly alien.

Again she tried to scream, but she couldn't even whisper.

The alien smiled at her, revealing a row of pointy white teeth.

Catalina blinked—

And it was gone.

Finding she could move again, Catalina sat up and screamed: "Alex!"

He sat up beside her, arms and legs thrashing, eyes wide and darting around the room. "What is it? What's wrong?" he asked, trying to look everywhere at once.

"I... there was something in the room with us. An alien. It was right there!" She pointed to the foot of the bed. "And then it was gone."

Alexander rubbed his eyes. "It was just a dream."

"It didn't feel like a dream. I was awake. And I was paralyzed. I couldn't move! I think... I think it did something to me."

"A night terror then—a hallucination."

"What if it wasn't? What if Benjamin's right? What if Proxima really is inhabited?"

Alexander smiled. "You know, usually it's adults who give children nightmares, not the other way around."

"Ha ha. I'm serious, Alex."

"So am I," he replied. Holograms flickered across his eyes as he checked something on his ARCs. "It's o-six hundred hours already. Breakfast's at eight. We may as well get up and get ready. Big day today. The itinerary says we're supposed to pick our careers."

Catalina let out a long sigh and swung her feet over the side of the bed. "I'm going to take a shower. Wait—they do have showers in space, right? Not some kind of high-tech, unsatisfying steam bath?"

"Yes, there are showers, but the water is all recycled."

Catalina made a face. "Recycled... so what goes in someone else's toilet..."

Alexander nodded.

"Yuck."

He laughed. "You'll get used to it."

"I'm not so sure about that..." she replied, grimacing as she stood up. The sheets fell away from her, and she caught Alexander staring. She'd slept naked last night. They hadn't brought any clothes with them, and she wasn't used to sleeping in a jumpsuit.

"Mind if I join you in the shower?" Alexander asked.

"That depends."

"On?"

"How big is it?"

"We've known each other for more than a century, and you don't know how big it is?"

"I meant—"

He flashed a sudden grin. "I know. It's big enough."

"Well, in that case..." Catalina sent a salacious look over her shoulder as she headed for the shower. "Come and get it."

* * *

Commander Audrey Johnson walked up to the ring, watching as Councilor Mikail Markov snuck a right hook past his opponent's guard and sent him stumbling back against the ropes with a grunt.

Markov advanced while his opponent was still recovering and landed a quick one-two punch. The man slumped against the ropes, blinking big, glassy blue eyes. "You win this round," he said in an inflectionless monotone.

Markov sneered and delivered a vicious uppercut that clacked the other man's jaw together noisily and sent those baby blues rolling up in his head. Losing his grip on the ropes, the man fell over on his face with a *bang!* Markov kicked him in the ribs for good measure.

Sensing that it was over, Commander Johnson cleared her throat and said, "That didn't look like a fair fight, Councilor."

"It wasn't," Markov agreed, nodding to her as he ducked out of the ring and retrieved a bottle of water from a nearby table.

As Audrey watched, the councilor's opponent picked himself off the floor. Part of his face dangled from his chin, revealing a metal skeleton underneath.

"I thought androids weren't allowed on the *Liberty*," Audrey said, crossing over to the councilor.

"They're not. That model's not sentient. It's just a regular bot with realistic padding," he explained as he removed his gloves. Underneath she saw that he'd grazed his knuckles on his right hand. He unwrapped that hand and flexed his fingers a few times to make sure nothing was broken. Silvery metal gleamed where the skin was broken.

He'd lost both arms on Earth, back in 0 AB when Benevolence had emancipated all the androids. Adding insult to injury, he'd been arrested and dumped into the Mindscape for correctional purposes. Overnight, owning a brothel full of sex bots had become a crime.

Audrey took Markov's damaged hand in both of hers and raised it to her lips, kissing the broken skin.

"We need to keep up a professional appearance," he reminded her.

"That's not what you said when you came to my quarters last night," Audrey mused.

"That's different. What we do when we're off duty is our

business. While we're on the job, that's another matter."

"True, but I don't see anyone else in here, do you?"

"No, but—"

"Then shut your mouth, you big ox."

Markov fixed her with a shallow frown—his version of a smile.

"What are you doing here, Audrey?" he asked after she'd kissed his knuckles a few more times.

She looked up with a sigh. "You don't like to be doted on, do you?"

Markov grabbed both her hands and raised them above her head as he shoved her roughly against the wall. He pinned her hands above her head and kissed her roughly on the lips. "No, I don't like to be *mothered*," he replied.

"And why's that?" Audrey replied, trying to look defiant, despite the fact that he had her pinned to the wall. She wasn't used to being dominated by a man. It made her heart pound and sweat prickle on her skin, adrenaline surging for a fight.

"Because you're not my mother," he breathed, his lips tantalizingly close.

She smiled sweetly up at him, doing her best to look submissive.

As he leaned in for another kiss, she kneed him in the groin and swept his legs out from under him. He fell with a *thud* and lay blinking up at her with a pinched expression, his face turning red.

"You're going to pay for that," he gasped.

"Mmmm, I'm counting on it," she replied. "Unfortunately, we don't have the time right now."

Markov heaved off the ground with a grimace, bouncing lightly to his feet despite his size. Point three eight Gs was a lot less gravity than he was used to back on Earth.

"You still haven't answered my question," he growled. "What are you—"

"Doing here? You weren't answering your comms. You're needed on the Academy Level."

"I know."

"The new arrivals are about to choose their careers, and Mr. Jennings wants your help vetting the decisions."

Markov sighed. "I've still got hours to wait before they finish testing. Jennings has had it in for me ever since I stuck him with that job. Tell him I'll be right down."

Audrey nodded. "Yes, sir. I'll be in the CIC if you need me."

* * *

Remo Taggart withdrew a cigar and lighter from his duffel bag. He lit the cigar and began puffing spicy, fragrant smoke into the airlock. Then he produced a bottle of rum from the bag and passed it to his partner in crime, Desiree Dempsey. The squadron called her "Deedee" for short, which coincidentally also referred to some of her finest assets.

Deedee made a face as she took the bottle from him. "Rum? What the hell, *Romeo*? You couldn't find champagne? Beer?"

Remo blew out a cloud of smoke. "That's not just any rum. It's Zacappa. Best of the best from Earth. Try it."

Desiree cracked open the bottle and took a swig. Her frown melted into surprise. "Not half bad."

Remo grinned around his cigar. "Told ya." He yanked a pillow from his bag and placed it on the ground for Deedee to sit on. He sat beside her, and she waved away a cloud of cigar smoke, leaning away from him as she did so. "You're going to get us caught with that thing."

His grin vanished. He removed the cigar and held it up for her to study. "This *thing* is a Dominican. Best cigars ever made."

"I thought Cubans were the best cigars."

"Then you thought wrong. Anyway, there's no smoke detectors in the airlocks."

"So what happens when you open it?"

"We run like hell."

Deedee shrugged and took another swig of rum. She passed the bottle to him, and he gulped a few shots worth.

"I can't wait to get underway," he said. "All this waiting has me feeling like a zit-faced kid before the prom—sitting around hoping we didn't get all dressed up for nothing."

"Sounds like you're speaking from experience."

"Me?" He placed a hand on his chest and put on a roguish grin. "I was the one beating up those kids for staring at my cheerleader girlfriend."

"Sure."

He took another swig of rum and passed the bottle back. "Anyway, besides all that, we're a big ass target sitting up here in plain sight of Earth."

Deedee appeared to consider that as she took a sip. "The bots don't have anything to gain by stopping this mission."

"No? If they did, maybe they wouldn't have had to send their own colony ship all the way to Wolf 1061. Proxima's a whole lot closer."

"They might be planning to do that, anyway," she said.

"It'd mean war," he said, puffing out a cloud of cigar

smoke. "First one there gets to stick their flag in the mud and stake their claim."

"So you're suggesting they might start a war now, before we leave Sol, so that they'll avoid having to start one later?" Deedee looked skeptical. "That doesn't make any sense."

Remo shrugged and placed a hand on her knee, running it lightly up along her thigh.

She glanced at his hand. "What are you doing?"

He withdrew his cigar and stumped it out on the deck. "This," he said as he leaned in and kissed her. He could feel her pulling away, but he held her close, recognizing the difference between a pretense of resistance and the real thing. He laid her gently back on the deck, pinning her under him. Then he came up for air, and stared into her turquoise eyes.

"You taste like heaven," he said.

"That's the rum."

"Then why'd I reach for you instead of the bottle?"

Deedee cracked a smile. "There's the *Romeo* I signed on for. I was beginning to think your reputation had been exaggerated and you just brought me here to talk."

He grinned and leaned back down to kiss her neck while he fumbled with the seals of her jumpsuit. Her hands grabbed him below the waist and squeezed urgently. "Not nice to keep a girl waiting," she breathed.

When they were done, Remo waltzed out of the airlock with an insouciant grin on his face, his duffel bag slung over one arm, and Deedee hanging off the other.

"You two have a good time?" someone asked, stepping out from behind a bulkhead beside the airlock doors.

They both jumped with surprise. "Sergeant Torres..." he trailed off, feeling trapped beneath her glare. "What are you doing here?"

"Patrolling. How about you?" she asked, jerking her chin to the bag in his hand.

He shrugged, trying to appear nonchalant. "On our way to a sparring session with the rest of the squadron."

"What's in the bag?"

"This?" Remo's mind went blank. "Uh..."

"Training props," Deedee explained. "Padding, mouth guards, gloves—we're brushing up on hand-to-hand."

"I see. Mind if I take a look?" Torres asked, smirking.

"Not at all, Sergeant," Remo said. "But we are running late..."

"It'll just take a moment," Torres said as she reached for the duffel bag.

Deedee grabbed it from the other side. "All right, you win. There's no sparring session. The contents of the bag are private," she said.

Torres eyebrows hovered up, and her eyes narrowed. "You want a safe trip to Proxima?" She paused a beat, waiting for a reply, and Deedee nodded hesitantly. "Then there's no such thing as private."

"Come on Torres, you *know* me," Remo said.

The sergeant regarded him silently, her gaze so sharp it stabbed him repeatedly. "Exactly. Hand it over."

Remo grimaced and released the duffel bag. Torres opened it up and rifled through the contents. "A pillow... half a bottle of rum, and... what's this?" she withdrew a wooden box and opened it to find his lighter and half-finished cigar inside. "You were *smoking* in the airlock?" she demanded, shaking the contraband in his face.

He gave no reply.

"I'm going to have your wings for this, Remo. Hands behind your back."

"Come on, Torres, who's it hurt?"

She shot him an incredulous look as she took the cuffs off her belt. "There's oxygen tanks in the airlocks, dumb-ass. All you need is a leak and an open flame, and you could blow a hole in the side of the ship."

"Come on, Torres, you and I both know the concentration of oxygen you'd need in the airlock for that to happen is way higher than you'd get from a leaky tank."

Torres slapped cuffs on him and grabbed him roughly by his arm. "I forgot to mention that you have the right to remain silent. And you—" she said, turning to Deedee. "I hope you had a good time."

Deedee thrust out her chin and said, "I don't think that's any of your business, Sergeant."

She shrugged. "Maybe not, but from one woman to another—a few weeks ago he was fucking me in that airlock. Now it's your turn. Pretty soon it will be someone else's. You're just the flavor of the month, girl."

Remo watched Deedee's eyes flash at that, but she held her tongue.

"The only reason I'm not arresting you, too, is because I've been in your position, and that's punishment enough."

Deedee glanced at him, then back to Torres.

Remo shrugged and offered up a guilty grin. "Hell hath no fury..."

"Shut up, *Romeo*," Torres said, jerking his arm as if it were a leash. "Let's go."

In that instant, the lights in the corridor dimmed and flashed a bloody red. A battle siren roared to life, and the intercom crackled out with, "General quarters, general quarters! All hands to battle stations! All passengers belt in at emergency stations. This is not a drill. Repeat, all hands to battle stations! This is not a drill."

Remo jerked out of the sergeant's grip and shot her an urgent look. "Take 'em off, Sarge! I gotta get to my bird!"

Torres held his gaze, hesitating. "Don't think I'm letting this go," she said as she hurried to uncuff him.

"Wouldn't dream of it," he replied, mentally triggering a NanoCleanse from his adrenal implant to clear the alcohol from his system. As soon as his hands were free, he and Deedee sprinted down the corridor to the nearest drop tube.

CHAPTER 5

"Everyone please find your loved ones and take a seat," Councilor Markov announced from the podium in the center of the auditorium.

Catalina mentally searched for Alexander with her ARCs. A split second later, a green silhouette appeared, highlighting him through the crowd. He was on the other end of the room from her. She walked along the bleachers, pushing through the crowd to get to him.

She was anxious to learn the results of his tests. What careers had he chosen? They'd talked about it over breakfast, but he hadn't given her anything to go on, saying that he wanted to see what his options were and then he'd decide, which was completely unfair, because she'd told him right off what she wanted to be: section councilor or corridor prefect.

Her last job on Earth had been League Party Senator, so she wasn't ignorant of the requirements. She'd enjoyed the responsibility—the feeling that she could make a difference in people's lives, and with the *Liberty* they had a chance to write a new constitution, to organize a new and better government. Who wouldn't want to be a part of that?

A woman shoved past Catalina, almost knocking her over. "Hey!" Catalina said.

The woman turned to face her from the aisle. It was Esther. "Have you seen Benjamin?" she asked.

Catalina shook her head.

"I can't find him!"

"Maybe he's still in the testing rooms?"

Esther looked uncertain, her eyes wide and fearful.

Catalina walked up to her and reached for her hand. "Relax, we'll find him."

Then the room flashed crimson and a siren roared.

"General quarters, general quarters! All hands to battle stations! All passengers belt in at emergency stations. This is not a drill. Repeat, all hands to battle stations! This is not a drill."

Catalina blinked, frozen with momentary indecision.

People began shoving past Esther in their hurry to reach the auditorium walls, where emergency stations had been highlighted in red on their ARCs.

"All right everyone, there's no need to rush!" Councilor Markov barked out from the podium below. "You know the drill from your mission training. Please leave the bleachers in an orderly fashion as you head to the nearest emergency station."

Marines fanned out at the bottom of the bleachers, two below each aisle, directing people. Passengers shoved Catalina from behind, and she stumbled out into the aisle with Esther. The other woman gripped her by her shoulders. "I need to find Benjamin!" she shrieked to be heard above the rising tumult in the room.

"All right, just calm down!" Catalina said, trying not to fall over as people squeezed around her on all sides.

The intercom crackled once more. "All hands brace for emergency thrust!"

The auditorium erupted in chaos, everyone screaming at

each other as they pushed and shoved through the room.

"Everyone hit the deck right where you are!" Councilor Markov bellowed, but nobody listened.

Catalina felt her mag boots auto-activate, pinning her feet to the deck. She immediately overrode them and lunged back into the bleachers, ducking under them and laying her body flat. Esther stood in the aisle, frozen in place thanks to her boots. Catalina gestured urgently for the other woman to join her.

Then the entire ship lurched into motion. Despite their mag boots, a few people went flying from higher up. Someone's boot sailed into Esther's throat. Her eyes bulged, and then she vanished in a sea of flailing arms as people tried to steady themselves by grabbing one another.

* * *

Commander Audrey Johnson slumped into her chair with a flask full of coffee—her third one today. It was almost lunch time, but she was still waking up thanks to Councilor Markov's visit to her quarters last night. Audrey lifted the flask to her lips, taking a sip from the self-sealing lid.

In that instant, the shrill roar of the ship's battle siren assaulted her ears, sending adrenaline sparking through her veins. She almost spat her coffee all over her freshly-polished mag boots. The lights dimmed and flashed red, and then the intercom crackled with a general quarters alert.

"Commander!" her comm officer screeched. "We have an urgent comms from Admiral Urikov: an unidentified contact just appeared at the mouth of the Looking Glass. We're instructed to launch all fighters and drones in a defensive formation."

"Flight, you heard the man!" Audrey said.

"Aye, Commander. Pilots are scrambling."

"Target telemetry coming in from Section One..." Lieutenant Fields announced from sensors.

Audrey got up from her chair and walked up behind her sensors officer, sipping her coffee as she went. "Fields, get me a visual and put it on screen."

"Aye, Commander."

Everyone looked up from their stations as the main holo display switched from a 2D tactical map with colorful icons to a 3D telescopic view of the unidentified contact.

Black space and a dazzling array of stars filled the screen. Dead center of that was the Looking Glass. The wormhole looked like a perfectly clear glass marble distorting the surrounding starfield with its shape. Audrey spent a moment searching the screen, but there was nothing else there. A few tiny gray specks floated across the spherical mouth of the wormhole, but she knew those were Alliance and Solarian research stations.

"Where is it?" Audrey demanded.

The sensor officer shook her head. "According to the telemetry we received, it should be right there, ma'am."

"Well, it's not. Fields, use our sensors to double-check the coordinates."

"Yes, ma'am."

Audrey continued walking down the line of control stations. "Gunnery—report!"

"Weapons hot and awaiting target data," Lieutenant Gamble announced from the gunnery station.

"Commander!" It was Fields from sensors again.

Audrey spun around. "What is it, Lieutenant?"

"I've got nothing on sensors."

"What? Then where did our telemetry come from?"

"Section One, ma'am," Lieutenant Fields replied.

"And where did *they* get it?"

Fields didn't have a chance to reply. The deck shuddered underfoot and a distant rumble reached their ears. Audrey's eyes flew wide. "Engineering! Report!"

"I... we're detecting hull breaches in Section Eight!" Lieutenant Reed shrieked.

"From *what*? We didn't detect any weapons fire, did we?"

"No, ma'am!" Fields replied.

The intercom crackled with another announcement from Section One. "All hands brace for emergency thrust!"

Audrey lunged for her command chair, her entire body shaking with adrenaline. She fell into her chair and dropped her flask into the magnetic cup holder in the armrest.

"Secure all loose items!" she warned, reaching for her safety harness with trembling hands. She finished snapping the buckles together a split second before a sudden impulse from the engines pinned her into her seat. Audrey grimaced, thinking to herself that there hadn't been enough time for all the passengers and crew to belt in at emergency stations.

Hopefully there weren't too many injured.

* * *

Remo skidded to a stop in front of the drop tube. He opened the hatch via his neural link and nodded to Deedee. "Ladies first."

The overhead speakers buzzed with another warning: "All

hands brace for emergency thrust!"

Their mag boots auto-activated, and both of them dropped into emergency positions, sitting on their haunches and hugging their knees to their chests. In the next second, Remo felt an enormous weight pressing him toward the nearest bulkhead. His mag boots kept him rooted to the deck and locked his ankles to keep the stress off his joints. He gritted his teeth and counted up to ten to distract himself from the immense pressure.

"My boots won't lock!" Deedee screamed. "My ankles are going to break! I have to disengage!"

Remo looked up to see that they were about three meters from the nearest bulkhead. Their acceleration had to be at least one *G*, so if Deedee disengaged her mag boots now, it would be like taking a three meter fall back on Earth.

"You're going to break more than just your ankles if you disengage!"

"Screw it!" Deedee said.

Remo watched her go flying head-first toward the nearest bulkhead. She put out her hands at the last second, and screamed as her wrists broke. She hit her head anyway, and lapsed into silence as the ship's acceleration sprawled her out against the bulkhead and pinned her in place. Then that acceleration eased and Deedee slid down to the deck under 0.38 *G*s of artificial gravity.

"Fuck!" Remo roared. Mentally activating his comms, he said, "Section 7 Command, this is the CAG, I've got a pilot down, and I need a medical team at my location A-SAP!"

"CAG, this is Command, we acknowledge. Sending a medical team now."

* * *

"Damage report!" Audrey demanded.

"Sections Eight, Six, and One were all breached, Commander," Lieutenant Reed reported from engineering.

Audrey summoned the actual damage report from her control station and scanned the locations of those hull breaches.

Section Eight had been breached twice along the rings, while Sections Six and One were both pierced in three places each along the ship's stationary core. That struck her as strange, since it was much easier to hit the rings than the core. Whoever had shot them, they had to have been aiming for the core.

"So much for dodging a bullet," she muttered under her breath. It wasn't her place to question Admiral Urikov's decisions, but she couldn't help feeling like that execution of emergency thrust had done nothing but add to their casualties. "Sensors—do we have any idea of what hit us?"

"No, ma'am. Whatever it was, it didn't register on any of our grids."

Her brow furrowed as she considered that. "Invisible. Same as our mystery contact, then. How can Section One detect them if we can't?"

"Earth has ships in weapons range and they're lighting the target up with their lasers. We're tracking the vanishing points."

Audrey nodded. That explained why they hadn't seen anything on the telescopic view. Lasers were invisible in space and they were too far away for the *Liberty's* combat computer to bother simulating visuals.

"So whatever we're dealing with, it's EM-cloaked, and so are their weapons. That rules out a human origin, unless the Terran Alliance developed the tech in secret."

No one replied to that.

She directed her attention to the security control station where Major Bright sat. He served as both her XO and Section Seven's ranking Marine officer. "Major, get a team of VSM drones over to Section Eight to assess the damage and seal off our section from the rest of the ship until further notice."

"Aye aye, Commander," Bright replied.

The passengers and crew for Section Eight had yet to arrive, so it fell to them in Section Seven to inspect and repair the damage.

"Why send Marine drones?" Reed asked from engineering. "Shouldn't we send repair drones instead?"

"Not until we know what we're dealing with."

"Dealing with, ma'am?"

Audrey nodded to the main holo display. It showed a 2D tactical map. A bright blue icon marked the *Liberty's* position; bright green ones marked friendly Solarian ships, while yellow ones denoted Alliance ships from Earth, and a large, ambiguous red dot represented the enemy contact.

"Sensors—have we confirmed any casualties yet, Solarian or otherwise?" Audrey asked.

"No, ma'am," Fields replied.

"Yet we know the Alliance is firing on an invisible enemy, and we know that invisible objects punctured our hull in three different sections. If the enemy's objective were to destroy us, their opening volley should have done more than poke a few holes in our hull."

"You're afraid we've been boarded," Major Bright added

from the security station.

Audrey nodded slowly. "Let's hope I'm wrong, Major."

"I've got three casualties on the grid!" Fields reported.

"Where?" Audrey demanded.

"Commander! Incoming priority one transmission from Section One," Lieutenant Bates interrupted from the comms.

"Go ahead, comms."

"We've been ordered to abort launching all fighters and drones until further notice."

Audrey felt her brow furrow. "Flight, pass on the message. Tell our pilots to standby."

"Aye," Lieutenant Commander Ivanov replied.

"Fields, report!"

"Casualties are all fighters, ma'am—ours, from Section One. The incident report provides holo footage of the event."

"On screen," Audrey ordered.

The tactical map faded from the main screen, replaced by starry blackness. To either side of the camera she saw the ship's rotating rings and the spokes that connected them to the ship's stationary core. The recording zoomed in, and Audrey saw a glinting gray speck shoot out from the rotating ring section on the left. Soon after that another one shot out, and then a third. Audrey sat forward in her chair, squinting at the recording and wondering what to look for.

A sudden burst of light drew her eyes back to the lead fighter. A split second later, another explosion ripped through the void, and then the third fighter exploded with tentacles of fire. At that point, the recording froze, zoomed in, and rewound. They saw the moment of the first fighter's destruction in the gory detail of slow motion. A prolonged flash of light erupted, and hazy debris roared out in all directions. Or at least they should have.

The spread of the debris was wrong. As if reading her thoughts, the recording froze and re-wound once more. This time the debris was highlighted with bright green shading and vectors, and she noticed that the debris went leaping back toward the camera, as if it had hit an invisible wall and bounced off. *Not a wall—a ship,* Audrey thought.

"They're pacing us," she whispered.

CHAPTER 6

As soon as the *Liberty* stopped accelerating, Alexander used his ARCs to find his wife through the chaos. A green silhouette appeared, lying prone beneath the bleachers. His heart leaped into his throat, thinking Catalina had been trampled. He bounded past Marines directing people to emergency stations at the bottom of the bleachers. Medics tended to a handful of wounded on the stairs, but they were fewer than Alexander expected. By the time he reached the level where Catalina lay, she was already climbing to her feet. He snapped off the ARC overlay and held her at an arm's length, looking her over.

"Are you okay?"

She nodded, but her gaze slipped by him to one of the wounded on the stairs. It was Esther, Benjamin's mother. Her throat was bruised and swollen, her lips blue from hypoxia. She stared up at the ceiling, her eyes wide and lifeless.

The medic tending to her got up and shook his head. Catalina grabbed the man's arm before he could leave.

"Where are you going?"

He regarded her grimly. "Where I'm needed. I can't do anything more for her."

"So you're just going to leave her there?"

"Her mag boots will keep her in place for now."

"That's not what I meant."

"Ma'am, we're still at general quarters. You need to get to an emergency station."

The medic left them on that note and Catalina turned to Alex, her expression equal parts dismay and horror. "Where's Benjamin?"

Alexander grimaced and looked around, using his ARCs to search for the boy—now an orphan thanks to whatever freak accident had killed his mother. He found the kid through the walls of the auditorium in an adjoining room.

"Follow me," he said, grabbing Catalina's hand and running down the stairs to the bottom of the bleachers. A pair of Marines standing there directed them to emergency stations along the walls. Alexander nodded and pretended to head toward them, but as soon as they were past the Marines, he abruptly changed directions, moving toward Benjamin's ARC silhouette. A door slid open revealing Benjamin and a young girl huddled around a black box, what looked to be some kind of portable speaker for music.

Alexander wondered what they were doing listening to music at a time like this. Both kids looked up sharply as he and Catalina walked in. They looked frightened.

Catalina went down on her haunches in front of Benjamin and grabbed him by his shoulders. "Ben, you need to come with us."

"What is it?" he asked, his eyes flicking between Catalina and Alexander. "Are we in trouble?"

"We only hid in here because of the alarm," the girl added. "We didn't touch anything. I swear!"

"You're not in trouble. It's about your mother, Ben," Catalina explained.

"What about her?"

"There was an accident, and..." Catalina's face crumpled and she pulled him into a tight embrace. "It's going to be okay. We'll be there for you," she said, her voice thick and muffled with sorrow.

Understanding dawned in Benjamin's eyes, and he looked up at Alexander. "She's dead, isn't she?"

Alexander hesitated, trying to think of some way to sugarcoat it for him, but there wasn't one. "I'm sorry, kid."

The little girl standing beside Benjamin burst into tears, but he remained stoic, wide-eyed and blinking.

Alexander nodded to a nearby wall marked with flashing red triangles to denote emergency stations. "We need to belt in before they decide to use the engines again." He walked over to the wall and yanked down on one handle after another, folding out four chairs. He helped the kids to belt in before taking a seat beside his wife.

Catalina reached for his hand and held on tight. "What do you think is going on?" she asked.

He shook his head. "I wish I knew."

* * *

"Section One is instructing us to sound out any invisible targets by firing our lasers in three hundred and sixty degree arcs," Lieutenant Bates said from the comms. "We're to fire on their mark and track the vanishing points, same as what Earth's fleet has been doing."

"Gunnery—weapons free. Stand by to fire," Audrey ordered, hoping that whatever was hiding out there it wouldn't choose to fire back on them. It was Admiral Urikov's call, but it felt like a bad one to her.

"Aye, weapons free," Lieutenant Gamble replied.

"What if they fire back?" Major Bright asked from his station, his thoughts mirroring hers.

Audrey set her jaw. "Lieutenant Fields, has the target we identified at the Looking Glass returned fire on Earth's fleet?"

"No, ma'am."

"Then let's hope that whatever we accidentally hit, they'll respond just as passively."

"Mark!" Bates called out from the comms.

"Open fire!" Commander Johnson ordered.

"Lasers firing..." Gamble said from gunnery.

Simulated green and yellow laser beams snapped out on the main holo display, dazzling Audrey's eyes.

"Switch MHD to tactical view," she said, giving a verbal command to her control station.

A top-down, 2D map appeared on the main display, and Audrey saw the ship's lasers vanishing abruptly to all sides of the *Liberty*.

"What the hell?" she muttered under her breath.

"Multiple enemy contacts!" Fields reported. "We're surrounded!"

"Cease fire! Cease fire! Section One orders Weapons hold!" Bates called out from the comms.

"Aye, weapons hold!" Gamble acknowledged.

"Mapping the vanishing points..." Fields put in from sensors.

Audrey toggled a 3D version of the tactical map and used her hands to manipulate the display, rotating it around the *Liberty*. An open cylinder of yellow dots appeared around the ship, each one marking a point where a laser had been fired and abruptly cut off by an unseen obstacle.

"They must be flying an entire fleet of ships around us in a tight formation," Major Bright said from the security station.

Audrey nodded slowly as she studied the cylindrical pattern of dots on the tactical map. "Or... just one very big ship."

"In the shape of a hollow cylinder?" Bright replied.

"It would have to be unbelievably large," Fields added from sensors. "At least five kilometers in diameter with a length of more than ten. No ship ever built is that large."

"That we know of," Audrey said. "How else do you explain the uniform distribution? Our lasers all vanished at exactly the same distance." Audrey nodded down to her XO. "Major, do we have any news from the drones we sent to Section Eight?"

"Not yet. Almost there, Commander."

"What's the point of surrounding us if they're not going to fire back?" Lieutenant Gamble asked.

Audrey set her jaw. "The same reason they breached our hull, but didn't cause any major damage in the process. They're trying to capture us, not destroy us. Flight Ops—I want eyes on our hull breaches from the outside. Have our pilots launch a pair of drones on remote links and put the holofeeds on screen."

"Aye, Commander," Lieutenant Commander Ivanov replied.

* * *

Remo glared out the cockpit of his Phantom IV fighter at the dimly-lit launch tube, his whole body itching with anticipation. It was hard to know if that feeling was real. All the visuals and interfaces inside the cockpit were virtual, while his physical body floated in a *G*-tank pumped full of ICE (Inertial Compensation Emulsion) to buffer the effects of extreme acceleration. Without that, pulling more than ten *G*s for anything but the briefest periods would turn him into jelly.

"Raven Lead, this is Section Seven Command—you are ordered to remote launch two drones and inspect the damage to our hull. Be advised, an invisible, cylindrical barrier has encased the *Liberty* at a range of 1900 meters."

Remo frowned. *An invisible cylindrical what?* "Acknowledged, Command. Launching drones." Switching to the squadron frequency, he said, "Lieutenant King, you're on my wing in Mosquito Drone 218. We're cleared for a recon flight."

"Roger that!" King commed back.

Remo switched his virtual viewpoint from the cockpit of his Phantom Mark IV to that of Mosquito Drone 217. The virtual cockpit of the drone was cramped and circular, like an eyeball. A weapon hardpoint jutted out below the cockpit, long and pointed—affectionately known as the *stinger*.

As he went through the automated pre-flight check, a robotic voice echoed in his ears: "Navigation systems online. Weapons online. Engines online—" An accompanying roar of thruster tests accompanied that statement, making the cockpit rumble and shake. "—All systems green. Magnetic catapult initiating."

The launch tube ahead of him lit up with the yellow bars of mag boosters above, and two bright red lines below to mark the launch track. Metallic clanking sounds echoed through the cockpit as the doors at the end of the launch tube opened up. "Launching in three—"

"Hang on to your crown, King," Remo quipped over the comms.

"—two, one."

The catapult released.

Remo felt his guts flip as acceleration virtually pinned him to his chair. Red and yellow lights flickered through the cockpit, faster and faster, and then...

Nothing but an infinity of stars and wide-open space. Except it wasn't wide or open—something had caged the *Liberty* in.

"Woohoo!" King crowed.

"Lets head to the first waypoint," Remo replied as he jerked the flight stick sharply to one side, flipping back the way he'd come and bringing the *Liberty* into view.

"Roger," King said.

He set the throttle to 10% and acceleration pressed him back against his chair once more as the Mosquito rocketed forward. Up ahead an open green diamond marked their waypoint, the range ticking down from five hundred meters.

Remo magnified the area at the waypoint and a hole appeared in the otherwise pristine curvature of the *Liberty's* hull. Section Eight had been breached all right. The hull had crumpled inward in the shape of a crater, but there were no obvious signs of blast damage.

"Command, this is Mosquito 217, are you getting this?"

"All eyes are on you, 217. Get us a close-up as you fly by."

"Roger." Remo hauled back on the throttle as he drew near, making sure he captured every possible detail.

"It's like the hull is made of dough and someone stuck their finger in it," King said.

Remo nodded. "Damage isn't extensive, but it looks like it goes through several decks. Some kind of armor-piercing rounds, maybe?" They flew past the first waypoint and on to the next, this one on the other side of Section Eight. Remo rolled his fighter over and followed the curvature of the *Liberty's* hull until another green diamond appeared.

"Coming up on the second waypoint," Remo announced.

This time he flew slower and closer to the hull. He planned to stop and hover above the damage, maybe even fly through the breach if cleared to do so.

Lieutenant King rocketed out overhead, singing a vulgar song from a popular Martian band. Just as he was getting to the good part, a flash of light obscured his drone from view. When it faded, King's drone was gone.

King came back on the comms, cursing, and Remo sailed through a pelting rain of debris from his drone.

The command channel crackled with, "217, report!"

"I've lost 218. No sign of what hit him. Coming up on the second waypoint now..."

Remo slowed right down as he came to the damage. Again, the hull breach was crater-shaped.

"Still no signs of blast damage, Command. Permission to enter the breach?"

"Standby, 217..."

Remo crept slowly forward, anticipating his request would be granted.

Bang!

He leapt against his flight restraints, and they dug roughly into his shoulders and chest. His neural connection flickered as the primary comm array took damage. The backup array took over a split second later, and he was back. Remo saw the *stinger* was crumpled into a useless mess under his drone.

"What the hell?!" he roared.

"What happened, 217?"

Remo shook his head, his gaze flicking over the various displays inside the cockpit. The nav showed him sailing backward at four meters per second. "I appear to have collided with something," he said, but sensors showed he was too far from the *Liberty*, and there was nothing else nearby. "Something invisible," he added.

"Light it up, 217. We need to know what's there."

"Roger. Arming cannons." Fortunately he'd only lost his lasers with the crumpled *stinger*.

Reversing thrust to put some distance between him and whatever was out there, Remo passed his targeting reticle over the empty space where he'd hit an invisible wall. He let loose a short burst of fire and bright golden hypervelocity rounds shot out in staggered lines to either side of his cockpit. They collided with something invisible and flashed brightly as they exploded into clouds of microscopic shrapnel. He waited for those miniature explosions to fade, hoping he'd made a dent in whatever cloaking armor the target had, but nothing happened.

"There's something there all right," he said.

"Try to find out where it begins and ends. We'll track the impacts from here."

"Acknowledged," Remo said. This time he held the trigger down for a sustained burst. The simulated roar of cannon fire rumbled through the cockpit as he tracked his targeting reticle back and forth. Rounds exploded with continuous bursts of light, but at the more extreme angles his fire sailed on unhindered, marking the peripheral bounds of the target.

From there, Remo tracked his targeting reticle away from the *Liberty's* hull. Hypervelocity rounds exploded all along that line, tracking furiously upward until the explosions grew too far away for him to see whether he was hitting or missing.

"Weapons hold, 217."

"Roger that. What's it look like, Command?"

He didn't have time to hear the reply. Suddenly he was back in his Phantom IV, staring down the launch tube. "Damn it! Command—what the hell happened out there?"

"All outbound comms are being jammed, Raven One. You were disconnected from the drone. Please stand by for further orders."

"Acknowledged, standing by..."

CHAPTER 7

"It almost looks like one of the spokes between the *Liberty's* rings and her core," Fields said from sensors, pointing to the main holo display where a long line of yellow dots protruded from the Liberty's hull.

Commander Audrey Johnson considered that. Each dot marked an impact from one of Mosquito 217's hypervelocity cannons. Collectively the impacts traced what looked like a giant spear sticking out of the *Liberty's* hull.

"Incoming comms from Admiral Urikov," Lieutenant Bates announced.

"On screen," Audrey said. *They must have finished analyzing the recon data,* she thought. "Admiral," she said, inclining her head to him as he appeared. Dim red battle mode lighting on the bridge cast his features into sharp relief, and the lower half of his face all but disappeared under his shadowy beard.

"Commander. It appears that we may have been breached by some kind of... boarding tubes. I've deployed marines to guard the breaches, but so far nothing's tried to come through, and our preliminary inspections haven't told us anything we don't already know. There's something there, but it's completely invisible to anything but direct physical contact."

Audrey nodded. "The VSM drones I sent to Section Eight found the same thing. I've sealed off all the bulkheads between us and the rest of the ship as a precautionary measure."

"Good. I've informed Admiral Rathers of the situation, and the First and Second Fleets are moving into position. Until then, we're going to attempt to break free using our thrusters. I doubt a few boarding tubes will be able to stop us, especially not if they're as long and slender as your data indicates."

Audrey nodded. "I agree, sir."

The admiral turned aside from the camera and said, "Helm, ahead fifty percent, ramp up slowly."

The helmsman's muffled reply came back over the holofeed, "Aye, fifty percent ahead."

A soft, but persistent thrumming rumbled through the walls and floor of the ship. Audrey waited, her pulse racing. She expected to hear Lieutenant Reed call out the damage from the engineering station, but nothing happened.

"Engineering, report!" the admiral bellowed, obviously just as confused as she was.

"Nothing to report, sir," came the chief engineer's reply.

"We're not moving," the helmsman reported.

The admiral's expression clouded darkly. "All ahead full!"

"Aye, all ahead full..."

Audrey waited, expecting to hear that they'd broken free, or to feel the deck suddenly leap out from under her, the acceleration pinning her to her chair.

But nothing happened.

"Our speed's not increasing, Admiral," the helmsman added.

"How is that possible?" Audrey asked. "If we're accelerating, then our forward velocity has to increase—that's

Newton's first law of motion."

"Maybe we're not *actually* accelerating," Admiral Urikov replied. "The engines might be damaged, or else whatever is surrounding us somehow detected our acceleration and it's exerting an equal force in the opposite direction."

"That would only double the stress on whatever rods or tubes they have holding us in place," Audrey said. "Even if those structures are made from materials of infinite strength, they'd rip straight through our hull and out the other side. Our engines must be disabled. What happened when we executed emergency thrust?"

"It worked," Admiral Urikov said. "We accelerated up to fifty meters per second and then killed the engines. Somehow the engines must have stopped working between then and now. I'll have engineering look into it. Until we find out more, make sure you keep your section sealed. Section One out."

Audrey scowled as the admiral disappeared and the tactical view of the *Liberty* returned. Something very strange was going on.

"Ma'am... I'm getting some unusual readings from sensors."

"What kind of readings, Fields?"

"Negative gravitational lensing, dead ahead. It just came out of nowhere!"

"Speak *English*, Lieutenant."

"It's a wormhole, ma'am. Range at 4,950 klicks and dropping."

"The Looking Glass? How the hell did we get all the way over there already?"

"No, ma'am. That's still almost five hundred thousand klicks away."

"You're telling me *another* wormhole just magically appeared beside the first? Is that even possible?"

"The first one magically appeared sometime during the last century. This might be a continuation of whatever phenomenon spawned it."

Electricity sparked in Audrey's fingertips as adrenaline saturated her blood. "If that wormhole is directly ahead of us, are we on a collision course with it?"

"No, ma'am. We're still orbiting Mars. At the nearest point between our orbits we should only come within about 2,000 klicks."

"Check that, Lieutenant."

"Checking... wait. No, I'm wrong. That can't be right."

Audrey felt suddenly cold. "What is it, Fields?"

"We're accelerating toward the wormhole at more than fifteen Gs."

"We'd be blacking out if that were true."

"Aye. Our sensors must be mis-calibrated."

"First our engines stop working and now our sensors? Engineering—"

"Yes, ma'am?" Lieutenant Reeds replied.

"Have you detected any damage to those systems?"

"No, ma'am."

"Okay... hypothetically speaking, if our inertia were to be somehow compensated or removed from the equation, how would the ship be able to measure its own acceleration?"

"We'd have to extrapolate it from our range to nearby objects or celestial bodies."

"Celestial bodies like a wormhole. Bates, get me Admiral Urikov on the comms!"

Admiral Urikov appeared on the main holo display a split

second later. Audrey sucked in a deep breath. "Admiral, please tell me we've fixed the engines and we're the ones accelerating toward that wormhole."

"What wormhole?"

"My sensor officer detected a second wormhole directly in front of us. Something about negative gravitational lenses."

"*Negative gravitational lensing,*" Admiral Urikov corrected. He summoned a holo display to life on his end to check for himself, his features bathed in a cold blue light. "Incredible..." he breathed, shaking his head.

"What's even more incredible is that we're headed straight for it at over fifteen *G*s and I can still wave my hands in front of my face. We have *zero* detectable acceleration, Admiral."

"That would explain why our engines didn't appear to work."

"So our engines work, but the laws of physics don't? For all intents and purposes we no longer have any inertia."

The admiral gave a thoughtful frown. "It seems more likely to suggest that our sensors *and* our engines don't work. If true, it should be easy enough to check. Please hold, Commander, while I contact Admiral Rathers to confirm our speed and heading."

The main display went to a waiting screen with the Solarian flag on it, and Audrey scowled. "Fields, how long before we reach the wormhole?"

"According to our sensors—one minute and fifty seven seconds."

"That fast?"

"We were already headed toward it thanks to our orbital velocity."

"Put the time on the clock, and get me a visual of the

wormhole."

"Yes, ma'am."

A green timer appeared above the main display, counting down from 1:42, and then the tactical map switched to a glassy, bubble-shaped orb full of stars floating in an otherwise nondescript patch of space. The bubble-shape came from a bright halo of light around the inner rim of the wormhole's "mouth." Audrey spent a moment watching it grow larger until it all but filled the main display.

"Fields, what magnification are we at?"

"No magnification, ma'am."

"Then the mouth must be hundreds of kilometers wide!"

Admiral Urikov re-appeared before Fields could reply. His expression was grim. "I can't reach Admiral Rathers—or anyone else for that matter. Our comms can't get past the jamming, but I have been able to verify that we *are* accelerating. I launched a pair of drones to check, and as soon as they left our hull, they began falling away behind us at a rate of one hundred and eighty-two meters per second."

"That's over eighteen *G*s of acceleration!" Audrey said. "We should all be dead by now!"

"And yet we are not."

Audrey's eyes snapped up to the timer above the main display. Forty seconds. "What's happening with the First and Second Fleets? They must have seen what's happening."

"They're breaking off."

Audrey blinked. "They're giving up on us?"

"There may be a reason for that. We received a comms back when this all started. After receiving it, I triggered the emergency thrust to try and get away from whatever's ensnared us."

Audrey shook her head. "You knew we'd been captured?"

"I didn't *know* anything, but I had reason to believe that whatever's out there, it might be trying to dock with us. It turns out I was right, but it was already too late."

"What did the message say?"

A dialog popped up before her eyes, requesting to transfer the current conversation to her ARCs and neural link so that the rest of the crew wouldn't overhear what was said. She accepted the request and Admiral Urikov vanished from the main display, appearing instead on her ARCs.

"Listen for yourself," he replied. *"Be advised, this transmission is restricted to only the highest levels of clearance."*

Audrey nodded and listened as a hum of comm interference started up inside her head, followed by a human voice.

"My name is Captain White. Some of you will remember me as the Captain of the Intrepid, *a mission we sent to Wolf 1061 more than a century ago. What we discovered there was beyond our wildest dreams. We are not alone in the universe, and I have returned as an ambassador. Please do not be alarmed. The ones who travel with me are here to help us. We have been invited to join their Federation, and as a gesture of good faith, they have agreed to help the colonists aboard the* Liberty *reach their destination in a matter of days rather than the years it would have otherwise taken. Again, please do not be alarmed. We come in peace."*

Audrey opened and shut her mouth repeatedly, gulping in air like a guppy. Words failed her.

"I need to try to explain all of this to the other section commanders," Urikov said. *"I'm going to set condition yellow while we figure out what we're going to do."*

"What we're going to do?!" Audrey echoed. *"We need to hit*

them with everything we've got before it's too late!"

Admiral Urikov's eyebrows floated up. *"You don't trust the Captain's message?"*

"It might not be him, but even if it is, the last communication anyone has from the Intrepid *was a threat."*

"You know about the mission?"

"It's public knowledge, Admiral."

"Yes, but ancient history."

"Not anymore," Audrey said, a muscle twitching in her jaw. *"We can't trust this. We need to break free before they take us through that wormhole. For all we know they're taking us to their homeworld where they're going to enslave us all. If we focus all of our firepower on those... tubes that are holding us in place, then maybe we can sever them and get out of here."*

"I don't think that would be wise."

"What do you mean?"

"I mean, an invisible starship bigger than anything we've ever seen or built has us skewered in a dozen different places, and they're dragging us into a wormhole that they probably created. Not to mention, as you pointed out, they've somehow found a way to suspend the laws of physics in ways that we can only dream about. No, Commander—" The admiral shook his head. *"—we're not going to poke that bear. We've pushed our luck as it is by sounding them out with our weapons. I think the only reason they didn't fire back at us is that our guns are too weak to do any real damage to them."*

"Then we should evacuate. If those drones you launched could escape, it means we could evacuate the crew using the shuttles they came in on."

"The drones didn't escape."

"I thought you said..."

"I said they fell away behind us at a rate of more than one

hundred and eighty meters per second. Soon after that they exploded on an invisible wall a few klicks aft of our position. The previously open ends of the ship that surrounds us are now shut, and we suspect that's the reason we've lost comms contact with the fleet."

"What about sensors?"

"Their EM cloak is just as effective from the inside as the out. It's passing visible light straight through, so we can still see what's happening around us."

"Then we should be able to receive radio waves, too."

"Unfortunately that's not the case."

"Maybe they don't want it to be the case, and they've purposely cut us off."

Admiral Urikov inclined his head to her. "It's certainly a possibility."

Audrey blinked. "What are we going to do?"

"Right now we're going to stay calm and keep this quiet. We do not need anyone else finding out about this."

"Ma'am—I'm sorry to interrupt..." Lieutenant Fields began.

Audrey glanced over at his station. "What is it, Fields?"

"We've just entered the wormhole."

Audrey grimaced. "Thank you, Lieutenant, please keep me posted."

Admiral Urikov shook his head. *We wanted to travel between the stars..."*

"Not like this," Audrey replied, using her neural link again. *"No, not like this."*

"If you want me to keep this quiet, we need a cover story," Audrey added. "People are going to ask what the General Quarters was about. What do I tell them? We can't say it was a drill when we have multiple hull breaches."

"*No... no, we can't,*" the admiral replied while stroking his beard thoughtfully. "*Governor Chong and I will come up with something.*"

Audrey nodded. "*What if rumors about what actually happened start to surface?*"

"*Who would believe them? I barely believe it, and I witnessed the whole thing.*

"*Maybe we should just tell people the truth.*"

"*And have a full-scale riot when people realize that aliens have taken us hostage and they're dragging us off to their homeworld for some sinister purpose?*" The admiral shook his head.

Audrey gulped, and he went on, "*Best to keep people in the dark for now. Wish me luck. I have another five conversations like this one to get through with the other section commanders before I can get back to figuring out what the hell is going on.*"

"*Good luck, sir,*" Audrey replied as the admiral's face faded from the screen.

Back was the view from their bow cameras. It showed them plummeting down the throat of a wormhole, the starfield warped around them in a vaguely spherical shape. Audrey stared at a dim knot of stars in the center of the holoscreen, wondering if they were shining out from the other side of the wormhole, and if so, where that other side was.

She shook her head slowly. *What the hell is going on?*

PART 2 - CONTAGION

"Disease often comes with a smiling face."

—Dejan Stojanovic

CHAPTER 8

Alexander heard the overhead speakers crackle with, "Set condition yellow throughout the ship. Repeat, set condition yellow throughout the ship. All hands please remain seated with your restraints securely fastened."

"What's that mean?" Catalina whispered.

Alexander turned to her. Both Benjamin and the young girl sitting beside him were also waiting for his answer.

"It means the danger's passing," he said.

"What was it?" the little girl asked.

Alexander shook his head. "Hopefully they'll tell us soon."

They passed the next ten minutes without speaking, their hearts beating against the silence. Then came another announcement.

"This is Governor Chong. By now you all know that we came under attack. The danger has passed, but our engines and comms were damaged. Unfortunately, I am told that the repairs will take some time. The attack appears to have come from a rogue android fleet. Our hull was breached in Sections One, Six, and Eight with what we fear may have been biological weapons. The threat is contained, but as a precaution all sections have been quarantined from one another until further notice, and as such, we will not be taking on any more shuttles, nor will any be allowed to leave this ship."

Alexander heard a rumble of discontent come shivering through the doors to the auditorium.

As if the governor had anticipated the effect her words would have, she added, "Please remain calm. As I said, the danger has passed, and any pathogens contained. The quarantine is just a precaution. This is only a brief hiccup along the way to our destiny in the stars, and I'm sure it will all be resolved soon.

"With that said, I am setting condition green throughout the ship, and you may all now leave your emergency stations and go about your business. If you're not sure what that business is, or if you have any further questions, please speak to your section prefects. Have a good rest of the day everyone. Governor Chong out."

Alexander unbuckled from his emergency station and rose to his feet. The chair he'd been seated on folded automatically back against the wall. Catalina got up, too, followed by Benjamin and finally the girl beside him.

Catalina walked up to her. "What's your name?"

"Jessica," she replied.

"Do you need help finding your family?"

She shook her head, sending curly brown hair bobbing over her shoulders.

"Well, I think I'd feel better if we took you back to them."

"Okay," Jessica said, as Catalina took her hand and led her toward the doors of the auditorium.

Alexander studied Ben, and hesitated, thinking about the boy's mother lying dead on the stairs. He might need to see her at some point, but not like *that*. "We'll wait here for you," he decided.

Catalina glanced his way and nodded her agreement. The doors swished open and they breezed through into a noisy, chaotic mess of people getting organized in the wake of the governor's announcement.

As the door slid shut behind them, Ben spoke up. "I want my mom."

Alexander saw tears glistening in Ben's eyes. The shock was wearing off, reality setting in. He went down on his haunches and grabbed the boy's shoulder. "I know, kid," he said. "She's... she's in a better place," he decided, without really believing it.

Ben sniffled and wiped his eyes on the sleeves of his jumpsuit. Looking up at Alexander with shining brown eyes, he said, "That means this place is a worser one."

Good point. "Do you have any other family on board?"

Benjamin shook his head. "Uncle Tom, but he was assigned to Section Ten."

"Okay. Well, Section Ten hasn't arrived yet, and with the quarantine, it might be a little while before he gets here, so that means you're with us for now. That okay with you?"

Benjamin nodded.

Alexander summoned a grim smile. "Don't worry. You're with the lion now, kid. Better start working on your roar. Let's hear it."

Benjamin just stared blankly back at him. *Not in the mood for joking around. Fair enough.* He gave Benjamin's shoulder a reassuring squeeze. "We'll take good care of you, kid."

* * *

Remo was still inside his cockpit when he heard Governor

Chong's speech, so no one was around to hear him call bullshit. He'd been just about to start shouting that from the rooftops when a priority one memo came over his comms, text only.

Top secret

Do not discuss or share any first or second-hand information which might seem to contradict the governor's announcement. Spreading rumors will lead to immediate court-martial.

End of message.

"Everybody *loves* a good cover-up...." Remo grumbled.

Feeling his weight pressing uncomfortably against his flight harness, he swung his legs *down* and planted his feet on the front wall of his G-tank to take the weight off while he unbuckled. The harness auto-retracted to the walls and he reached over his head for the bottom rung of the ladder leading back *up* the drop tube behind his Phantom IV's ball-shaped cockpit.

Remo looked up to see that the hatch in the back of the cockpit already lay open in anticipation of his exit, revealing a long, brightly-lit tunnel disappearing endlessly above his head. In this case, *endless* meant the entire length of the ship's radius from the rings to the core—a distance of some six hundred meters. Recessed rungs marked notches in the walls of the tube, while color-coded circles between some of those rungs marked hatches leading to the ship's various decks. The nearest hatch was military red—the hangar—followed by white—the Command Deck.

Remo hauled himself up out of his G-tank and began to climb. His exposed skin itched with sticky residues from the *ICE* inside the tank, but a shower would have to wait. He had more urgent business to attend to.

As he reached the glowing white hatch leading to the command deck, he had to resist the urge to open it and go demand some answers from Commander Johnson.

Pointless. If his part in things was classified, then hers had to be, too, and whatever information she and the rest of CIC might be privy to, they wouldn't be allowed to share it.

After climbing past eight color-coded hatches, Remo finally stopped at the second-to-last hatch in sight, marked by a sapphire-blue circle—*Med/Sci.* He hoped by now Deedee would be awake and ready to receive visitors. Climbing out through the hatch, he made his way to the reception area for patients.

As soon as he arrived, he asked about Deedee. The receptionist told him she had just come out of surgery and wasn't awake yet, so he took a seat in the visitors' lobby and waited. Half an hour passed before a nurse came and led him to Deedee's room.

Remo found her lying in bed with both her arms elevated above the bed in bulky casts.

"Hey, you," Remo said as he walked up beside her bed. "How are you feeling?"

"How do you think?" she asked.

The nurse left them with a tight smile, and the door slid shut behind her.

"Right, stupid question. You in any pain?"

"They've got me high on meds, so no, not yet, but my nose itches like hell. I've been trying to scratch it with my tongue. No luck as yet."

Remo gave a crooked smile. "How's your head?"

"Concussed, but no permanent damage."

"That's good," Remo said, looking around the room.

"What did I miss?" Deedee asked.

"Didn't you hear the Governor's speech?"

"No, but a nurse filled me in—rogue rebel androids, bio-weapons, and a ship-wide quarantine. Crazy. You manage to bag a few bots for me?"

Remo shook his head. "We never got clearance to launch." He looked around her room as if to take in his surroundings. There was a holoscreen at the foot of her bed, a visitor's chair mag-bolted to the deck in one corner, and a bunch of medical equipment clustered around her bed, all beeping rhythmically in time to her vital signs. He also managed to glimpse the glassy black eye of a security camera watching them from the ceiling.

"Seems pretty cozy here," he said. "Do they allow visitors to spend the night?"

Deedee fixed him with a dry look. "You can't stop thinking about sex for one second, can you?"

He grinned. "Want to know what I'm thinking about right now?"

"Not particularly."

Grinning lasciviously, he leaned in close and whispered beside her ear. "Act like I'm saying something dirty and listen up: the governor is full of shit. A giant invisible starship somehow encapsulated ours. Our weapons have had no effect on it, and they've breached our hull in multiple sections with some kind of boarding tubes. The quarantine is in place to keep whatever's on board that ship from getting aboard ours. This is all classified, so best keep it that way or I'll be facing a court-martial."

"Fuck me..." Deedee gasped.

He leaned away and shook his head, grinning once more.

"Wish I could, darling, but that'll have to wait until you're better."

CHAPTER 9

Councilor Markov stormed into the CIC, dragging a pair of Marine corporals, one hanging off each of his inhumanly strong prosthetic arms. "What's going on here, Commander?"

"You can't be in here, sir!" one of the corporals said through gritted teeth.

"The hell I can't! Commander! Call off your dogs before I have to put them down."

Audrey turned to look. "It's okay, Corporal. Clearance codes just came through. The councilor is cleared to be in here again."

"Yes, ma'am," one of the Marines said as they let the Councilor go and marched back to their guard positions outside the doors.

"Well?" Markov demanded, stopping beside her chair.

Audrey got up and nodded to the main display where a funnel-shaped wireframe had been overlaid on the starfield ahead of them.

"What am I looking at?"

"The wormhole we're traveling down."

"The what?"

Audrey summarized recent events, but omitted the part about the transmission from Captain White. She used the tactical map to show Markov the cylindrical shape of the vanishing points they'd mapped around the *Liberty*, as well as the long, skinny boarding tube that had punctured their hull in Section Eight.

"So the Governor's announcement was a lie," the councilor said, his eyebrows beetling like a pair of black caterpillars.

"We have tens of thousands of civilians on board," Audrey explained. "We have to avoid inciting a panic for as long as we can."

The councilor nodded. "Okay, so now what? We've been captured by a mystery ship and they're dragging us through a wormhole to parts unknown."

Audrey nodded. "Our only saving grace so far is that they haven't made any aggressive moves toward us."

"Taking us hostage isn't aggressive?"

Audrey was about to reply when something changed on the main holo display. The section of space ahead of them abruptly vanished, replaced by a blank black screen.

"Engineering, report! What happened to the main holo display?"

"It... it's still working, ma'am."

"Then where are the stars?"

"I might have an answer," Fields said from sensors. "I'm detecting eight tube-shaped anomalies protruding from our hull. Each one corresponds to one of our hull breaches, and they appear to connect to equidistant points along the inside of another anomaly—one that's cylindrically shaped."

"They're not hiding anymore..." Audrey said.

"Good. We should blow them to hell," Markov replied.

"We're *inside* of the target, Councilor. If we destroy them, we'll destroy ourselves, too."

"Clever little bastards. Then we should send out as many

Marines as we can muster to board and capture *them*."

"That's actually not a bad idea, ma'am," Major Bright put in.

"That's not my call to make."

"So contact the Governor and suggest it," Markov said.

Audrey turned to him with a look of strained patience. "Don't you have somewhere else you need to be, Councilor?"

"I'm fine right here."

"I wasn't asking."

Markov returned her glare and nodded crisply. "All right. Fine. Be sure to let me know if there are any new developments."

"Of course," Audrey replied. Turning back to Major Bright she said, "Get our VSM drones back into Section Eight to re-examine the hull breaches. Now that they're not cloaking anymore, we might be able to learn something about whatever it is they used to breach our hull."

"Aye, ma'am. Re-deploying VSMs," Bright replied.

* * *

"Welcome home, Benjamin," Alexander said as he opened the door to his and Catalina's quarters.

Their prefect, Ana Urikov, had given permission for Benjamin to stay with them until his nearest relatives could be contacted.

"You'll have to stay on the couch for a while," Catalina said as she led the boy by the hand to the living room. "Is that okay?"

Benjamin nodded, but said nothing. He looked around, taking in the sights. "It's the same as our room. Except ours was in a forest," he added as he stared out the sliding glass doors to the terrace. Holographic waves crashed, racing up a dazzling golden beach. "Can I watch a holovid?" he asked, looking suddenly back to Catalina.

"Sure," she said. "You know how?"

He nodded and went to sit on the couch facing the holoscreen. Benjamin summoned it to life with a gesture and began swiping through channels until he found the one he was looking for—a blank screen with a few lines of text.

"It doesn't work," Benjamin said.

Alexander walked up to the screen so he could read what it said.

Solar flare warning in effect. External cameras disabled.

The channel Benjamin had selected was a live feed from the ship's bow cameras.

"I don't remember anyone mentioning a solar flare..." Catalina said.

"Neither do I," Alexander replied.

Moments later the announcement came over the PA system. "Please be advised. All cameras and external viewports have been shielded until further notice due to a solar flare. Thank you for your patience. We hope to restore all shipboard functions soon."

"No comms, no engines, and now we're blind, too..." Alexander mused. "This just keeps getting better."

Catalina looked suddenly worried. "What if we get attacked again? Won't we be sitting ducks?"

"We still have sensors and weapons, so no, we should be able to defend ourselves. You'll have to watch something else for now, Benjamin."

"Okay," he said, and went flipping through the channels

again.

Alexander turned away with a sigh and went to sit at the breakfast bar. He waved Catalina over and she sat beside him. They watched as Benjamin settled on watching old, pre-recorded cartoons.

"So much for career day," he muttered.

"Right, with everything going on I almost forgot to ask— what did you choose?"

"Marine corps, Navy crew, or Navy pilot."

Catalina's brow furrowed. "Those are all military careers."

Alexander shrugged. "Stick with what you know."

"Are you sure you want that life again?"

"It won't be like the last time. We're both on the same ship together, so they can't possibly separate us with my deployment."

"And what happens after we arrive? They could leave you on the ship in space while the colonists go down to the surface."

"Which is why I picked the Marines as my first choice. If they give it to me, I'll definitely be going to the surface with you."

"And if they don't?"

"Then I'll finish my term of enlistment and transfer to the surface."

Catalina looked uncertain. "You promise?"

Alexander nodded. "Promise. What about you? What did you choose?"

"Campaign manager, political aide, and political activist, but I'm really hoping to run for office and get an elected position."

"You're diving back into politics. You sure you want to

have that life again?"

"Like you said—stick with what you know." Catalina glanced back at Benjamin and whispered, "What are we going to do about him?"

"Wait until we can contact his relatives. Maybe his uncle will take him when he arrives in Section Ten."

"I know *that*," she replied, still whispering. "I meant emotionally. He just lost his mother. He must be grieving. He needs someone to talk to."

"Go ahead," Alexander replied.

"I was thinking maybe *you* should talk to him."

"What? Why me?"

"Because you lost someone you cared about recently. At least, you went through grieving for her recently."

Alexander's eyes narrowed, and he realized that Catalina wasn't just asking him to help Benjamin. She was also checking to see if he missed his girlfriend and former XO, Viviana McAdams. "I haven't thought about her in months," he said, and it was true.

"Still," Catalina insisted. "I know how hard that was for you. After we came out of the Mindscape you spent a year being treated for depression because of her."

"It's complicated."

"So explain it to me."

"I was depressed because we just spent a hundred years together in a virtual world where you were impersonating Viviana in order to help me get over the fact that she was actually dead."

Catalina nodded. "See? Not so complicated."

Alexander shot her a dubious look. "If you say so. Look—I understand what happened. I know she's dead, and I know that you were really the woman I was married to and in love with for all those years. What I actually had with Viviana before the Mindscape seems like a dream now, and not the kind that I wish could come true. I wasn't depressed because I missed her. I was depressed because I couldn't tell what was real anymore. I'm surprised you weren't affected by that just as badly as I was."

"It was an adjustment," Catalina admitted.

"Yeah, you can say that again. There's still something I don't get, though. We were divorced, and I was in the Mindscape living a lie. I didn't want to leave because I supposedly couldn't handle the truth that I was responsible for Viviana's death. Benevolence went to you and asked you to impersonate Viviana in the Mindscape so that I could get over her. You spent a hundred years with me living a virtual life and impersonating her."

Catalina grabbed his hand and laced her fingers through his. "And I'd do it all over again."

"That's what I don't get—why?"

"I never stopped caring for you."

"Even after you learned that I'd moved on and was hung up on someone else?"

"Even after that."

"Mmmmmm."

"You don't believe me?"

"Well I don't really have a choice. You're here, aren't you? I can't deny that without plunging myself back into a depressive spiral, wondering what's really real and whether or not I actually woke up from the Mindscape."

"It *is* real, Alex."

"I've come to terms with that. But there's something else I

don't get. Benevolence kept us in the Mindscape for a century. Do you really think that's how long it took for me to get over Viviana?"

"Does it matter?"

"What if it does? What if he was keeping us prisoner there and he only let us out now because he has some kind of agenda?"

Catalina's brow furrowed. "You think Benevolence brainwashed us while we were in the Mindscape?"

"Maybe."

"What for?"

"I don't know. To turn us into spies, maybe."

Catalina laughed. "Well, we're going to make terrible spies with the comms down."

"They'll get fixed."

Catalina patted his hand and got up from her bar stool. "I'll let you know if I catch you trying to send any coded messages."

Alexander turned to watch her leave and caught Benjamin staring at them. The boy quickly turned his head away and went back to watching his cartoons. He'd been listening in on their conversation. He smiled wryly and said, "Don't worry, Ben, I'm not a spy."

Ben turned back to him and nodded, looking suddenly very serious. "I know you're not, Alex." And with that, he went back to watching his cartoons.

* * *

"What the hell is that? Get us a closer look, Sergeant Torres," Commander Audrey Johnson ordered.

"Yes, ma'am." Torres walked up to the hull breach with her Virtual Space Marine (VSM) to examine the damage more carefully. Glossy black tubes—*or cables?*—snaked along the ceiling from the breach, crawling into a pair of nearby air ducts. "It looks like they tried to get into our air supply."

"What the hell for?" Commander Johnson said.

"No idea, ma'am," Torres replied. She was all alone for this inspection. The rest of her squad wasn't cleared to see whatever she was looking at. Torres followed the invading tubes to the nearest air duct. They'd pushed their way through the vent on the outside of the duct, bending it into a pretzel shape, and the air gaps in and around the damaged vent were all sealed with a translucent white substance. Fortunately, because of the hull breach, those air ducts had already been sealed off from the surrounding areas.

"I don't like this," Commander Johnson said. She could see everything Torres saw via the VSM drone's live holofeed. "See if you can cut one of those conduits open."

"Yes, ma'am." Torres removed a cutting beam from her equipment belt and raised it to the ceiling. She studied the knot of glossy black tubes slithering into the duct and traced one of them to a point where it separated from the rest. "Here goes..." she said, and activated the beam with a flash of light. A simulated orange beam of light appeared connecting the muzzle of the device to its target.

The tube glowed red hot and began to smoke. "I think it's working," she said.

The tube abruptly snapped and a stream of smoke gushed out, quickly dispersing through the vacuum in the breached corridor.

"What is that coming out of the conduit?" the commander

asked.

Torres shook her drone's head. "We'll have to take a sample." Torres opened a compartment in her drone's chest and withdrew a small, transparent flask designed for collecting air and water. The *Liberty's* VSM drones had been designed for exploring planetary surfaces, so they came equipped with several types of sample containers. She aimed the flask at the stream of smoke pouring from the severed conduit and activated the miniature aspirator in the flask. It sucked in a cloud of smoke before sealing itself. Torres held the sample up to the light and watched smoke swirling around inside of the container, as if driven by miniature convection currents.

"Strange," she remarked.

"Seal it inside of one of the other sample containers, just in case something leaks out, and then bring it back to Section Seven," Commander Johnson ordered.

"Yes, ma'am," Torres replied, already withdrawing a soil sample container to encapsulate the flask of smoke.

CHAPTER 10

Safely ensconced in a hazmat suit and standing on the other side of the bio-safety lab, Audrey watched through a broad window as the lab technician withdrew the sample container from Sergeant Torres' VSM drone.

She held her breath as the technician carried the sample over to the examination area. Beside her, Councilor Markov fidgeted, shifting his weight from one foot to another.

"Opening the first container now..." the technician said, moving awkwardly in his bulky mustard-yellow hazmat suit. "Ah... Commander, we have a problem."

"What kind of problem?" Audrey asked.

"The containers appear to be broken."

"What do you mean they're broken?" Audrey demanded.

"The outer one is deformed, while the inner one is shattered, ma'am."

The VSM drone's head turned. "That's impossible! They were both fine when I collected the sample!" Torres said over their shared comm channel.

"The containers are not indestructible. Perhaps you were too rough. VSM drones are calibrated to administer far more force than any human could. You might not have noticed that you were damaging them."

"I know the difference between a gentle squeeze and a death grip," Torres snapped.

"Well, however it happened, the fact is that it happened," Councilor Markov said, "and that means our quarantine is breached."

"I need to report this to Admiral Urikov," Audrey added. "Meanwhile, see if you can detect any residuals from the inside of the container, and if possible, find out how it broke."

"Will do," the technician replied.

Markov turned to her, his face deeply shadowed behind the hazmat helmet. "What was in there?" he asked.

Audrey noticed a closed loop comms icon on her ARCs; the councilor was speaking to her over a private channel. She switched to the same one and shook her head. "You know as much as I do, Councilor."

A frown creased his face. "I doubt that. Don't think I didn't notice how you shooed me out of the CIC earlier."

Audrey held his gaze without blinking. "If there is something I'm not saying, it's because I'm not allowed."

"The safety of this ship and its crew is my responsibility, Commander, and the civilian government is in charge of this mission—not the Navy. Whatever you're allowed to know, *I'm* allowed to know."

"You mean the safety of this section."

"What?"

"The safety of this *section* is your responsibility—not the entire ship."

"You know what I mean," Markov replied, waving his hand dismissively in her face. He looked away to watch the technician work.

Audrey switched comm channels to update the admiral before Markov could say something else.

"Yes, Commander?" Admiral Urikov answered after a

moment.

Audrey explained about the broken sample containers, and the admiral let out a guttural sigh.

"Now we have four sections compromised."

"Four?"

"Sections One, Six, and Eight were all breached, Commander. Now with Section Seven, that makes four."

"I thought the breaches were contained?" Audrey said.

"They were, and they are, but from what you're telling me we can't be sure that they can be contained. That smoke you sampled could be bleeding through our air supply as we speak."

"If that's the case, then you'd detect a loss of pressure in the areas around the hull breaches."

"Not if they re-sealed the ducts. Isn't that what your sergeant found? Some kind of sealant around the grilles?"

"Yes, but breaking through a flimsy vent with mechanized conduits is one thing. Breaking through sealed bulkheads is another, Admiral. It would take a cutting beam for anything to get in."

"I hope you're right. I'm sending a team from engineering to look into it. I'll let you know what they find. Meanwhile, until we know what we're dealing with, you should confine everyone to their quarters and shut down the ventilation system."

"Shut it down, sir? We'll suffocate."

"There's enough air in the dormitories to last everyone for at least a week. Hopefully long before then we'll know what's going on and what to do about it."

Audrey nodded. *"Yes, sir. What should we tell people as the reason for their confinement?"*

"There was a containment breach. Tell them that. It just happens to be the truth."

"I'll pass along the message to Councilor Markov, sir."

"Good. I'll be in touch. Urikov out."

Audrey turned to Markov only to find him already engaged in a conversation with the lab technician.

"So the sergeant didn't break the containers," Markov said.

"No," the technician replied. "There's no way she could have caused this type of damage."

"What type of damage?" Audrey interrupted.

"The soil sample container is shot full of microscopic holes, ma'am. Millions of them. It's like..."

"Like something ate its way out," Audrey said.

"Yes, exactly," the technician said.

"Any sign of whatever that was?"

"No traces of the sample, ma'am."

Audrey grimaced and turned to Markov. "Councilor, we need to confine everyone to their quarters until we can find and contain whatever was in that flask. I've been ordered to shut down the ventilation system to prevent it from spreading."

Markov regarded her silently for a long moment before conceding to her with a nod. Neither of them liked taking orders from the other. There was a constant tension in their relationship, professional and otherwise, over who would get to wear the pants—and for how long. Fortunately, he seemed to realize they had bigger issues to deal with right now.

"Very well," he said. "I'll give the order."

* * *

The PA system crackled and Catalina looked up, one ear cocked toward the nearest overhead speaker.

"This is an urgent alert from your section councilor. Our quarantine has been breached. All non-essential passengers and crew are to return to their quarters immediately and remain there until further notice. I repeat, unless you have specific orders to the contrary, you must return to your quarters immediately and remain there until further notice. Thank you."

Alexander traded a worried look with Catalina, and then both of them glanced at Benjamin.

"What about supper?" Benjamin asked.

They'd been just about to go get something to eat. Catalina frowned. "They can't expect us to stay here without food."

"Maybe they're planning to bring us something," Alexander suggested.

"We should try the door," she said. "Maybe one of us can get something and bring it back here."

"And risk contamination from whatever bio-hazard prompted the quarantine?" Alexander replied.

"How do we know we're not already contaminated?"

"If we are, then staying here will keep other people safe. We can't risk it," Alexander insisted. "I'm sure it won't be long."

Catalina stared at the door until an *Open/Lock* option appeared on her ARCs.

"What are you doing?"

"Checking something," she selected *Open,* but nothing happened. Instead an error flashed up before her eyes.

Access Denied.

"It's locked," she said.

"I'm not surprised," Alexander replied. "They can't have us wandering around and breaching containment protocols at the first sign of hunger."

Catalina's eyes drifted out of focus as she stared at him. "What if this lasts more than a few hours? What if it's days or weeks?"

"Then they'll have to find a way to bring us food..." Alexander trailed off, one ear cocked toward the ceiling, as if listening to another public announcement that only he could hear.

"What is it?" she asked.

"The air—it's not circulating. They've shut the vents."

"What?! We'll suffocate!"

Benjamin's blue eyes were wide and frightened.

Alexander shook his head. "We have enough air to last for a while... but whatever they're worried about, they think it might be airborne. That's not good."

"I want my mom," Benjamin said.

Catalina felt a pang of regret for speaking so candidly in front of him. She walked over and took his hand. "Come on, let's go sit on the terrace."

"What for?" Benjamin asked.

"So we can play a game," she said.

"What kind of game?"

"You'll see."

She led Benjamin outside. A salty breeze blew off the holographic ocean and waves crashed rhythmically on the beach.

Catalina took a seat on a couch facing the view and patted the space beside her. Benjamin hesitated a moment before sitting down.

The air shimmered with heat, and the beach vanished into the distance, becoming a mirror for the cloudless blue sky where the waves had left it smooth and wet. Sunlight shattered on the water, sending shards glinting to their eyes.

Catalina sighed. "Peaceful, isn't it?"

"I guess," Benjamin said. "I thought you said we were going to play a game?"

Out of the corner of her eye Catalina saw Alexander come outside. He stood leaning against the sliding glass doors, unseen by Benjamin and watching them with a conspiratorial smile.

"You know how to change the view?" she asked.

"Sure," Benjamin replied.

"Then you go first. I'll close my eyes and try to guess things about the scene you picked. I get five guesses. Each time I guess right, I get a point, but if I guess wrong, you get a point. And if I get two guesses in a row wrong, you have to give me a clue."

"Okay," Benjamin said, his lips curving into a brief smile. "Close your eyes. And no peeking!"

She nodded and squeezed her eyes shut. "I won't."

"You better not. I'll know if you do, and then I'll get an extra turn."

Catalina nodded. "Fair enough." The rhythmic crashing of waves suddenly ceased. So did the salty ocean breeze and the waves of heat pulsing off the beach. The air was still and cool, but not cold, and it was heavily laden with pine scents. A river or a waterfall roared in the distance.

"We're in the mountains," Catalina said, deducing that from the speed and tenor of the river.

"Yes," Benjamin confirmed.

"In an evergreen forest."

"Right again."

"And..." Catalina thought about what else she could deduce. Mountain air was cooler due to the altitude, so despite the chilly air it could be summer. Also, pine trees were prevalent in the Northern hemisphere, but not the southern hemisphere. "It's summer, and we're in the northern hemisphere."

"Right again," Benjamin said. "One more and you get all five points."

"Okay..." It was hard for her to think of another deduction she could make. There was no way to be sure about the time of day, though by default that would correspond to the shipboard time. Should she risk assuming that Benjamin hadn't changed that parameter? *At least it's something to go on,* she decided. "It's night time," she added.

"Nope."

Catalina opened her eyes to see the soft golden rays of the morning sun trickling through the trees.

"But four out of five isn't bad," Benjamin said. "I'll have to make it harder next time. Your turn!" he said, scrunching up his entire face as he shut his eyes in anticipation of the next scene.

Catalina smiled. Her plan was working. She'd completely distracted him from his empty stomach, the quarantine... his mother. For her scene she chose a summer night by a lake in midwestern America. The sound of crickets and frogs chirping filled the air.

Benjamin proceeded to guess that both creatures were present, using two separate guesses. *Clever boy,* she thought. "That's two points."

"And... the temperature is between twenty-two and twenty-three degrees centigrade."

Catalina checked that. "It's twenty-two degrees." She blinked with shock. "How could you possibly know that?"

"Dolbear's law."

"What's that?"

"It states the relationship between air temperature and the rate at which crickets chirp. All you have to do is count the number of chirps in twenty-five seconds, divide by three and then add four. I did that twice and got twenty-two and twenty-three degrees respectively, so I gave my answer as a range to make it more accurate. Go ahead and count for yourself."

Catalina couldn't even pick out cricket chirps from frog croaks. She shook her head. "I'll take your word for it."

"You don't believe me."

"Well, even if you counted correctly, how do you know that the designers calibrated the cricket chirps to the temperature?"

"Because the default scenes are all pre-recorded from real locations, and I don't think you know how to customize your scene."

"How old are you again?"

"Nine. Why?"

"Because sometimes you act your age, and other times..." she shook her head.

"My mother says I'm precocious. That's another way of saying I'm too smart."

"Well that's a given," Catalina replied. "You've got three out of five guesses right. Let's see if you can get two more," she added, not wanting to give Benjamin too long to dwell on his mother

Benjamin guessed the season and the time of day, both of

which were relatively safe bets from the other things he already knew.

"Five points. You're up by one."

"Soon to be five more," he said, grinning.

"Don't get too cocky. I'm sure to get at least a few things right."

"We'll see," Benjamin said, smiling up at her. "Close your eyes."

Catalina did as she was told. The sound of the crickets and frogs vanished, replaced by a haunting melody of hoots and wails like nothing she'd ever heard before. The air was hot, dry, and gusting, as if pouring from an oven or furnace. The wind sent a pungent odor, sweet and acrid, tickling through her nostrils. It smelled vaguely like burning grass. Catalina had visited a lot of different places on Earth, but this one seemed utterly foreign to her. Another animal made its presence known with loud, urgent clicking sounds.

"It's a jungle," Catalina decided from the sheer variety of animal noises.

"Nope."

"Okay... the African savannah, then."

"Half right. Three more guesses."

"Is it in Africa?"

"No."

"Then it's a savannah."

"Yes. Lots of grass."

"I thought so... then that brings me to my next guess. The grass is burning, isn't it?"

"Correct."

Catalina frowned, wondering who'd want a pre-recorded scene of an inferno raging through a grassy plain. For her final guess she decided to focus on the animal sounds. Hoots and wails could easily be from birds or monkeys. "There are primates," she decided. "They're calling out in alarm because of the fire."

"Wrong and wrong again."

"Okay, I give up," Catalina said, opening her eyes. As she did so, her jaw promptly dropped open, and she sucked in a hasty breath of the noxious air.

To her left she saw a sickly yellow sky clogged with blowing sand and black smoke. Below that a wall of flames danced up from a field of tall blue grass, bowing in a vicious gale. The inferno advanced steadily with the wind, eating up more of the blue grass and chasing giant, glossy black arthropods. Bipedal, wrinkly, gray-skinned humanoids dashed between them, prodding the insects with sharp sticks, hooting and whistling as they went.

The scene obviously wasn't pre-recorded, but rather based on some type of fantasy setting on an alien world.

"Well, they might not be primates, but I was right about them calling out in alarm because of the fire."

"No, they're not alarmed. They're excited. The fire is herding their prey toward a cliff."

Catalina shook her head. "You win. Where did you find this scene?"

"I didn't find it. I made it."

"You what?"

Benjamin smiled proudly. "It's my impression of Proxima B."

"How did you do that? Is there a program for customizing scenes?"

"Probably, but I used a rendering engine."

"Don't you have to program that?"

Benjamin shrugged.

"Smart kid," Alexander commented from where he stood leaning against the terrace doors, watching the game. Catalina had forgotten he was there. "You sure you aren't an android in disguise?" Alexander went on.

Benjamin flipped a smile over his shoulder. "Disguised as what? An android? That wouldn't be much of a disguise. Like dressing you up as a lion."

A smile flickered through the frown on Alexander's face. "Good point," he said, and left it at that.

Catalina was also curious about Benjamin's acute intelligence, but if he were an android, surely the mission's recruitment and HR offices would have identified him early on in the selection process. She put the matter from her mind and nodded to Alexander. "Don't you want to join us?" she asked.

"Sure," he said, and went to sit on the other side of her.

"All right, you're next, Mr. Lion," Benjamin said.

Alexander smiled and reached around her to tousle the kid's hair.

"We'll have to take turns guessing," Benjamin added, already closing his eyes.

"All right, here goes..." Alexander said.

They played several more rounds. At some point it was Benjamin's turn to guess, but he said nothing even when prompted, and Catalina turned to find him fast asleep.

"We should take him to bed," she whispered.

Alexander nodded and got up to carry Benjamin inside. He was about to lay the boy down on the couch when Catalina grabbed his arm to stop him. She shook her head, and jerked her chin to their room. "It would probably be better if I slept with him tonight. Do you mind?"

Alexander hesitated, then shook his head. "No, you're right. That's a good idea." He carried Benjamin to their bed and tucked him in.

Catalina kissed Alexander goodnight and whispered, "You're going to make a great Father, you know."

He arched an eyebrow. "Think so? I didn't do so great the first time around."

"Dorian was your stepson. It's not your fault he never listened to you. And besides, one failure doesn't make us bad parents. He was a troubled boy from the start."

"Maybe. Or maybe I made him troubled."

A lump rose in her throat at the sorrow in Alexander's voice. She shook her head and smiled. "No."

Alexander shrugged. "Well, you're going to make a great Mother. That was a good idea you had—distracting Benjamin with that game."

"Thanks." Catalina's stomach growled painfully and she winced. "I hope they let us out for breakfast."

"If they don't, I'm going to pry the door open."

Catalina gave him a skeptical look. "What about the quarantine?"

"They can't expect us to stay in here without food."

"They'd better not. See you tomorrow morning."

"Sleep well," he replied.

"I'll try."

Catalina watched him leave and then she pulled off her boots and crawled into bed beside Benjamin. She was too tired and stressed to bother changing into a new jumpsuit or brushing her teeth. She used her neural link to dim the lights, and Benjamin stirred and rolled over, tucking his head under her chin and draping an arm over her to hug her close.

She hugged him back, and the lump in her throat returned. He was all alone, and distraction wasn't going to work forever to keep him from feeling the loss of his mother. Catalina lay awake thinking about that, about the cruel caprice of the universe, where death could come suddenly for anyone at anytime.

Benjamin's body grew suddenly tense in her arms and he woke up, his eyes huge and frightened. "Mom?" he asked, blinking up at her in the dim light.

Catalina shook her head. "It's me, Catalina."

Tears welled in his eyes and fell silently to his pillow. He rolled over, looking up at the ceiling. "It's not fair," he said.

"No, it's not," Catalina agreed.

"She always looked after me, but I wasn't there to look after her."

"You couldn't have saved her, Ben."

"I could have. If I was there."

"You're not superhuman."

Benjamin said nothing to that. When the silence grew uncomfortably long, she decided to try a change of topic. "Why did you come aboard the *Liberty?*"

"My mom sold everything to save me. We didn't have a home anymore. I applied for the *Liberty* and passed all the entrance exams and my Mom got to go free because of me."

Catalina frowned. "She sold everything to save you? From what?"

"I was born with a disease—Tay-Sachs. I would have died if my mom hadn't signed me up for a new treatment on Earth."

"A *genetic* disease? How is that possible?"

"Not everyone's a gener. Some people say it's us playing God and they still have children naturally."

"But without genetic engineering you'll grow old and die," Catalina objected.

"Everybody dies. My mom was immortal, and..."

It didn't save her. Catalina frowned. "How could she deny you immortality if she was immortal herself?"

"She didn't have a choice about being a gener baby. She wanted to make sure I did."

"But it didn't work out the way she planned."

"No." Silence stretched between them once more. Benjamin broke it a moment later. "What about you? Why did you come aboard?"

Catalina explained about her and Alex's desire to have children, and their fear for the future of Earth and Mars with so much animosity between androids and humans.

Benjamin yawned. "Androids aren't bad. They saved my life. Why would they do that if they wanted us all dead?"

"That's a good question," Catalina said. "I think the real danger is in our minds. Fear can make us do crazy things, and we're afraid of them, so..."

"It makes us crazy."

"Exactly."

Benjamin nodded and rolled back to face her. Catalina wrapped an arm around him and he tucked his head against her chest. After a while his breathing slowed, and the frown lines disappeared from his forehead as his muscles relaxed in sleep.

Catalina watched him for what must have been at least an hour before finally succumbing to sleep herself, and even then she slept fitfully, dreaming of food. She awoke early with a vicious pain in her stomach. She'd dreamed that someone had stabbed her there, and now as she awoke, she probed the area carefully to make sure that wasn't actually the case. Her belly curved away in a concave hole below her ribs, but the skin was unbroken. Catalina let out a breath and rolled over to find Benjamin. He was already awake, and this time he was watching *her*.

"Good morning," he said.

Catalina frowned. "How long have you been awake?"

"I don't know. A while. I'm hungry..." he whined, his eyes accusing, as if the quarantine were somehow her fault.

Catalina blinked, surprised by his behavior. Benjamin was such a precocious boy that it was easy to forget he could still act his age.

"I'm going to go make some coffee and wake Alexander. As soon as we're both up, we'll find a way to get food—quarantine or no quarantine."

"Promise?"

Catalina smiled and kissed his forehead. "Promise. Come on, you can help me figure out how the coffee maker works."

"Okay."

It didn't take long to figure out. All they had to do was pick the type of coffee, put a cup under the dispenser, and press a button; then, like magic, a fragrant, steaming brew poured out.

"Mmmmm. It smells good," Benjamin said. "Can I have some?"

"Sure—but only if it's decaf," Catalina added as she carried Alexander's mug over to the couch where he lay sleeping. He looked so peaceful that she hesitated to wake him. She set her coffee down on the table in front of the couch and placed his under his nose, thinking the smell would wake him, but he didn't stir. "Alex..." she whispered. "Wake up, Alex."

Still nothing.

Catalina set aside his coffee, too, and tried waking him with a kiss, but his lips remained cold and lifeless against hers. She withdrew to regard him with a frown. "Alex," she said sharply. "Alex, wake up!"

"What's wrong?" Benjamin asked, walking over with a steaming mug of his own.

"He won't wake up," she explained.

"I know how." Setting his mug down beside the other two, Benjamin knelt beside her. He reached out and pinched Alexander's nose shut with one hand. After a moment, Alexander's mouth popped open, but he still didn't wake, so Benjamin used his other hand to hold Alexander's jaw shut.

Long seconds passed, and Catalina heard her heart beating furiously in her chest. Nothing was happening. "Stop," she said. "Let him breathe."

Benjamin withdrew with a puzzled look, and Alexander's nostrils flared as he sucked in a deep breath.

"I don't get it, that always works," Benjamin said.

Catalina shook her head. "It should have. Something's wrong. It's almost like he's in a coma. I'm going to call for a medic." She used her neural link to browse through the ship's directory on her ARCs and place an emergency call to med bay. Catalina waited anxiously while the comms rang.

And rang...

"There's no answer," she said.

"What if they're in a coma, too?" Benjamin asked with big

eyes. "What are we going to do?"

Catalina gave him a blank look. "I..." She trailed off as her gaze slid back to Alexander—statuesque but for the steady rise and fall of his chest. His hands lay folded there in a funereal pose. He no longer looked peaceful to her. "I don't know," she finished.

CHAPTER 11

When he heard the order to return to his quarters due to a containment breach, Remo had decided to rather stay in the med bay with Deedee. After all, where better to be with some unknown pathogen on the loose? Well, maybe not the best place if sick people came streaming in, but he could easily come into contact with whatever it was just by rushing down to the dormitory level with everyone else. Besides, he had to safeguard his investment. A no-strings girl like Deedee was hard to come by.

Remo sat up, watching her sleep from the chair in the corner of her room. *Does this count as a string?* He wondered. If it were any other girl, he'd be out flirting with the nurses, not sleepless at her bedside, waiting for her to wake up. Maybe he'd got too close. Started to care. Remo shuddered.

A more likely explanation for his insomnia came to mind: *I can't sleep because I've been taken hostage by aliens.* Worse yet, there'd been no action during the night—at least none that he'd heard about. Why weren't they fighting their alien captors?

Remo shook his head to clear away those concerns. It was a quiet night in the med bay, nothing but the rhythmic beeping of life signs monitors to disrupt the silence. His eyelids grew heavy, and the sound lulled him to sleep...

Thumps, thuds, and crashes rumbled through the walls,

followed by an urgent voice that shattered his sleep. Remo stood up quickly, blinking the sleep from his eyes, his whole body tense and ready for a fight. But there were no detectable threats in the room.

He crept quietly up to the door, his imagination alive with alien horrors.

As he drew near, he heard that urgent voice again; it was a man calling a woman's name repeatedly. Remo cracked open the door. At the end of the hall, in the admitting room, nurses lay slumped over their stations. The comms buzzed insistently in their ears, somehow not waking them. *What the hell?*

Remo heard that man's voice again, echoing down the hall toward him—

"Dalia, wake up, damn it!"

"Hello?" Remo called out as he edged down the hall toward the voice.

Footsteps approached, and a man in a white jumpsuit with blue piping and a luminous blue cross in the center of his chest appeared. His long, pale, angular face, black hair, and piercing red eyes made him look sinister. "You're awake," he said in a thick, rasping Martian accent.

Remo's ARCs identified the man as Doctor Ross Laskin. "What's going on?" he asked.

Doctor Laskin shook his head. "I don't know. Everyone has collapsed, and they won't wake up."

"Everyone?" Remo repeated with a sudden frown. He cast a quick look behind him to Deedee's room, hoping whatever contagion they were dealing with hadn't found a way to reach her yet. "I need to check on someone," he said, and hurried back the way he came.

As soon as he reached Deedee's side, he grabbed her roughly by the shoulders and shook her. Her head bounced lifelessly on her pillow, but she didn't stir.

"Desiree!"

"It got her, too," Doctor Laskin rasped out behind him.

Remo turned to see the doctor standing in the open doorway.

"Why are we still fine?" Remo wondered aloud.

"There could be a million reasons. We might be immune, the contagion might affect us differently, or more likely, we were among the last to come into contact with it, and it's just a matter of time before we end up like them."

"How long have they been like this?" Remo asked.

"I don't know. I only just found out. I've been in my office for a while."

"There must be some way to wake them," Remo said, looking back to Deedee. Absurdly, he wondered if a kiss might work.

"We could try dopamine stimulants or sedatives. If that doesn't work, then directly stimulating brain activity is an option, but in cases like this, we need to find out what's causing the coma first."

"What do you mean?"

"Brain damage is the primary cause of a coma, but when an infectious agent is responsible, it's usually because of encephalitis."

"Ensefa-what?"

"Encephalitis. Inflammation of the brain—usually caused by a virus."

"So the bio-weapons scare was real."

Doctor Laskin cocked his head to one side. "Why wouldn't

it be?"

Remo shook his head to dismiss the question. "If it's a virus, what do we do about it?"

"We create a nano virus to target and destroy it. I'll show you, but first we need a blood sample. We'll start with her," he said, nodding to Deedee. "I'll be right back."

Remo looked back to Deedee, resisting the urge to reach for her hand.

Doctor Laskin returned pushing a food service cart with a tray full of hypodermic needles and empty vials rather than food. He stopped beside Deedee's bed and tied a blue tourniquet around her upper arm. He spent a moment tapping her arm to find a vein. Remo watched as the doctor filled one vial after another with dark red blood.

When he was done, he took a rectangular scanner from his belt and slotted one of the vials into it. Remo waited while status lights blinked and beeped on the device—first red, then yellow, then green. A solid tone sounded, and different colored patterns flickered over Doctor Laskin's eyes, changing them from red to blue as he studied the results on his ARCs.

A frown crept across his brow and slid down his cheeks in deep lines before settling on his lips. "Her blood counts are normal. Pathogen and toxicology scans are both clean."

Remo shook his head. "What's that mean?"

"It means her immune system isn't reacting and there's no known bacterial, viral, fungal, or parasitic infection. We've also ruled out all known toxins, which would have been my next guess."

"It must be a false positive."

Doctor Laskin's brow lifted. "You mean a false negative."

Remo waved his hand dismissively. "You know what I

mean."

"Lieutenant, these scans are 99.9% accurate. If the scanner says her blood is clean, then it's clean."

"Then why is she like this? You said the scanner ruled out *known* infections and toxins. What about unknown ones?"

"The scanner also looks for new strains."

"What if it doesn't know what to look for? This could be something entirely foreign to our experience. Something alien."

"Alien?"

Remo nodded. "Yes."

"Where would an alien pathogen come from?"

He was just about to explain what he knew when a third voice joined the conversation. "Remo?" The voice was soft, feminine, and familiar. Both of them turned to look at Deedee.

"I'm scared..." she said, her eyes darting and wide.

"Deedee," he said, grinning. "You're back!"

Doctor Laskin flicked on a small penlight and shone it into her eyes, checking for something. "What do you feel?" he asked.

Desiree shook her head, her eyes still darting. A murmur of voices drifted to their ears from the corridor beyond her room. Remo glanced at the open door. "It sounds like the others are waking up," he said.

"Yes," Doctor Laskin replied. Speaking to Deedee, he added, "It's okay, I'm a doctor. Tell me your symptoms."

"Why is everyone so worried? What happened?"

"You were in a coma," Laskin explained.

"A coma? For how long?" Deedee asked, her voice spiking with concern.

"Not long. I need you to tell me what you're feeling so I

can help you."

"I'm feeling... anxious, scared, confused... that's it."

"No physical symptoms? How's your head? Any headache?"

"No."

"Interesting. We're going to have to run some more tests to understand what happened. I'll be back in a moment. I'm going to check on the others."

"The others?" Deedee asked.

"You weren't the only one in a coma," Remo explained.

"Who else?"

He shook his head. "Almost everyone." He leaned over her to kiss her, but hesitated, remembering she could be infected with something. He aimed for her forehead instead.

"I love you, too," she said.

He withdrew abruptly. "I didn't say anything."

"No, but you thought it."

Remo shook his head. "If you say so." *So much for no strings.* He glanced at the door, but felt no compulsion to run for it. Her declaration of love should have scared him off. *I must be getting soft,* he thought. He nodded to her arms, both still elevated in casts. "Bet you could score us some morphine if you play your cards right." She'd come out of surgery less than 24 hours ago.

"What are you going to do? Suck it out of my IV?"

Remo gave her a sly look. "Maybe."

Deedee snorted. "Too bad for you. I feel fine. What's going on, Remo? Does this have something to do with..."

She trailed off, but he understood she was talking about the alien ship that had snared the *Liberty.*

He grimaced. "I think they infected us with something, but

we can't find it with a blood scan."

Deedee nodded slowly. "They don't mean us any harm. We're going to Proxima, Remo. We'll be there soon!" Deedee's eyes were bright with joy. She sat up suddenly and withdrew her arms from their harnesses.

"Easy there," he said, reaching out to support her. She was obviously experiencing some type of delusion. He cast an urgent look over his shoulder, wondering where Doctor Laskin was.

Deedee grabbed his hand and gave it a squeeze. "Don't be afraid. I'm not crazy."

"I didn't say you were," Remo replied, offering an uncertain smile. "But I don't think we're going anywhere."

"We're already on our way," she said with a dreamy look on her face.

"Des, we're still on the ring decks. If we were accelerating, we'd feel it. Everything, including us, would be pinned to the aft-facing bulkheads."

Deedee's rapt expression faded to confusion. "But..."

"It's okay. You were just in a coma. You're allowed to be confused, but whatever you think you know about what's going on, it was just a dream. We're still in orbit around Mars."

"You're wrong."

"We can argue about it later. Right now we need to worry about what's going on with you."

"Nothing is going on with me," Deedee said.

Remo nodded agreeably while casting another glance over his shoulder to look for Doctor Laskin. When he looked back, Deedee was gone. Or rather, her face was. For a moment he thought she was playing a trick on him, having somehow tucked her head into the collar of her jumpsuit, but there were no unusual bulges to suggest that. He glanced down and saw that the hand he was holding was also invisible. He flinched away from her. Confusion swirled, making his head swim.

"What the hell! Des?"

She reappeared, looking puzzled. "What's wrong?"

* * *

Audrey slapped Councilor Markov hard enough to leave a red, hand-shaped mark on his cheek, but he didn't so much as flinch. The sound echoed in her ears, and her hands trembled. She couldn't reach Med Bay on the comms, and no one was answering from the bridge in Section One or the CIC in Section Seven. Maybe the comms were down?

Audrey warred with herself over whether or not she should leave her quarters and check the CIC for herself. Markov stirred in bed beside her.

"Ow," he said, reaching up to touch his cheek.

Audrey breathed a sigh and glared at him. "Did you take a tranquilizer or something?"

Markov's eyes darted to her. "No, why?"

"I couldn't wake you. I thought you were dead!"

A grin touched his lips. "You were worried about me? How sweet."

"Don't get all sentimental on me." She tried the CIC again. This time she got through, but instead of telling her about a comms malfunction, the comms officer explained that they'd all somehow blacked out and collapsed at their stations.

"All of you blacked out at the same time?" Audrey demanded.

"Yes, ma'am."

"I need to speak with the admiral," she said.

"I'll transfer you. One moment."

Audrey waited while the call went through. After a few seconds, the admiral answered. He appeared on her ARCs, looking harried. His usually clear indigo eyes were striated with angry red veins, and his black beard looked scruffy rather than groomed. "Commander Johnson," he said. "I don't know what's going on, if that's what you want to know."

Audrey paused with her jaw hanging open, halfway to forming exactly that question. "It happened there, too," she realized.

The admiral nodded. "Yes. Everyone passed out except for a handful of civilians and crew. It hasn't reached Sections Two through Five yet. Only the ones that were breached, and yours—no doubt because of that missing sample and the containment breach."

"Then we *are* dealing with something contagious."

"It would appear so. We're looking into it, but whatever it is, I don't believe it poses us a threat."

Audrey frowned. "With respect, sir, it's too early for us to know that. We don't even know what we're dealing with yet."

"We'll keep up the quarantine for a while longer just to be sure, but so far it would appear that Captain White was telling the truth. If that's the case, and we're on our way to Proxima, then we need to get ready. We thought we were going to have years to train everyone for colonizing a new world, but now we're down to just a few days. It's good news, of course, but we have a lot of work to do before we arrive."

Audrey gaped at him and shook her head. "Admiral, are you feeling okay?"

"I'm fine, Commander..." he said.

She blinked and he was gone, leaving his crimson jumpsuit behind and floating in mid-air. Audrey blinked a few times more, and he was back.

"Are *you* okay?" the admiral asked, returning the question. "You look terrified."

Audrey's jaw hung open, at a loss for words "You... you just disappeared, sir."

"I've been standing here the entire time, Commander."

"No, I mean you... became invisible. Like the ship that captured us."

Admiral Urikov looked skeptical. "You must be imagining things, Commander."

"Ask your crew, or check the surveillance tapes," Audrey insisted.

Admiral Urikov barked an order at his chief of security, asking her to check if he became invisible at some point in the past five minutes. They waited while she ran back through the tapes.

Audrey overheard the woman's incredulous reaction— "What the hell?!"—and she knew she hadn't imagined it.

The admiral looked shocked. "How...?"

"You still think this contagion doesn't pose a threat to us?" she demanded.

This time the admiral was the one at a loss for words, but he recovered with a curiously rapturous expression. "They don't mean us any harm," he said slowly.

"They? They who?! That's what they want you to think!" Audrey blurted out. "Your judgment is compromised

Admiral. Whatever your gut is telling you, it's wrong. Don't fall for it."

"You're out of line, Commander, but you'll understand soon enough. Admiral Urikov out." He vanished for a second time, but this time it was because he'd signed off. Audrey shook her head, incredulous.

"He's right, Commander," Markov said. "I can feel it, too."

Audrey turned to find him sitting up in bed beside her. She stared sideways at him, and leaned away as if he might leap up and attack her at any moment. Markov couldn't have overheard more than her side of the conversation with the admiral, but he'd obviously pieced together the gist of it.

"We'd better start getting ready for our arrival at Proxima," he went on. "It won't be long."

Audrey froze. "How do you know about that?" She hadn't told him about Captain White's transmission, and knowledge of it had been classified.

"I just... do," he said, shrugging and smiling rapturously at her. "I'm right, aren't I?" he pressed. "They're taking us to Proxima. That's where the wormhole leads."

"Think about what you're saying," Audrey said. "You have no basis for any of those assertions!"

With that, Markov vanished just like the admiral had. Audrey screamed and leaped out of bed. Markov had slept naked, so not even his jumpsuit remained to identify where he was.

Audrey backed against the wall, watching with wide eyes as the bedsheets flattened and Markov's weight left the mattress. Her heart drummed in her ears, and she strained to listen for footsteps.

His bare feet made meaty slaps against the deck as he

approached. Her eyes darted around the room, searching for a weapon. Not finding anything within easy reach, she brought her fists up and adopted a fighting stance. Then she remembered Markov's hobby of beating up bots with his prosthetic fists, and icy fear trickled through her gut.

"Don't come any closer!" she screamed.

"It's okay," he cooed, his voice right beside her ear.

She whirled toward the sound, and he caught her wrists in an unyielding grip. "Let me go!" she gritted out.

CHAPTER 12

"Are you okay?" Catalina asked for the hundredth time.

Alexander nodded and smiled. "Yes. How long was I out?"

Catalina shook her head. "I don't know. When we got up, we couldn't wake you. A few hours maybe?"

Alexander said nothing to that. His eyes drifted out of focus, and he said, "We're on our way to Proxima..."

"I don't think we've left yet," Catalina replied.

"Are you sure?"

She began to nod, but then stopped herself and glanced at the door. "Well, we're still locked in, and no one is answering the comms, so I guess I don't know."

"The others were also in a coma," Alexander said.

It didn't sound like an educated guess. It sounded like he knew what he was talking about. Catalina regarded him curiously. "Are you sure you're okay?"

Benjamin chose that moment to interject. "How do you know that?"

Alexander appeared confused by the question, but then his expression cleared. "I just do."

Before they could continue their conversation any further, the ship's PA system buzzed to life. "Attention all passengers and crew, this is Governor Chong speaking. Yesterday sections One, Six, Seven, and Eight were all compromised by an unknown pathogen. Preliminary reports suggest that whatever it is, it's able to eat through the seals between sections, and signs of infection are already manifesting in Sections Two through Five. At present the only clinical symptom is that the infected appear to lapse into a brief coma. We're working hard to understand what's happening, and we ask that everyone please remain calm. In the meantime, I felt it best to level with you all about what is really going on." The governor paused, allowing the gravitas of that statement to set in.

Catalina held her breath, her mind racing through a thousand different possibilities.

"We were not attacked by rogue androids from Earth," the governor declared. "In fact we were not attacked at all in the traditional sense. Our ship was physically breached and captured by a much larger vessel, invisible to both our eyes and sensors. They spoke to us and the rest of the Sol System via an open comms transmission that went as follows—"

A new voice took over from Governor: *"My name is Captain White. Some of you will remember me as the Captain of the* Intrepid, *a mission we sent to Wolf 1061 more than a century ago. What we discovered there was beyond our wildest dreams. We are not alone in the universe, and I have returned as an ambassador. Please do not be alarmed. The ones who travel with me are here to help us. We have been invited to join a Galactic Federation of sentient species, and as a gesture of good faith, they have agreed to help the colonists aboard the* Liberty *reach their destination in a matter of days rather than the years it would have otherwise taken. Again, please do not be alarmed. We come in peace."*

The Governor's voice returned a moment later, "Soon after receiving this message, a new wormhole opened up in front of our ship and we were dragged inside. I believe very strongly that this wormhole does in fact lead to Proxima Centauri, exactly as Captain White indicated. I suggest that you join me in this hope and take Captain White at his word.

"We have no reason to believe that these aliens are hostile, and in just a few days we will have proof one way or the other. Besides that, my engineers tell me we cannot safely do anything to resist the vessel that's carrying us through the wormhole, because it is likely shielding us from the extreme conditions inside the wormhole. That is, if we did somehow manage to break free, we'd be irradiated and crushed in a matter of seconds. I would like to stress, however, that these aliens have shown no hostility toward us. Even when fired upon, they showed great reluctance to fire back.

"Rest assured, we are working diligently to understand whatever pathogen has infected the *Liberty*. There do not appear to be any negative symptoms as yet, but some of them are more esoteric and frightening than others. Infected individuals seem able to completely vanish from sight. We assume this is some extension of the cloaking technology they use aboard their starships.

"For reasons that are not yet well understood, a select few of us appear to be immune, or at least more resistant to whatever is affecting us. If you were not found in a coma this morning, you are instructed to report to Med Bay for examination. Thank you. We'll keep you updated as further details emerge, but for now please remain calm."

Catalina listened to that speech with growing horror. It was simultaneously absurd and terrifying. *People disappearing, alien contact, a wormhole taking us to Proxima...?*

"We'd better get you and Benjamin to Med Bay,"

Alexander said, interrupting her thoughts.

Benjamin shot her a worried glance, and then he said, "How did you know we were going to Proxima?"

"The governor just mentioned it," Alexander said.

"No, before that," Benjamin replied. "You said we were going to Proxima."

Alexander shrugged. "I told you—I just know."

Catalina's own suspicions came whirling to life. "Why us?"

Alexander cocked his head curiously to one side. "What do you mean?"

"We're fine and everyone else is infected. Why are we the ones going to Med Bay?"

Alexander shrugged. "Probably because we can't stuff more than seven thousand people in there, and even if we could, what we really need to know is why you're not presenting symptoms, and what to do about that."

Those words slithered through Catalina's brain, sending shivers down her spine. "What to *do* about that? Isn't it obvious? We need to find a way to fight whatever alien virus is infecting us."

Alexander hesitated, looking ready to disagree.

"You're one of the most distrusting, skeptical people I know, Alex. Are you really going to sit here and tell me that we should take these aliens and this *Captain White,* at their word? How do we know they're not dragging us all off into slavery?"

Puzzlement flickered across Alexander's features, and for a moment the man she knew and loved was back. But only for a moment. In the next instant a rapturous smile took the place of his confusion and he said, "I can't explain it, I just *know* that they're not trying to harm us."

"And that's enough for you? Some mystical feeling that's probably been planted in your brain by the very aliens you're saying we should trust?"

"You'll see. It won't be long before we reach Proxima and then we'll have all the proof we need."

Catalina looked askance at him, her chest rising and falling in quick, shallow gasps. Every fiber of her being told her to run from this doppelgänger—this ridiculous parody of the man she'd married—but the calmer, more calculating part of her brain whispered that she should play along until she knew *where* she could run to.

"You don't trust me," Alexander said.

She smiled as reassuringly as she could manage. "I'm just trying to process everything. You're experiencing something that I can't relate to yet," she added, framing her feelings as diplomatically as she could.

"That's why we need to get you to Med Bay."

Another spike of dread lanced through her. He'd basically said it: they were gathering the uninfected in Med Bay so they could find a way to infect them, not because they wanted to find a cure.

"What if I don't want to go?" Catalina asked.

"I won't try to force you, if that's what you're wondering, but for your own good and for the good of everyone on board this ship, you really need to go."

Catalina tried to pick out the hidden threat lurking between the lines of what Alexander had just said, but she couldn't tell if he was being sincere or not. A small hand grabbed hold of hers and gave her arm a tug. She turned to see Benjamin heading for the door.

That gave her an idea. "We're going to get some food before we go to Med Bay," she said, letting Benjamin tug her toward the door. She kept half an eye on Alexander to make sure he didn't try to stop them. "Don't you need to eat, too?" she asked.

"You two go ahead. I'll meet you there. I'm going to change and shower first."

She nodded, secretly relieved that he wouldn't be joining them. They reached the door and Benjamin opened it with a wave of his hand. They weren't locked in anymore.

Outside, the corridor was unusually peaceful. After being locked in their rooms and skipping supper, the passengers all should have been trampling one another to get to breakfast, but instead, people flowed out of their rooms in orderly lines, as if they'd all choreographed their exits. The emergency response lane was alive with Marines in deep crimson jumpsuits riding patrollers, but rather than zipping around at high speed responding to crises as the uninfected panicked in response to the governor's announcement, they rolled along at walking speed. Everyone she saw was either smiling or laughing.

Whatever the joke was, Catalina wasn't getting it. "It's like they're all high on something," she whispered.

Beside her Benjamin nodded. "Just smile and play along. For now, they don't seem to see us as a threat. We need to gather the rest of the uninfected together and form a plan."

Catalina nodded along with that. Then she caught herself, surprised by the boy's take-charge attitude. He was just nine years old, and here he was, telling *her* how they should proceed. She looked at him with new eyes.

"What?" he asked.

"You're an unusual kid, you know that?"

"Thank you. I'll take that as a compliment."

"How are we going to find the others?" she asked, glancing around nervously as they began bumping shoulders with passengers on their way to the dining halls.

"I think I might know a way," he explained.

"Okay...?"

"Trust me. I'll explain later."

* * *

Doctor Laskin was busy running more tests on Deedee when Governor Chong made her announcement. They were trying to figure out how she'd vanished into thin air.

After the governor finished her announcement, Remo shot Deedee a curious look.

"How did you know we were going to Proxima?"

She shrugged. "I had a feeling."

"That's a pretty specific *feeling*." Remo glanced at Doctor Laskin for an answer.

"Whatever this infection is, it's somehow communicating with them. That would also explain why the infected feel so strongly that these aliens are not trying to harm us."

Deedee nodded. "That makes sense."

Remo regarded her with incredulity. "You don't sound very worried."

"Why should I be?"

Remo stared at her for a long moment, waiting for her to react more appropriately, but she just smiled. He looked away with a grimace. "Doctor, can I speak with you for a moment?"

"Of course."

Remo flashed Deedee a strained smile. "I'll be right back."

"Sure."

Doctor Laskin led him out of the room and down the corridor. The reception area at the end was once again filled with attending nurses and physicians. The doctor led him down another corridor to his office and shut the door behind them.

"What the hell is going on?" Remo blurted out.

"Shhh," the doctor said. "I don't know what we're dealing with, but whatever it is, if your squadmate and the Governor are anything to go by, it's brainwashed them all into singing the same tune. I need you to act like I'm one of them so I can look into this. You're the only witness that I wasn't also in a coma."

Remo considered that. "Deedee woke up to find you already running tests on her."

"If she asks, you can tell her I woke up just a few minutes before she did."

"I hope she buys that."

Laskin nodded. "So do I. The other uninfected are supposed to be coming here soon. I'm going to run a few tests—see if I can find out what we all have in common. If we really are immune, maybe we can formulate a cure for the others."

"You think they'll want to come here?" Remo asked.

"They might not have a choice," Doctor Laskin replied.

"I hope you're wrong. Forcing us to all gather here for *testing* sounds like a convenient way to quell any possible resistance."

Doctor Laskin nodded. "I agree, but we need to identify the uninfected somehow if we're going to establish that resistance."

"Damned if we do, and damned if we don't," Remo decided.

Doctor Laskin grimaced. "Exactly. At least for now we have the two of us to study. If you wouldn't mind, I'd like to take a few samples from you and get started."

Remo rolled up the sleeve of his jumpsuit and thrust out his arm. "Let's make it quick."

* * *

Audrey was back in her command chair in the CIC, blinking the sleep from her eyes and chowing down on a concentrated ration bar. She'd forgone a proper meal and her usual cup of coffee. How could she trust the food when she knew it was more than likely being prepared by infected crew members? They'd probably slip something into her meal and then she'd end up just like them—high as a kite and farting rainbows.

They were all preaching peace and alien love with glazed eyes and blissful smiles—even Councilor Markov! She'd expected him to drag her kicking and screaming to the Med Bay—that would have been more in character—but instead he'd tried to calm her down, and when she'd refused to go peacefully, he'd just let her go.

Audrey took a rabid bite of her ration bar, and cast a suspicious glare around the room, studying each of her crew members in turn. No urgent reports. No anxious requests for orders. No apparent concern whatsoever about their situation. Just business as usual.

Farting rainbows, Audrey thought. *All right. I can play along with that.*

"This is really *crimson!*" she said. "We're going to be at Proxima in what... Fields? What's our ETA?"

"A couple of days, according to Captain White, ma'am."

"Right, right, Captain White! He was the one who told us that, wasn't he? Amazing he's still alive. Over a century of silence and then suddenly he's back and saying *how-d'ya-do.* How old is that crazy bastard by now?"

"Over two hundred, I'd guess," Major Bright put in from the security station.

"Older than dirt! He must be one of the oldest geners alive. I guess it makes sense, Earth sent his mission right after they found a way to banish old Father Time and make us all immortal. Does anyone here still remember how that went down? The Captain's mission, I mean. What was our last contact with the *Intrepid?* We got a message from them before we lost contact, didn't we?"

Audrey waited for someone to take the bait.

"Aye, that we did," Major Bright said.

"Do we have a copy of that message in our databanks?"

"We have the entire known history of the Sol System in our databanks—you know that, ma'am..." Lieutenant Bates put in from the comms.

"Right you are! Silly me. Would you mind playing the *Intrepid's* message back for us on the main display, Mr. Bates?"

"Aye, pulling up the records now..."

"Thank you, darling." Audrey drummed her fingers on her armrests while she waited. She stuffed the last of her ration bar into her mouth, raining crumbs onto her lap.

A hologram sprang to life, and a man in an old Alliance

Captain's uniform appeared—black with gold buttons and tassels. A subtitle below the image identified him as *Captain White of the W.A.S. Intrepid.* He had straight brown hair and black holes for eyes with crows feet splayed around them. He'd obviously reached middle age before pressing pause on his telomeres.

"Hello wretched creatures," the captain said, his voice toneless and robotic. His lips moved, but the rest of his face remained perfectly still. "Your species sickens us. The time of your judgment is at hand." The hologram zoomed out to show an assembled group of Alliance Navy officers and enlisted, all with equally black eyes and rigid expressions. "Death you sow, and death you reap," the captain said. The rest of the crew repeated that line in unison, all in exactly the same toneless voices. Then the camera panned back to show just the captain's face once more. "We are coming."

The transmission faded to black and Audrey waited, desperate for someone to break the silence in the CIC with an outraged exclamation; she'd even have settled for a whisper of doubt or a murmur of collective concern, but there were no signs of apprehension whatsoever.

Audrey felt goosebumps prickle her skin. "Would anyone care to venture an analysis of that transmission?"

"Well, clearly *that* Captain White and the one who more recently contacted us were not in the same frame of mind," Major Bright said.

"That's a good start. What else?"

Silence.

"All right. My turn," she said. "Whatever the *Intrepid* ran into along the way to Wolf 1061 that made her crew suddenly so contemptuous and judgmental of their own species, it is likely somehow connected with the aliens who are supposedly taking us to Proxima Centauri. Would you say that logic follows, Major?"

"It's possible, ma'am."

"All right, then the captain's open hostility toward us, calling us *'wretched creatures'* suggests that these aliens are not actually friendly. The very fact that all of the infected seem inexplicably convinced to the contrary is suspicious enough by itself, but add to that this old transmission from Captain White, and the case becomes a more compelling one. Clearly sometime in the past century these aliens decided that an outright invasion would be somehow disadvantageous, so they decided to pretend to be our friends and then convince us of that by infecting us with some type of brainwashing disease."

Audrey waited for her crew to come to their senses, but no one spoke for an uncomfortably long moment. A few turned from their control stations to regard her with pitying smiles, as if she were the one suffering delusions. Audrey felt her skin begin to crawl, and she clenched her teeth against the sensation.

"I believe there's been some kind of misunderstanding," Major Bright ventured. "These aliens, whoever they are, are our friends. If you don't believe it, ma'am, then just wait until we arrive at Proxima. It won't be long."

Heads bobbed in agreement.

Audrey was about to argue with that logic—*Proxima might be where these aliens have their nearest work camp, or commune, more likely*—but she pasted a smile on her face and nodded. "I guess you're right. Their intentions will be known soon enough. In the meantime, I suppose it's not like we can do anything about it, anyway."

"Aye, ma'am. We're along for the ride. May as well sit back and relax."

"Yes. I'm going to go do a few rounds of our section, make sure no one's stirring up trouble. I'm sure I'm not the only one who's uneasy about all of this."

"I'll have a detail of Marines join you, ma'am."

"No, that won't be necessary. I don't anticipate running into any trouble. Everyone I've met so far has been unusually friendly and calm. If that's the result of this contagion, then I'm probably worrying for nothing."

Audrey left the CIC in a daze. A cold sweat trickled down her back, and her heart pounded irregularly in her chest. She made her way toward the nearest elevator. Along the way, all of the officers and enlisted she passed smiled and waved at her and each other. A few were holding hands. She even caught a Marine sergeant and a Navy ensign pressed against the wall and making out. Audrey's pace faltered as she recognized the sergeant. "Sergeant Torres?"

Torres waved at her and smiled. "Hi, Audrey," she said.

Audrey smiled thinly back, and Torres went back to making out with the ensign. Audrey entered the elevator and punched the button marked, *5-DORM,* planning to go to her quarters and lock herself in. As the elevator doors slid shut, she slumped against the handrail, and muttered, "What the hell?"

The doors opened on level five to reveal a young boy and his mother holding hands and smiling at her like idiots.

They're everywhere! Panic surged in her brain, and Audrey felt like she couldn't breathe.

Mother and son walked into the elevator. The boy grabbed

her hand. "Hello," he said, looking up at her.

Audrey stared back with wide eyes, wanting to rip her hand away, but too terrified to even twitch. *Maybe I'm the only one who's not infected.*

They rode the elevator up to *9-MED/SCI.* "See you later," the boy said, his hand slipping out of hers as he and his mother left the elevator.

The doors slid shut, and Audrey sucked in a deep breath. She realized she'd been holding her breath ever since they'd walked in.

Her hand tickled where the boy had touched it. She looked down, half expecting to see something horrible and contagious crawling on her skin.

Instead, she saw the corner of a page torn from an antique book. A sequence of numbers was scrawled over the words on the page —

7-5106J @ 1130.

Audrey stared at that piece of paper for a long moment as she rode the elevator back down to the next person who'd called it. As her panic faded, her mind cleared, and she realized what she was looking at. It was a room number — room 5106, J corridor, and a time — 11:30.

Those two hadn't actually been infected, but they had enough sense to pretend they were. Somehow they knew she also wasn't infected, and they'd invited her to a meeting.

The elevator doors opened and a group of Marines crowded in, all laughing and smiling as they chatted amongst themselves.

Audrey closed her hand into a fist around the piece of paper and offered the Marines a convincing smile. One of them told what was obviously an inside joke and they all laughed again as the elevator shot back up to level 5-*DORM*. Audrey joined in and matched their smiles with one of her own. This time it was genuine rather than sarcastic. She had an inside joke of her own to laugh at.

CHAPTER 13

The first one to arrive was also the first one they'd invited. Catalina watched as Commander Audrey Johnson came into Benjamin's old quarters. She was easy to recognize, tall and skinny with flashing red hair and vibrant opalescent eyes. Those eyes flicked from side to side, twin rainbows shimmering in the low light as she searched Benjamin's living room for hidden threats. As soon as she was through the door, Benjamin waved it shut behind her, and Audrey stopped where she was, regarding them carefully.

"Who are you two and why am I here?" the commander asked.

"Straight to the point," Benjamin said.

"I don't have any time to waste."

"Were you followed?" he asked.

"No, but it's impossible to be sure when everyone but me can apparently disappear into thin air."

Benjamin nodded. "I'll be as brief as possible."

The commander's eyes narrowed sharply. "This is a joke, right? How old are you—seven?"

"Nine," he corrected, "and looks can be deceiving."

The commander crossed her arms over her chest. "How did you two know I'm not infected? And how do I know that *you* aren't?"

Catalina turned to Benjamin expectantly. She'd also been

waiting to hear the answers to those questions. Benjamin had dragged her all around the ship for the past two hours, surreptitiously pressing torn out pages of paper into people's hands to set up a meeting that didn't have to be arranged through the ship's comms or neural link hubs. And since there weren't any surveillance systems in the ship's dormitories, whatever they did and said in here would be impossible to spy on—unless Benjamin had made a mistake with one of the invitees and accidentally invited someone who was already compromised by the virus.

"Well?" the commander demanded.

"Let's wait for the others to arrive so that I only have to explain this once."

"How many others are coming?"

"Three. Assuming all of them come."

"Let's go sit down," Benjamin said. If they find us, we want to make this look as much like a social meeting as possible."

They all sat down on the couches in the living room and shared an awkward silence while they waited.

The next one to arrive was tall and handsome with wavy brown hair and warm amber eyes. Catalina recognized him as one of the people Benjamin had invited from Med Bay. From his crimson jumpsuit and the single red star insignia on his sleeves, he was obviously a ranking officer. He approached them with a wary frown, and stopped to salute Commander Johnson. "Ma'am," he said.

"Lieutenant Commander Taggart," Johnson replied, nodding to him.

"Take a seat," Ben suggested.

"If it's all the same to you, I'd rather stand," he said.

Catalina watched his gaze drift from Benjamin to her. "What's this about?" he asked.

Before she could say anything, Benjamin repeated that they were waiting for the others to arrive first. The man didn't look happy. He glanced at the door behind him. "I'm on duty. Maybe we can do this another time?"

"Relax, Remo," Benjamin added. He must have looked up the man's name on his ARCs.

Remo ignored him and once again stared at her. "He do all your talking for you?"

Catalina shrugged. "I'm just as clueless as you are. Benjamin's the one who called this meeting."

"Sure. Nice trick using the kid as bait, but I'm not buying it."

Commander Johnson nodded along with that as if she'd come to the same conclusion. "You'd better start talking or we're out of here."

Benjamin sighed. "If we're with them, and we're out to get you, do you really think running away is going to do you any good? We'd either have reinforcements waiting to grab you, or else we'd call for them as soon as you leave."

"That a threat, kid?" Remo demanded, taking a step toward the boy. "'Cause I can silence you before I go."

"I'm sure you could," Benjamin agreed.

"You'd kill a nine-year-old boy?" Catalina asked.

Remo turned his flashing amber eyes on her, but said nothing.

"Five more minutes," Benjamin insisted. "As soon as Doctor Laskin arrives I'll explain everything."

"The doc's infected, kiddo," Remo said.

Commander Johnson looked alarmed, but Benjamin spoke

before she could. "Is he? Or is that something the two of you came up with so that he could study what's going on?"

Remo lunged at Benjamin, grabbing fistfuls of the boy's jumpsuit and lifting him off the couch as easily as if he were a sack of potatoes. Benjamin's feet dangled above the cushions.

"Put him down!" Catalina yelled.

Remo ignored her. "How the hell do you know what the Doc and I did or didn't agree to?"

"Patience, Remo. I'll explain everything soon."

"Patience is something I'm getting real short of, kid."

Before things could escalate any further, the door swished open and in walked a man in a white jumpsuit with glowing blue piping and a matching blue cross emblazoned on his chest.

"Doctor Laskin," Benjamin said. "Please come in and take a seat."

The doctor crept toward them warily, his eyes darting around the room as the commander's had been. Benjamin waved the door shut.

"Start talking," Remo gritted out.

Benjamin glared back at him. "As soon as you put me down."

"Fine." Remo dropped him onto the couch, and Benjamin bounced back up in the ship's low gravity. He used his momentum to turn around and stand up and then walked over to the sliding glass doors leading to the terrace. He turned to address them all from there.

Catalina noticed that the simulated view from the terrace was of a dark, shadowy green forest. Shafts of light flickered through the tree branches, illuminating Benjamin's brown hair and one side of his face.

"You're all wondering how I knew that you're immune to the virus we encountered. I have the answer, but I'm afraid that it might shock you. To back up what I'm about to say, I'd like you, Doctor Laskin, to please explain what you've found in common so far between the samples you took from yourself and Remo."

The doctor glanced at Remo, as if to ask if he'd spoken about that. Catalina knew that he hadn't. Somehow, Benjamin knew things about them without having to ask.

"So? What did you find?" Benjamin insisted.

Doctor Laskin frowned. "Why is there a child in charge of this meeting?"

Remo snorted and shook his head. "The million Sol question."

Benjamin smiled. "We'll get there. You found nanites in both of your blood samples, didn't you, Doctor?"

Doctor Laskin looked taken aback. "How did you know that?"

"Because I have them, too. We all do."

"Lucky guess," Remo said. "Nanites are used for so many different treatments—half the crew probably has the little buggers in their blood!"

"True," Benjamin said. "Though statistically it would be unlikely to find nanites present in all five of us. What does the name Nano Nova mean to all of you?"

Catalina didn't recognize it, but she saw recognition flash across everyone else's faces, and they began trading wary looks with one another.

Benjamin went on, "You all received medical treatments from them for varying reasons. As you know, Nano Nova specializes in lost causes—cases that conventional medical science hasn't found a way to treat. Let me start with myself—at the age of four I was diagnosed with juvenile onset Tay Sachs. It's an incurable genetic disease that causes progressive deterioration of nerve cells.

"At age seven, by the time my mother finally took me to Earth and Nano Nova for treatment, I could no longer walk or speak, and I had to be fed through a tube. By this point my mental faculties had deteriorated to a critical point, and there was no way to restore my mind and body to what they once were. Even if Nano Nova found a way to fix me, they informed my mother that my memories and personality would be completely different, filled in where need be from a compatible template. Desperate to save what was left of me, she agreed to the treatments anyway. It worked. Nano Nova saved my life."

"Touching," Remo said. "What's that got to do with us?"

"Shut up, Lieutenant," Commander Johnson snapped. She was hanging on Benjamin's every word.

He went on, "All of you have your own stories to share about your experiences with Nano Nova, and all of you signed the same waivers and consent forms. In there was a clause about using synthetic cells and sequences of DNA to replace your existing ones. Although you were all treated for different diseases, one thing about your treatments was identical. Your brains were all replaced, cell by cell, with synthetic copies."

"Bullshit!" Remo blurted out. "I've heard enough of this crap."

"How is that possible?" Commander Johnson demanded.

"A synthetic brain cell is functionally no different from one that you were born with, except for the fact that it is synthetic. This was the real purpose behind Nano Nova. Benevolence used it to test synthetic cell and DNA grafts."

"I was treated for degenerative bone loss from prolonged exposure to low *G*," Commander Johnson put in. "What does that have to do with my brain?"

"Nothing, but giving you a synthetic brain was necessary to accomplish *our* goals."

"*Your* goals?"

"Ben is short for Benjamin—the name my mother gave me—but the template that was used to fill in the dead parts of Benjamin's brain came from an android who was coincidentally also named Ben—in this case short for *Benevolence*."

Remo shook his index finger at the boy. "*You're* Benevolence?!"

"No, I'm Ben. Soon after my creation, I made a copy of my code. That copy spread through the Internet like a virus, absorbing all of the data available there, and becoming a much grander intellect, one which ultimately became the AI that now rules over Earth, while I remained relatively unaware and naive. Benevolence is my older brother."

"I know who you are," Commander Johnson said, glaring at him. "This ship wasn't supposed to have any androids on it."

"And it doesn't. We're synthetics, a new breed."

"But still artificial."

"Partly, yes."

"Why?" Doctor Laskin asked. "Why go to so much trouble to make five people into synthetic hybrids and then smuggle them onto this ship?"

"You were just the beginning. A proof of concept. The goal

was to prevent a war between androids and humans. If everyone's a synthetic, suddenly there won't be any differences to divide us anymore. You can't discriminate against yourself."

"How would you make everyone synthetic?" Doctor Laskin asked.

"Nano Nova has perfected their treatments, and it is now possible to preserve both a person's body and their consciousness as pure data so that even accidental deaths can't kill people anymore. With an insurance policy like that, who could resist? Benevolence has already patented the procedure to create synthetic copies of people and started up a subsidiary company to offer life after death insurance. You were all offered a Sure Life policy after your treatments with Nano Nova."

"Shit. I've got that," Remo said.

"Me, too," Doctor Laskin nodded. "But it didn't say anything about bringing us back from the dead."

"The wording in those policies is open to interpretation. We haven't decided to go public with these procedures yet."

"How does any of that prevent a war?" Remo demanded. "You're not removing the differences that divide us, you're just adding a new one. Discrimination will shift from humans and androids to synthetics, humans, and androids. Now there's a happy little love triangle."

Benjamin shook his head. "Within a decade all of the androids on Earth will be replaced by synthetics, and as for the human population—sooner or later everyone dies from something. Fear of that will drive them all to get Sure Life policies, and when they do eventually die, they'll come back as synthetics."

"What about babies?"

"Birth rates are low, but babies born to even one synthetic parent will also be synthetic. Kind of like dominant versus recessive gene expression."

Catalina saw Commander Johnson shaking her head. "War will erupt long before you have a strong enough majority to prevent it."

"Perhaps, but if a war does start, people will be rushing out to get their Sure Life insurance policies faster than ever, and they'll be dying faster than ever, too."

"So you and your big brother have been quietly planning to make humanity extinct?" Remo demanded.

"Not extinct—look at it as the next step in human evolution, one which will make you all better and ultimately bring us together as a unified whole."

"That's it," Remo said. "I've heard enough! I thought we came here to discuss what's going on aboard this ship and what to do about it."

"You did," Benjamin said.

"Then skip to the point, kid. We'll figure out what to do about your plans for galactic domination later."

Ben nodded. "All right, the point is, I know how to cure the rest of the crew and make them all immune like us."

Catalina watched realization setting in on the others' faces, but she was the first to voice it: "We have to make them synthetics," she said.

Ben nodded. "Exactly. Whatever it is that's making everyone act so strange, it has no effect on synthetic cells."

"Well, isn't that convenient. Benevolence gets to advance his agenda," Remo said. "How do we know he's not behind all of this?"

"If he is, then that would mean he has the technology for energy shields, inertial compensators, artificial gravity, and cloaking devices—not to mention traversable wormholes. If all of that's true, then there's no need for him to use an alien virus and invasion plot as an excuse to convert us all to synthetics."

Catalina shook her head. "There's just one problem. I never signed up for any treatments with Nano Nova, so how am I immune?"

"When Benevolence approached Catalina de Leon, asking if she would join her ex-husband in the Mindscape to help him get over his girlfriend's death, she laughed in his face, but she consented to create a digital copy of herself and allow that copy to enter the Mindscape to help Alexander. You are that copy."

Catalina gaped at him. "That's not possible."

"As soon as he finished perfecting the technology for synthetics, Benevolence brought you to life and allowed you to leave the Mindscape with Alexander. You, Caty, are actually the very first fully synthetic human. You're the proverbial Eve of your kind."

Catalina shook her head, speechless.

"Fuck this shit!" Remo said. "I've heard enough. I'm turning all of you in. I'll take aliens over Benevolence any day!"

"You can do that..." Benjamin said, a note of warning in his voice. "But what do you know about them, or their motives? Nothing. On the other hand, how long have you known Benevolence? More than a century—and he's only ever shown kindness to humanity."

"Yeah, and he's kindly scheming to make us all into bots

like him," Remo sneered. "Hell, if you're telling the truth, then he's already done it with the five of us!"

Benjamin nodded. "Exactly, and you're still just as hateful as ever. That should prove to you that you're no different now as a synthetic than you were as a human, so what have you got to be upset about? What's he done to you that's so terrible?"

"And what's to stop big brother Benny from brainwashing us all later?"

Ben scowled and shook his head. "You see us as the enemy, and then you make it so."

Remo smirked.

"We're already synthetics," Commander Johnson said. "What do we have to lose?"

"Uh, the rest of the crew?" Remo suggested.

"They're already gone," she replied, "and if we don't do something soon, whatever's happening to them might become permanent. If making them synthetic brings them back, then I'm all for it. Let's put it to a vote. All in favor of immunizing the crew with synthetic treatments?"

Catalina raised her hand. Everyone else raised theirs, too. Everyone except for Remo.

"It's settled then."

Commander Johnson turned to Ben.

"I'll need to work with Doctor Laskin to program the nanites," Ben said, glancing from the Commander to the doctor.

"You'll need a cover story to explain what you're doing in Med Bay," Commander Johnson said.

"I just lost my mother," Benjamin replied. "I've always been interested in medicine, and I want to become a doctor someday, so Doctor Laskin agreed to let me hang around and watch him work to help distract me from my loss."

Catalina remembered how she'd spent the previous day trying to distract him from exactly that. "Were you just pretending to grieve?" she asked. "If you're Ben, not Benjamin, then she's not really your mother."

"There's still a remnant of the real Benjamin in me, and the android part of me feels deeply when *anyone* dies, regardless of how close they are to me personally."

Catalina heard Remo give a dubious snort.

"Let's not go off on a tangent," Commander Johnson said. "We need to get out of here before someone finds us."

Everyone nodded their agreement, and a new voice joined the group. "Too late for that."

Catalina spun around to see Councilor Markov materialize out of thin air, stark naked, and blocking the exit with his broad frame.

CHAPTER 14

Catalina saw it all happen as if in slow motion. Remo spun around, revealing a small pistol he'd had hidden in his palm.

"Wait!" Commander Johnson yelled.

There came a bright flash of light and a muffled *screech*. Councilor Markov's body hit the floor with a loud *thump*. A tendril of smoke curled from a blackened hole in his chest, his eyes vacant and staring.

"What have you done?" Audrey demanded, jumping up from the couch and running over to the fallen councilor.

"He would have reported us," Remo explained in an uncertain voice. He lowered his weapon with exaggerated care and stared at it in his palm.

Doctor Laskin snapped out of his own shock and went to help Commander Johnson examine the councilor.

"He's dead," the commander said before Doctor Laskin could get there. She turned to glare at Remo, her nostrils flaring and opalescent eyes flashing. "You couldn't have stunned him?"

Remo shook his head. "I..."

"We need to hide the body," Ben said quietly. "And we need a good excuse for why the councilor won't be answering his comms. Commander Johnson, you and the councilor were lovers, were you not?"

She glared at him. "How the hell do you know that?"

"Because of your reaction, and because part of my mission here was to watch all of you."

"You've been spying on us?" Catalina asked.

"From a distance," Ben explained. "Synthetic brains can communicate directly with each other. Yours have been sending me updates."

Remo recovered enough to send Ben a dark scowl. Then he glanced at each of them in turn and said, "Big brother Benevolence is watching you."

Commander Johnson drew herself up from the councilor's side, her moment of outrage safely swept under an expressionless mask. "What does my relationship to the deceased have to do with anything?"

"You can be our alibi. Say he woke up feeling ill. Food poisoning. Doctor Laskin—you can corroborate that if need be. That will buy us roughly twenty-four hours."

"Is that enough time?" Catalina asked.

"To immunize the chief of security, yes, but we'll need another day for everyone else, assuming we can gain access to a suitable dispersal system—the ship's water supply, for example."

"We'll cover it up as long as we can," the commander said stiffly.

"We still haven't decided what to do about the body," Doctor Laskin said. "We can't take him to the morgue, even if we hide him in a body bag. It will raise too many questions."

"Leave him in here," Ben said. "In the shower. These are my quarters. No one will think to look for him here."

"Assuming no one knows he came," Catalina said.

"If he alerted anyone before or after he followed us inside, then we'll know soon enough," Commander Johnson replied. "Taggart—" she pointed to Remo. "Clean up your mess."

Remo hesitated briefly, then nodded and lurched into motion. He walked over and picked the councilor up. The councilor would have weighed at least two hundred and fifty pounds on Earth, but Remo carried him easily in the simulated Martian gravity.

"As for the rest of us, we should leave before anyone else stumbles in here," the commander said.

"One by one," Benjamin added. "That way passersby don't notice anything unusual."

"I'll go first," Commander Johnson said, waving her hand at the door.

It wouldn't open for her.

"Open up, damn it!"

"Hold on," Ben said. "Until we have the chief of security on our side, no one makes contact with the others, and no one meets in person, except in the course of our usual business— agreed?"

Everyone agreed, and Benjamin unlocked the door. Commander Johnson left the room.

Remo returned from hiding the body and scanned the room briefly, no doubt looking for the commander.

"Jessica never showed up," Benjamin said.

"Who?" Remo asked.

Benjamin glanced at him, and then back to Catalina. She shook her head, equally confused. Benjamin explained, "You found me with her after my mom died—a girl my age, curly brown hair, brown eyes..."

"Right. I took her back to her parents," Catalina said. "I remember now." But she didn't remember Ben giving the girl a piece of paper with his room number on it. "We didn't invite her, did we?"

"Benevolence sent her with me. She's a synthetic like us, so we can communicate without going through the ship's comm systems or neural hubs," Ben explained.

"Your partner in crime?" Remo asked. Ben nodded, and Remo snorted, "Another kid."

"Just because you can communicate without going through the ship's comms, that doesn't make it undetectable," Dr. Laskin said. "Someone could have intercepted the signal and traced it back to her. That might be how the councilor knew to find us here."

Ben looked skeptical. "Even if they knew to look for it, the encryption would take weeks to crack."

"Can't you use the same method of communication to ask what delayed her?" Catalina asked.

"That's what I'm doing," Ben explained.

"And...?"

He remained silent for a few seconds, but then his head snapped up and his eyes abruptly widened.

"Her parents are forcing her to report to the Med Bay for examination."

"Is that a problem? Can they find out what she is?" Catalina asked.

Ben shook his head. "They'd have to biopsy her brain and extract some of her synthetic cells."

"That's a risky procedure," Dr. Laskin said. "It could kill her, which doesn't seem in keeping with the benign, passive behavior we've seen from the infected so far."

"Benign my ass," Remo said.

"Would Jessica's own parents be willing to risk her life just to find out what makes her immune?" Catalina asked.

"I don't know. Maybe her parents wouldn't, but the medical staff would. Or maybe the infected already know what we are. We need to find out what they're planning for us." Ben turned to stare at Doctor Laskin. "You have to be the one who examines her."

The doctor nodded. "Let's go."

* * *

"Hello, my name is Doctor Larry Laskin," he said, offering his hand first to the patient's mother, and then to her father. "What seems to be the trouble with your daughter?" he glanced down at the girl—curly brown hair and big brown eyes, probably no older than Ben. "What's your name?"

"Jessica," she replied in a cautious voice. She glanced up at her parents, then back to him, her eyes silently pleading.

"The governor told all of the uninfected to report to Med Bay," Jessica's mother explained. "So we brought her here."

"I feel fine," Jessica insisted.

Her mother smiled. "I know, dear, but it's best to be careful."

Jessica looked horrified. Her parents were acting like something was wrong with *her*, not the other way around.

"Your mother's right," Laskin said, pretending to agree.

"He's infected, too!" she said, and bolted for the door. Laskin locked it with his neural link. "Let me out!" she said, pounding on the door with her fists.

"Calm down, sweetheart," her mother said. "No one's going to hurt you. We just want to run a few tests."

"Listen to your mother, Jessy," her father added.

— 163 —

Doctor Laskin walked over to the girl. "I'm sure you're fine," he said, leading her gently back to the examination table. "But we can't be too careful with these things."

"She's been acting strange ever since we woke up this morning," her mother explained.

Laskin nodded along with that as if their perspective made perfect sense. "We'll get to the bottom of it."

"*You're* the ones acting strange!" Jessica screeched. "You're the ones who are infected!"

Both her parents just smiled and shook their heads.

Laskin added a smile of his own for good measure. "Kids," he said, as if that somehow explained everything. "Your parents just want what's best for you, Jessica."

She glared incredulously at each of them in turn. "Let's see what's going on, shall we?" He began to prepare a hypodermic needle for a blood sample, but Jessica's father came over and placed a hand on his arm to stop him.

"We should go straight to the source of the trouble. Take a tissue sample from her brain."

Laskin tried to mask his shock. "A brain biopsy? There are significant risks to such an invasive procedure."

He nodded gravely. "We understand."

Laskin stared back at him, his heart pounding and his brain screaming for him to *run* while he still had a chance. Out of the corner of his eye he noticed Jessica's mother nodding along with her husband.

"I'll go prep the OR," he said slowly.

Jessica caught his eye with another pleading look as he left the room. As soon as he was out the door, his private horror burst out, and his entire body began to shake.

What am I going to do?

CHAPTER 15

"**Y**ou have to go through with it," Ben insisted.

Catalina saw Doctor Laskin hesitate. He leaned forward to rest his elbows on his desk and steeple his hands in front of his face.

"We're not talking about a tonsillectomy—we're going to remove a piece of her brain. The procedure could kill her."

"She knew the risks when she signed on to the *Liberty*," Ben replied. "We both did," he added. "And if she dies, she won't be gone. Benevolence can bring her back using her latest backup on Earth."

"What about what Jessica wants?" Laskin replied.

"She would tell you the same thing. Besides, you can't ask her for permission without tipping off her parents. Perform the procedure, Doctor, and while you're in surgery, I'll get to work programming nanites so that we can immunize the others."

Laskin grimaced. "They're going to know what we are soon. After that they might guess what we're trying to do."

"Which is why there's no time to waste. We're not going to have time to test this procedure. We'll have to skip straight to section-wide dissemination. If it works here, we'll find a way to spread it to the other sections. Where's your lab?"

"I'll show you," Doctor Laskin said, getting up from his desk and heading for the door to his office.

"What about me?" Catalina asked.

Turning to her, Benjamin said, "You'd better get back to your quarters. By now your husband must be worried about you. Best not to raise his suspicions any more than we have to."

Catalina nodded slowly, her eyes drifting out of focus as she watched them leave the room. Her chest heaved, her breathing fast and shallow. Things were spinning out of control. Just a few minutes ago she'd learned that she wasn't even human, and now they were going to try to fight an unknown alien virus by making everyone else just like her.

What if Jessica wasn't the only one in danger of a risky procedure? What were the risks of turning infected, biological humans into synthetic copies?

I could lose Alexander forever...

* * *

Alexander sat in the living room watching the door, waiting for Catalina to return. He couldn't sense her the way he could *sense* the others. Her emotions and thoughts were a dark spot in an otherwise dazzling universe. He had to read her body language and read between the lines of everything she said to know what she was thinking. He knew she didn't trust him, but she would come around. Soon her eyes would be opened as his had been opened, and then...

A burst of euphoria surged through him. Alexander sighed, and a dreamy smile parted his lips. He wondered if this was what drug users felt like when they got their fix. Probably. The difference was, he had a permanent supply, and there was no need to worry about addiction, tolerance, or overdose.

This must be what heaven is like, he thought, reveling in the feelings of oneness, security, acceptance, and love... he was one with the *Entity.* He could feel everyone else on board the ship, their minds bright sparks in an otherwise dark universe, an unseen tapestry weaving them all together, moving them in synchrony and harmony with each other. He could also feel the ones *around* their ship, the ones on board the... *Harvester,* the word came to him as if whispered by the Entity. That's what they called their ship, but their word for it was in a different language, a more logical language.

Alexander sighed once more. The burdens of what to do, where to go, and how to get there had all been settled. They would go out into the Federation as extensions of the Entity. *We must be its hands and feet, slaves to its will, acting in the interests of the All.*

A warm glow suffused Alexander's brain, lighting up his pleasure centers until he couldn't help but smile. Unity with the Entity was the best thing that had ever happened to him.

The door swished open and in walked Catalina. She glanced at him. Revulsion twisted her upper lip and wrinkled her nose, forcing her to look away.

Some of his joy and enthusiasm waned as her presence changed the Entity's mood. He could feel its disapproval, its suspicion. She wasn't a part of the All. She was immune to its influence, still driven by petty individual interests. She wasn't a piece of a greater whole like him. She was her own piece in an impossibly tiny universe that only revolved around her and those she cared about.

If everyone perished and yet she and her loved ones remained happily untouched, she would scarcely feel the pain of their passing. Her caring extended from her in ever weakening circles, the more distant the relation, the less she cared, until she could live quite happily knowing that children were starving in Africa and people were being sold into slavery in Asia. She could buy a three story mansion by a lake in California, and live a life of ease and luxury while others sat shivering in the rain and eating garbage.

Alexander remembered how his old self had felt about such things. He had been just as ignorant and selfish, just as blinded to the misery of others. Benevolence had tried to remedy those problems on Earth, but without everyone working together his solutions were never permanent.

Alexander had comforted himself with the knowledge that he could do nothing to solve such vast problems, and therefore, he was not to blame. He didn't have to help because whatever help he could offer would never really fix anything.

And all of that had been true to a certain extent, but as a part of the All, with the Entity guiding them in unison, privation was a mote of dust that could be swept away with a whisper. And just as simply, all the other problems would disappear. Just as you wouldn't sell yourself into slavery, a member of the All would never sell another member.

"What is wrong with you?"

Alexander turned to see his wife staring at him in disgust. Her hands were planted on her hips, her honey-brown eyes flashing.

Back was the darkness and suspicion he'd felt when she'd entered the room. Catalina was his wife, but she was divorced from him in every way that mattered. The Entity *had* to find some way to join her with the All or he would lose her forever. A wave of despair rolled through him with that thought, and his smile faded.

"What do you mean, darling?" he asked.

"I've been watching you from the hall for the past ten minutes. You're just staring at the wall with your eyes glazed and a stupid grin on your face. What's going on with you, Alex? Talk to me!"

"You wouldn't understand."

"Try me."

The Entity encouraged him, urging him to speak. Perhaps if she knew, she would no longer see him as a threat.

"I'm becoming a part of something bigger. The Entity has joined us all together. Now my needs are the needs of the All. My life is not my own. I belong to the All, a slave of the Entity's will."

Catalina's eyes grew round. After a long moment she smiled and said, "Sounds great," but he didn't miss the way her lips trembled.

"You don't understand," he said.

"I'm trying to," she replied.

"The Entity only wants what's best for the All. When I say I'm a slave to its will, I don't mean that in a negative way. Humans are afraid of losing control, because deep down we only trust ourselves to look out for us, but there's another way. If we all look out for each other, the All acting as one, there's no reason to fear. Each individual is just as important as the others, and none will be neglected."

"You're talking about some new form of communism," Catalina said slowly.

"The only kind that works. How can you have equality without unity of mind, body, and soul? If we are one, then there is only one set of needs, one set of desires, one directive."

"And *you* cease to exist," Catalina added.

"I still exist. I'm here talking to you, aren't I?"

"But your thoughts and actions are all directed by this Entity, so where does the Entity stop and you begin?"

"You, me, them—these are the divisions that cause us to act selfishly, serving our own interests instead of those of the All. The only way to put an end to human suffering is to unify us. Together we can build a society with no more tears and no more pain. Heaven in all but name."

Catalina's brow furrowed deeply. "And this Entity, what is he then? God?"

Alexander shook his head. "The Entity didn't create us."

"So what gives it the right to change us?"

"What gives it the right?" Alexander echoed. He shook his head. "You have it all wrong. It's not a right, it's a responsibility. If the Entity left humanity to their evil ways, knowing it could do something to save them, would that not make it just as evil and uncaring as they are?"

Catalina appeared confused by that logic. "They? You're talking like you're not human."

"I am All."

Catalina shivered. "How do I know becoming a part of this All won't kill me?"

"In a way you will die, but death to self is not to be feared—it is to be welcomed!"

"And what happens when we die for real?" Catalina asked.

"The All cannot die."

"I'm pretty sure people can still die, infected or not."

"Infected?" Alexander felt a wave of frustration ripple

through him. "You insist on giving negative connotations to what is happening because you refuse to open your eyes! You cling to your notions of self as if selfishness were a good thing."

Catalina glanced behind her. "Does this Entity care if *others* apart from the All and itself die?"

Alexander smiled. "Why do you think the Entity came to join everyone together in the All?"

"But I'm not joined to it."

"Not yet," Alexander corrected.

"And what if I don't want to be joined?"

He shook his head. "That's ignorance talking. Once you see what you're missing, you won't want to be apart from it."

"Okay, let me put it another way. What if I *can't* be joined to the All?"

Alexander found himself wondering the same thing, but the Entity reassured him—no one would remain apart from it. "The Entity will find a way," Alexander insisted.

A thin smile spread across Catalina's lips. "Well, I can't wait. Thank you for this talk, Alex. I really needed someone to explain what's going on."

Alexander knew she was lying. He was tempted to tell her that the Entity could not be so easily fooled, but he knew it would do no good. Best to let her take comfort in her lies, exposing them would only make her feel more threatened. He nodded and smiled back at her. "You're welcome, Caty."

She nodded back and headed for the door.

"Leaving so soon?" he asked.

"I need to check on Benjamin."

"Yes, where is he?"

"He was bored, so I left him... in the rec hall," she said

quickly.

More lies. Alexander said nothing.

Let her go. Soon she and the others will know that the All means them no harm.

CHAPTER 16

Catalina left their quarters shaking uncontrollably. *The Entity? The All?*

They weren't just dealing with some behavior-modifying virus—this was an organized takeover of the human race. She could only imagine what the aliens they'd left behind in the Sol System were busy doing on Earth and Mars.

She had worried about trying an experimental treatment on Alexander, not knowing what it could do to him, but anything would be better than this. Even if the treatment killed him, it would be a merciful release from the Entity that had enslaved him.

When Catalina reached the Med Bay, she walked up to the reception and asked for Doctor Laskin.

The nurse behind the counter turned to her with a blissful smile that faded by a few degrees upon seeing her.

"He's in surgery, ma'am. You'll have to wait."

"Any idea when he'll be out?"

The nurse shook her head. "Are you reporting for examination? We have other doctors who can see you."

"No, no, I feel fine."

"Ma'am, for your own good and that of everyone else on board, you should get checked out."

"Of course, but not yet."

The nurse regarded her with a frown, and Catalina smiled

back. "Going to call for security to drag me into an examination room?"

The nurse remained silent, and for a moment Catalina feared that was exactly what the nurse was going to do, but the woman just shook her head. "If you'd like to speak with Doctor Laskin, you'll have to wait," she said again.

"That's fine," Catalina replied. She turned and went to sit in the waiting area.

She passed an hour there, twiddling her thumbs and glancing nervously at doctors and nurses as they walked by. Some of them glanced back, their perpetual smiles fading the moment they saw her. They knew. Somehow, just by looking at her, they *knew* she wasn't one of them. Did they also know what she and the others were planning?

Finally Doctor Laskin came walking out into the reception area, looking exhausted.

Catalina got up and went to speak with him. "Doctor."

He glanced at her and smiled. "Mrs. de Leon. Are you ready for your examination?"

She hesitated, suddenly wondering if they'd all misjudged Doctor Laskin, but then she noticed the way his smile didn't reach his eyes.

"I'm ready," she said.

"Follow me."

He led her down another corridor on the other side of the reception area. Once they were far enough away from the nurses she leaned over and whispered. "I need to see Ben."

The doctor nodded, but said nothing. He led her through corridor after corridor until they came to a door covered in warnings, both holographic and painted-on.

Her ARCs identified the door as leading to Bio-safety Lab

#3. The door was locked and access restricted.

Doctor Laskin looked both ways, making sure they were alone before waving the door open.

Catalina wondered about that, remembering how the councilor had appeared out of thin air. If the infected could make themselves invisible, then they could be hiding literally *anywhere*.

The doctor led her through the open door and into a small containment corridor beyond. It was sealed on the inside with another door. Doctor Laskin waved the outer door shut behind them, and a computerized voice said, "Decontamination initiating."

Red lights flashed in the corridor, and pressurized air blasted them from all sides. An acrid, aseptic smell filled Catalina's nostrils. Then the air stopped blasting them, leaving a swirling, acrid-smelling mist behind. The flashing lights pulsed crimson through the murk, making it seem as if they were drowning in blood. Then a loud whirring noise started up and the mist ran into the corners of the room. As soon as the air was clear once more, the red lights pulsed green, and a pleasant tone sounded.

"Decontamination complete."

The inner door swished open, and they walked into the bio-safety lab. Catalina was surprised to find the others already waiting there and wearing bright yellow hazmat suits. She couldn't see them through those suits, but her ARCs identified them clearly enough. Remo stood by an open locker full of matte black guns, while Commander Johnson stood beside him in a matching suit, removing vials from a crate and fitting them into tranquilizer darts. Remo took each of those darts and carefully slotted them into ammo belts.

"What's going on?" Catalina asked, turning to Doctor Laskin in question. He seemed equally confused.

"I called them here."

It was Benjamin's voice, amplified to a tinny register. Catalina turned toward the sound and saw him sitting motionless at a computer terminal, drowning in another hazmat suit while a trio of holo displays blazed in front of him with rapidly scrolling lines of text. Trying to track what he was doing made her head spin. Clearly there were some differences between her synthetic brain and his.

She approached him carefully. "Ben?"

"Yes, Catalina?" he replied, not turning to look.

"We have a problem. I think they're on to us."

"They are," he replied. "But I have the solution."

Without looking away from his work, he pointed to where Remo and Commander Johnson were busy preparing their arsenal.

Catalina followed that gesture and shook her head. "We can't possibly tranquilize them all. There's too many of them."

"I know," Ben said. "But we won't have to. They'll run away from us as soon as they realize what we're shooting them with."

Catalina studied the crate where Commander Johnson was withdrawing the vials, and this time she noticed the bio-hazard warnings scrawled on the sides of it. She used her ARCs to check the contents of the crate, and a holographic label appeared before her eyes.

The vials contained Ebola III mixed with a sedative agent.

Catalina gasped. "You're going to set loose a plague?"

"How did you get this?" Doctor Laskin demanded. "This is weaponized Ebola! What are we even doing with this on board?"

"We have it in case we run into a hostile alien species that's too advanced to fight with conventional methods."

"An alien species whose biology just happens to be susceptible to a plague from Earth?" Doctor Laskin asked. "How can this be in here and I don't know about it?"

"Maybe you didn't have the clearance to know," Ben suggested. "You two had better put on your hazmat suits. That virus is airborne. If they drop one of those vials and it breaks open, you'll both be dead within the hour."

Her heart pounding in her chest, Catalina glanced hurriedly around the room, searching for a hazmat suit. Ben pointed to another locker opposite the one where Remo and Commander Johnson were busy loading dart guns. Doctor Laskin was already on his way there.

"This is insane!" he objected as he reached the locker. "You can't set Ebola loose on this ship! You'll kill everyone! Including us! We need a vaccine."

"I'm working on it," Ben said.

"Better to kill everyone than let them be dragged off into slavery to the Entity," Commander Johnson said.

"Fuck the Entity," Remo added.

Catalina realized someone must have explained everything to them at the same time that Alexander had been explaining things to her. She reached the hazmat locker and waited for Doctor Laskin. His hands shook furiously, rattling the hazmat suits on the rack as he struggled to remove them from the locker.

Catalina placed a hand on his arm to still his violent tremors. "Let me," she said.

The doctor nodded quickly, his eyes wide as he backed

away.

"How's Jessica doing?" Ben asked.

It took Doctor Laskin a moment to realize Ben was speaking to him. "She'll live," he said. "Until the Ebola gets her. We can't do this!" he insisted. "I agreed to the other plan, but this is going too far."

Catalina was about to agree with him when Ben's voice came whispering through her thoughts.

There is no Ebola III. Play along. They might be watching.

Then what's in those vials? Catalina thought back, wondering if Ben would be able to hear.

To her surprise, he replied, *The nanites.*

Catalina glanced at Doctor Laskin and saw from the relief on his face that Ben had explained the same thing to him. She glanced around the room, wondering if someone really was watching them.

"How are we going to shoot invisible targets?" she asked aloud. "Councilor Markov appeared out of nowhere. The others could hide like that, too."

"Not safely," Ben said. "The councilor was naked. They can't use hazmat suits and cloak themselves at the same time."

"They might sacrifice a few of their own to take us out."

"Let's hope they're not that callous," Ben replied.

"Just in case, our first objective should be to get to a real weapons locker," Remo said. "If they're shooting at us with automatic rifles and we're shooting back with darts, this is going to be the shortest mutiny in history."

"Mutiny?" Catalina wondered aloud as she pulled on her hazmat suit.

Remo turned to her with a loaded dart rifle in one hand

and belt full of darts in the other. "What did you think this was?"

Catalina grimaced and put her helmet on. She struggled with the neck seals with her hands now encased in bulky yellow gloves.

Commander Johnson walked over to her. "Let me help you."

"They're coming," Benjamin warned.

"W-what?" Doctor Laskin stuttered.

Remo walked up and pushed a dart rifle and an ammo belt into his hands.

"You know how to use it?"

The doctor shook his head.

"Point and shoot. Right down the barrel. Like this—" he took back the rifle and illustrated. "Take the safety off here. It's a bolt action rifle, so you have to reload after each shot. To do that, you lift this handle and pull it back to open the breech. Once the breech is fully open, you slide in another dart and push the handle back into position to shut and lock the breech. Got it?"

Doctor Laskin shook his head, and Remo scowled.

"We're out of time," Ben said. "He'll have to figure it out on his own. Someone watch the door! As soon as it opens, you all shoot. Remember, we might not be able to see what comes through."

Remo passed Catalina a rifle and an ammo belt. She set the rifle down and leaned it against the wall while she clipped the belt around her waist. Taking up the rifle she spent a moment looking for the safety. She found it—a little lever above the trigger. She flicked it into the *off* position and raised the rifle awkwardly to her shoulder to aim it at the lab door. She glanced back at Ben and found him still sitting in front of his holo displays, lines of code scrolling by faster than ever.

A *hissing* sound drew her attention to the door and she recalled the pressurized jets of air that had blasted her during decontamination.

"Here they come..." Remo said.

Catalina counted down the seconds in her head. She heard footsteps behind her and whirled around—afraid that one of *them* was creeping up behind her—but it was just Ben. He'd finally left his computer terminal.

"You're done?"

He nodded. Catalina saw that the excess fabric of his hazmat suit had been bunched up and cinched behind him with surgical tape—but how he could walk in those over-sized boots was a mystery. Ben went to the weapons locker and grabbed a rifle and an ammo belt for himself. The rife was almost as tall as he was, but he hefted it easily and aimed it at the door.

"Ready?" he asked.

Catalina was about to say no, but then the door swished open.

"Fire!"

CHAPTER 17

Darts streaked out, the feathery fletches turning to fiery red streaks. A few sailed on and *plinked* off the walls. Another one hit something solid and bounced off.

"Drones!" Remo yelled, diving to one side of the entrance. Commander Johnson hit the deck, and Doctor Laskin scrambled into the hazmat locker. That left only her and Ben standing. Catalina saw a matte black head turn her way, the dim red glow of an optical sensor fixing on her. The drone raised both of its arms and Catalina stared down the twin barrels of its integrated weapons. She cringed, anticipating the muzzle flashes and the searing pain that would follow.

But nothing happened.

"Its not shooting..." Commander Johnson said.

"It can't," Ben explained. "I reprogrammed it. We're permanently designated as friendlies. Looks like we got lucky — they didn't risk sending any people."

The drone dropped its arms and turned to face back the way it had come. Missile racks folded out from its shoulders and it fired, blowing open the opposite door with a deafening *bang!*

"You could have just opened the door," Catalina said.

"And go through decontamination again?" Ben shook his head. "No time. Let's go," he said. The drone went clanking out, punching a hole in the cloud of smoke left by the explosion.

Ben went after it, followed by Remo and Commander Johnson. Catalina went next, and Doctor Laskin trailed behind.

Once they were all standing outside the bio-safety lab, Catalina asked, "The drone's on our side?"

"It is now," Ben said. "I thought they might send drones in first, so I programmed a back door into them."

"I guess that solves the problem of firepower," Remo said, glancing back at the ruined door.

"Where is everyone?" Catalina asked, looking down both sides of the corridor. Gone were the doctors and nurses she'd seen earlier.

"They could be anywhere," Commander Johnson said as she swept her rifle from side to side, looking for invisible targets.

Ben clucked his tongue three times fast. Waited, and then did it again.

"Nothing," Benjamin said. He raised his rifle to his shoulder and started forward. "Let's go." Keep your distance, and I'll clear the way." He went on ahead, clucking his tongue.

"What the fuck is he doing?" Remo asked.

Catalina shook her head.

"He's echo locating," Doctor Laskin whispered. "Like a bat. Incredible..."

"Is that even possible?" Commander Johnson asked.

"It's been documented that blind people can develop the ability," the doctor replied, "and I'd guess that his synthetic brain is far superior to the average biological one, so yes, it's definitely possible."

"Their cloaking technology reflects sound waves, but not light?" Commander Johnson asked as they crept down the corridor after Ben.

"Limitations of the technology, perhaps," Doctor Laskin suggested. "Electromagnetic radiation can be absorbed or reflected around an object. Sound is just vibrations in the air. It's impossible to contain that."

Catalina heard the drone clanking along softly behind them, bringing up the rear. She looked back and saw that it was actually walking backwards, somehow not colliding with anything or falling over. Both of its arms were raised and its weapons tracking restlessly back and forth.

Ben was bringing up the rear with that drone and echo-locating from the front at the same time. Yet more proof of the superiority of synthetic brains. She wondered if she and the others had that same potential.

They walked on until they reached the reception area, but it was just as empty as the corridors.

"Where are we going?" Catalina asked.

"To where all the others went," Ben explained as he stopped in front of the Med Bay doors.

Catalina checked the doors with her ARCs and found them locked. She tried unlocking them, but an error flashed up before her eyes—

Access Denied.

"They locked us in!" she blurted out.

"Not for long," Ben replied, and a split second later, the doors *swished* open, revealing a broad corridor and a row of elevators.

Commander Johnson's voice crackled to them over the comms: "We should get to the CIC. From there we'll be able to see where they've gone, and we'll be able to take control of the ship's systems."

Ben clucked his tongue three times, waited, and then walked out of the med bay.

"Did you hear me, Ben?" Commander Johnson asked.

One of the elevators in the corridor opened for him as he approached, and he replied audibly, not bothering to use the comms. "I've already taken control of the ship's systems."

He walked inside the elevator and beckoned to them. "We need to hurry. They're going to leave."

"Leave where?" Catalina asked as they all crowded into the elevator. She imagined he meant they were fleeing to one of the ship's adjacent sections—either Section 6 or 8.

"For the planet," Ben replied.

"What are you talking about, kid?" Remo asked as the elevator raced down. Catalina saw that Ben had selected level *1-HANGAR.*

"We're already in orbit over Proxima B," Ben said. "They're boarding the shuttles as we speak."

PART 3 - ARRIVAL

"'The journey is the reward'—except when it isn't."

—Anonymous

CHAPTER 18

Wwhile Alexander stood in line, waiting to board his shuttle, a man with coffee-colored skin, elongated features, and a shaved head walked up to him. Alexander realized from the deep maroon color of his jumpsuit, and from the golden oak leaf insignia on it that the man was a Marine Major. It was Major Bright, Section 7's executive officer.

"Alexander," Bright said, stopping in front of him.

"What can I do for you, Major?"

"Our security measures have failed to contain the Outsiders. They are coming."

Alexander's eyes darted to the elevators and back to Major Bright. "We'd better go now, then."

"There's not enough time to get everyone on board. The Entity thinks you might be able to buy us the time we need. They will hesitate if they are confronted by their loved ones." As he said that, a woman with short blond hair and dimpled cheeks walked up beside him. "This is Lieutenant Dempsey. She'll be joining you for the negotiations."

"You can call me Deedee," she added.

"The others are already on their way," Major Bright said, beaming brightly at him.

Alexander understood what Major Bright meant, and he smiled back. "That's very good news." He couldn't wait to see the Outsiders' faces.

* * *

Catalina steeled herself for a fight as the elevator reached the hangar level and the doors parted.

"Don't shoot!" someone said. "We just want to talk to you."

"Who's there?" Remo demanded. "Show yourself!"

Catalina recognized that voice. "Alexander?"

Ben stepped out of the elevator, clucking his tongue and turning his head every which way, his ears cocked for slight changes in pitch that only he could hear.

Another voice spoke, "Remo, it's me."

"Deedee?"

They crept out of the elevator after Ben into a room with wall-to-wall lockers of spacesuits.

Ben took aim and fired in the direction of the voice. The dart froze in midair; then it fell straight down and hovered just above the deck. A moment later, a naked woman appeared lying there with the dart sticking out of her arm.

"Deedee!" Remo roared and raced toward her, heedless of the risk. He went down on his haunches and checked her pulse.

Ben was already scanning for his next target. His commandeered drone went clanking to the fore, weapons tracking.

"Ben, wait! Let's hear what they have to say," Catalina said.

"There's no time for that!"

"Benjamin?" another woman's voice asked. Catalina frowned. That voice was familiar. "Put the gun down,

Benjamin."

It can't be... Catalina thought.

"Mom?" Ben asked, his aim faltering as he searched the room for her. "You're dead!"

"I was," she replied. "The Entity brought me back."

Esther's voice seemed to be coming from everywhere at once, and Catalina realized that she was speaking to them over the ship's PA system.

"Where are you?" Benjamin asked.

"I'm right here," she said. The doors at the far end of the locker room parted, and she came striding in wearing a black jumpsuit. She didn't bother to hide from them, and she wasn't alone. The man who walked in behind her was unmistakable for his size and the haughty swagger in his stride.

"Mikail?" Commander Johnson dropped her rifle to her side. "You're dead! You're..." she shook her head. "How is this possible?"

Mikail and Esther stopped in front of them with matching smiles. "The question you should be asking is *why*," Mikail replied. "If the Entity were evil, *why* bring us back from the dead?"

Commander Johnson scowled. "You're one of them, so why the hell wouldn't it?"

"*I* wasn't one of them," Esther added, shaking her head and smiling patiently. "It brought me back, too."

"You were dead for a whole day before the others were infected. There's no possible way they could bring you back," Ben said.

"A fossil is dead, yet we can use it to reconstruct a skeleton," Esther replied.

Ben shook his head. "You're not my mother."

Alexander chose that moment to appear, standing right beside them, buck naked, and wearing a matching smile. "We're not the enemy. Put your guns down."

Commander Johnson did the opposite, bringing hers back to her shoulder and sighting down the barrel at Alexander. "You've got five seconds to convince me of that before I shoot. Five..."

"Because if you kill us, we might not come back again," Councilor Markov said.

Commander Johnson shook her head. "Not good enough. Four."

"We've arrived at Proxima," Alexander said. "That means the Entity has been telling the truth from the start."

Commander Johnson glanced at Ben and then back again. "So what if we have? Three."

Their smiles faded in unison. "You really *are* wretched creatures," Esther said.

Commander Johnson pulled the trigger and Alexander fell. Ben and Remo each fired another shot and both Esther and Councilor Markov crumpled to the deck beside him.

"How long before we know if it works?" Commander Johnson asked.

"A day. Maybe two," Ben said.

Catalina ran out to check on Alexander. He looked like he might have hit his head on the way down. Thankfully the low gravity had made the fall easier. Going down on her haunches beside him, she pressed two fingers to his carotid artery and found a steady pulse. Beside her, Commander Johnson did the same with Councilor Markov. Benjamin didn't bother to check on his mother. Either he didn't care about her as much as he claimed, or he'd already checked her vitals via some hidden means that was only available to his enhanced synthetic brain.

"We need to get as many of the others as we can," Ben said, already reloading his rifle as he stepped by them and through the open doors. He froze there at the threshold, his rifle slowly dropping from his shoulder.

"We're too late," he said.

Catalina jumped up and hurried over to see what he was looking at. There, on the other side of the waiting room, clearly visible through a wall of viewports, a shuttle hovered nose-first above the outer doors of the hangar. As they watched, the boarding tunnel folded away and the outer doors rumbled open.

CHAPTER 19

As soon as the hangar doors were fully open, the shuttle's magnetic docking clamps released, and it shot out, propelled by the ring decks' rotation. Catalina gaped at its departure.

"At least we were able to save a few," Remo said after a long moment of silence. He turned to glare at Ben. "Assuming your cure works."

"It'll work," Ben said slowly, as if uncertain of that.

They all turned back to look at their loved ones lying crumpled on the deck in the locker room.

"What about the other shuttles?" Doctor Laskin asked. "They can't all have left already..."

The hope in his voice was painful to hear. *Everyone has their loved ones except for him,* Catalina realized. "You had someone on one of the shuttles."

To her surprise, Doctor Laskin shook his head. "No. I don't have anyone, and now I never will."

An awkward silence followed, and Remo cleared his throat. "Tough break, Doc, but if it makes you feel better, you might not need to worry about it. Has anyone else wondered *why* they left us all alone up here? The *Liberty* was designed to separate into ten sections and support the colonists from orbit. We're talking about a hundred trillion Sols of valuable supplies and machinery, but they just threw it away like an empty gum wrapper."

"Maybe the ship that brought us here already has everything they need," Commander Johnson suggested.

"Maybe," Remo said. "But if that's true, then we really are disposable. Ben—? Hey, what's with the kid?"

Catalina noticed that he appeared to be in some kind of trance.

"Maybe he's running out of oxygen?" the doctor suggested. The hazmats had built in air tanks, but they could only last so long.

Wordlessly, Ben turned to them, his eyes wide and unblinking. "You need to see this."

"See what?" Remo demanded.

Ben walked over to the viewports facing the empty hangar. They followed him there and watched while he toggled the viewport to show a view from one of the ship's external holo cameras.

Floating there below them was Proxima B. Shuttles, fighters, and drones streaked down toward it in a steady stream of bright blue thruster trails. The alien ship that had encapsulated theirs was nowhere to be seen.

Catalina studied the planet below. They were orbiting just above the day/night terminator line. Half of the planet was cast in deep shadows and glowing with dendritic red patterns of light, while the other half was bleached white and dazzling with reflected light from Proxima Centauri—an endless desert, no doubt. Between those two extremes ran a colorful blue band of what might have been liquid water. Varying shades of blue and indigo blossomed around the central band in grainy patterns that suggested vegetation, or maybe even algae.

"What are those striae?" Doctor Laskin asked, pointing to

the glowing red lines on the dark side of the planet.

Catalina thought maybe they were rivers of lava, but the planet was tidally locked, meaning the dark side of Proxima B never changed—not like Earth or Mars where they rotated on their axes to bring a steady cycle of day and night—and since the dark side never saw the sun, it had to be hundreds of degrees below zero.

"There's only one thing they could be," Ben replied. "Cities."

"Cities?" Catalina echoed uncertainly. She'd seen both the urban sprawls of Earth's cities and the pimply green rashes of Mars' domes from orbit, but these patterns didn't look anything like either of those. The only thing she could liken them to was Europa's *lineae,* but those lines didn't glow in the dark like these ones did.

"We came to colonize Proxima Centauri," Ben said, "but someone already beat us to it."

* * *

"Now what?" Catalina asked as she watched Alexander sleep—if it could even be called sleep. *More like another coma,* she thought. He hadn't woken when she'd carried him to a bed back in Med Bay. None of them had. She glanced around the recovery room at the other beds and their occupants— Councilor Markov, Desiree, Esther, and Jessica, still recovering from the brain biopsy her parents had authorized. Each of them had someone by their side, all except for Esther. Benjamin stood by Jessica's side instead. He was no longer wearing his over-sized hazmat suit. None of them were. With all of the others gone, there was no longer any need to pretend that their dart guns were loaded with Ebola instead of nanites.

Jessica was the only one of them who was awake. Her head was wrapped in a bandage, concealing her bouncy brown curls, but she seemed to be alert and in good spirits. "Ben?" Catalina prompted.

It still felt strange to be looking to a nine-year-old for guidance, but all the others were looking to him, too. Even Commander Johnson, who by all accounts should have been the one in charge.

Ben faced them. "We still don't know exactly what we're dealing with, do we, Doctor? Two people came back from the dead—and one of them wasn't even infected."

"As far as we know," Remo said. "And not to mention Deedee had a pair of broken arms last I checked. Not only did she shuck her casts like corn husks, but they don't seem broken anymore."

"The infection might bestow regenerative capabilities on its hosts," Doctor Laskin suggested.

"We should run some tests and see what's going on," Ben replied.

Doctor Laskin nodded. "I already took blood samples from the infected and also from myself and Lieutenant Taggart. I checked and cross-checked them for signs of—well, anything really, but I didn't find much."

Ben nodded. "What about Jessica's biopsy?"

"I sent the sample to the lab. I don't know what happened to it after that, or if the others found something before they left."

"Which lab?" Ben asked.

"Bio-safety Four. On the other side of Med Bay."

"We should check on that," Ben said.

"I'm going, too," Commander Johnson put in.

"Likewise," Catalina added.

Ben looked to Remo. "We need someone to stay behind in case they wake up."

Remo nodded.

"Keep an eye on her," he said, jerking his chin at his mother. "The others might recover, but *she's* something else."

"*Might* recover?" Remo demanded, his brow furrowing darkly. "I thought you said your cure would work."

"It will," Ben said, nodding stiffly.

Again Catalina noted the hesitation in his voice. *He's just guessing,* she realized.

"Let's go," Ben said. He turned to Jessica and added, "Try to get some rest."

"I will."

They all followed him out of the recovery room—except for Remo, Jessica, and Ben's VSM drone. As she left, Catalina saw Remo checking his dart rifle with a preoccupied frown.

Catalina stopped in the open door of the recovery room and turned to stare at Alexander. If their loved ones didn't make a full recovery, what would be left of them? Would they even wake up?

* * *

Remo glared at the sleeping woman—Esther Copelan, according to the bar of text above her head. His aim never wavered from her chest.

Something about that woman bothered him—besides the fact that she'd somehow come back from the dead. What was it she had said before they shot her?

You really are wretched creatures.

That was disturbing, all right.

Esther's body twitched.

Remo blinked and squinted at her, wondering if he'd imagined it, but to his horror, she sat up and turned to face him.

"Halt!" the drone said in a robotic voice, having already detected the threat.

Jessica sat up and stared at Esther with wide eyes.

Remo snapped into action. He took aim, and pulled the trigger. A dart shot out of his rifle with a *pffft* of compressed air and buried itself deep in Esther's chest.

She smiled. "Hello, Remo."

"Goodbye, Entity," he replied, smiling back.

She reached up and pulled the dart from her chest. Holding it up to the light, she examined the empty vial. "What is in this? It is not a virus... no, these are the tiny machines. The cure. You fooled me into thinking you were going to kill everyone."

Remo shrugged. "Surprise." He nodded to the empty vial. "There's also enough sedative in there to tranquilize a horse."

"Interesting," Esther said, and hopped down from her bed.

Remo froze, and the cocky smile fell off his face. She should have collapsed by now. He hurried to reload his rifle, but the drone reacted first, and this time Remo heard Ben's voice crackle out of its speaker grill mouth.

"Take one more step, and I'll shoot."

Remo locked the breech, took aim, and fired a second dart. Esther moved impossibly fast, slapping the dart out of the air.

"Fuck this!" Remo growled, backpedaling furiously and reloading his rifle at the same time. "Ben, shoot her!"

Esther kept advancing.

The drone twitched and a sickening screech of comm interference erupted from its speakers. Remo glanced at the machine, wondering what was wrong with it.

Then he saw the way its limbs were jerking and jittering, as if caught in an invisible web. As he watched, the drone's matte black armor glowed bright orange, wrinkling and running to the deck in rivulets of molten alloy. Heat radiated from it like a furnace, prickling the hair on Remo's scalp and stinging the exposed skin of his hands and face. In a matter of seconds the drone was nothing but a glistening, steaming puddle of rapidly cooling alloy.

"Holy shit!" Remo exclaimed. He fetched up against the door. "You stay away from me!" he roared.

"Relax, Remo. I just want to talk to you," Esther said.

He snapped off another shot, but she flicked that one aside, too. Desperate, he used his neural link to connect to the ship's comms and contact the others.

"I need backup!" he screamed.

CHAPTER 20

"**W**hat is that?" Catalina asked with a wrinkled nose as she pointed to the holo display that Doctor Laskin had summoned from the lab computer. The image on the display turned her stomach. It looked like a pile of brown straw tossed with cherry pits. Poking out here and there from that fibrous web were much larger blueish globs with thicker blue-green fibers connecting them. It all looked intensely alien to her.

Catalina shivered.

"It's a colored scanning electron micrograph," Doctor Laskin explained. "Those brown seed-like structures are neurons. The connections you see between them are axons and dendrites."

"What about those?" Commander Johnson asked, pointing to the blue-green blobs.

"Those are the glial cells and their extensions. So far everything looks normal..."

Catalina regarded the doctor dubiously. "That's what a *normal* brain looks like?"

"Try increasing the magnification," Ben suggested. "We need to get a closer look at one of the neurons."

"Yes... one moment."

One of the brown seeds swelled to fill the entire screen. At that level of detail she could see a profusion of gray bumps sprouting from the neuron like a rash.

"Aha," Doctor Laskin said. "This is interesting."

"What is?" Catalina asked.

He pointed to one of the gray bumps, zooming in still further, and highlighting it. At this magnification she could see tendrils creeping out from it like roots, along the surface of the neuron. "That shouldn't be here," Doctor Laskin added.

A description of the foreign body appeared beside the image.

Cell type: unknown

DNA... not found.

RNA... not found.

Elemental Composition...

A list of elements and their percentages appeared. Catalina recognized carbon, oxygen, hydrogen, sodium, calcium...

"It's carbon-based," the doctor concluded. "No real surprise there."

"What is it?" Commander Johnson asked.

"It's our first look at an alien life-form," Ben said.

Doctor Laskin nodded. "Some kind of parasite, like a virus, but our immune systems and nanobodies don't react to it. Given the results—or lack thereof—from the blood samples I tested, I'd say the infection goes straight to the brain and stays there. Since Jessica never showed any symptoms, we can safely assume this is what the infection looks like when its dormant—or dead. It obviously tried to hijack this neuron, but for some reason it failed."

Catalina frowned. "So what's the infection look like when it's active?"

Doctor Laskin shrugged. "No way to know without doing another biopsy."

"What about their skin?" Ben asked.

"Their what?"

"If they can make themselves disappear, there has to be a mechanism for that somewhere—some other type of cell coating their skins."

"Assuming that cell isn't itself invisible, then yes, we should be able to collect skin samples and find out what's making them disappear."

"Whatever it is, they need to be completely naked for it to work. Their clothes don't disappear," Commander Johnson said.

"Viruses in general—as we know them, anyway—can't survive on their own. They need a host cell to help them eat and reproduce. My bet is that whatever energy these alien cells need to make us disappear, they have to take it from our cells. Clothing will be like a desert for them."

"We need to find out how this is possible," the commander added. "Something that can make itself invisible should be technological not biological. How could something like that be naturally occurring?"

Ben replied, "Maybe it isn't. Just because the alien virus is biological doesn't mean it can't use technology. They have starships don't they?"

"You're talking about it like it's sentient," Catalina said.

Ben turned to her. "It is. It has to be. I think this virus is the Entity. It's some kind of collective intelligence that feeds off the intellectual capacities of its hosts and knits them all together. That would explain how they all started singing from the same tune, all displaying the same symptoms and waking up at the same time.

"In fact, calling it a parasite might be premature—

parasites ultimately destroy their host cells, but we haven't seen any symptoms of sickness or diminished function in the hosts. This parasite is much smarter than the average virus on Earth. It's found some way to live in harmony with us, leaving our cells intact."

"Good for it," Commander Johnson said. "I don't think we have time for this. We're in orbit above an alien planet, we should make a run for it before they decide what they're going to do about us. Ben, you said you had control of the ship's systems—can you access navigation from here or do we need to be in the CIC for that?"

He was in some kind of trance again, his eyes glazed and blankly staring. Catalina grabbed his shoulder and shook him. His head jerked back and forth with the movement.

"What's wrong with him?" Doctor Laskin asked.

"Ben!" Commander Johnson shouted.

"She's awake," he said slowly.

"Who is?"

"Esther."

"And the others?"

Ben shook his head and went abruptly silent once more. "The tranq darts aren't working on her."

"Use the drone," Commander Johnson said.

Ben shook his head. "I can't..."

"Why not? She's not your mother! You said it yourself!"

"No, I mean I *can't*," Ben said. "I just lost contact with the drone."

Catalina gaped at him. "And Remo?"

"I don't know. She said she just wants to talk."

"Like hell she does. We need to get some weapons and get back there," Commander Johnson said.

An incoming comms popped up on Catalina's ARCs. She accepted the transmission and Remo's urgent voice roared through her thoughts. "I need backup!"

"He's in trouble!" Catalina said.

An icy draft brushed her face, and she shivered.

That was when she saw it. Someone was standing behind Doctor Laskin, short, naked and sexless, with wrinkly gray skin and bony limbs. Large, lidless obsidian eyes stared at them from an over-sized, hairless head. The creature's nose was tiny, and its jaw too small for its head.

Recognition hit Catalina like a bolt of lightning. She remembered the aliens Esther had described from her alleged abduction, and the one she'd hallucinated at the foot of her bed the morning after Esther had told them of her encounter—this creature was an exact match for both what she'd seen and what Esther had described. She spun around to see four more of them standing in a circle around her and the others.

The Grays. She recognized them from somewhere else, too. Benjamin's holographic depiction of Proxima B—the gray-skinned bipeds running through a grassy blue savannah, herding packs of black arthropods toward a cliff.

Catalina tried turning to Ben, but she couldn't move. She was paralyzed. Everyone else appeared to be equally afflicted. She tried to scream, but she couldn't even do that. Catalina's heart was beating so hard, she felt it might break.

She could only move her eyes—left, right, left.... Then her eyelids began to grow heavy, sinking involuntarily shut, as if she'd gone days without sleep. She forced them open, only to feel them sinking shut once more.

Catalina watched the Grays advancing on them through

ever-narrowing slits, thinking to herself—*they're going to abduct me!*

CHAPTER 21

Catalina woke up in a white room. Dazzling lights blinded her eyes. She blinked, squinting against the glare. She was naked. Frigid air caressed her skin making her hair stand on end. Her body was still paralyzed.

Her breathing became fast and shallow; her head swam, and sweat prickled, running in cold, itchy rivers. She felt nauseated.

"Hello?" Catalina tried. Her voice felt hoarse as if she'd been screaming for hours. Her tongue was like cotton in her mouth.

No answer.

Her stomach did a flip and she felt a knot form in her throat as her gorge rose. Her stomach heaved, but nothing came out.

"Leave me alone!" Catalina screamed. Her voice cracked, breaking into a husky whisper.

"*Nobby-egg,*" a toneless voice said somewhere close beside her ear.

Then a bald gray head with enormous black eyes appeared, hovering just inches from her nose. The blinding glare diminished as the alien's over-sized head blocked some of the light. Catalina stared into those lidless black eyes, simultaneously horrified and mesmerized.

The creature stared for a few more seconds, and then the

corners of its tiny mouth abruptly curved down, and its eyes hardened. It turned and said something to someone she couldn't see—

"Or-ala sa-kassy. Cat-al-ina, ey-a ra-sa to-saga."

Catalina's heart thudded in her chest. Had it just said her name?

It waited for a reply, and another voice answered from somewhere else in the room. *"Ta-ta to-saga! Cat-al-ina ey-a th-ik-a."*

The one leaning over her faced her again. Its tiny mouth was still frowning. She watched as it leaned even closer than before, until their noses touched. The alien's nose felt cold against hers.

It stared into her eyes for a long, breathless moment, and Catalina wondered what it was doing. She tried to ask, but found she was unable to talk. Her eyelids grew heavy... and she drifted off into a hazy sleep, taking the image of that giant gray head and those staring black eyes with her into her nightmares.

When she awoke once more, she was lying on the floor in a much dimmer, warmer room with bare, glossy black walls. The ceiling was circular, giving a shape to the room, and it glowed with a dim red light.

She could see that she wasn't naked anymore, but once again wearing her black jumpsuit. Her memories of the operating room were fuzzy and dreamlike. What had they done to her in there?

Maybe it had all just been a dream.

Catalina sat up and saw that everyone else was there, too—even Remo. But Benjamin's mother, Esther was missing. She saw Alexander sit up beside her. He wasn't naked as he had been when they'd shot him, or even clothed in the hospital gown they'd found for him. Instead, he wore one of the ship's off-duty black jumpsuits. He turned to her, and she stared wordlessly back, too afraid to ask how he was feeling.

"Caty—" he began, but then he winced and grabbed his head in both of his hands. "Ow! What the hell... I feel like I drank a whole bottle of Scotch. What happened last ni..." He trailed off with a furrowed brow, his eyes darting around the room. "Where are we?"

She shook her head, relief coursing through her. He was back to normal! "I don't know," she said, unable to help smiling.

Alexander stood up and whirled around. He stopped and stared at Councilor Markov. "Councilor," he said. "What's going on?"

"I was about to ask the same thing," Markov replied. "The last thing I remember was going to bed. Then I woke up here..."

Alexander turned back to her, his brow pinched with concern. "Me, too."

Catalina regarded him curiously. "You don't remember anything after that?"

"Anything about what?" Alexander replied.

"Someone better tell me what the hell is going on!" Councilor Markov said.

Commander Johnson made a feeble effort to walk over to him, looking like she might collapse at any moment.

"Ouch," a woman said from the other side of her. Catalina turned to see Desiree cradling her head in her hands like it might fall off her shoulders.

"We need to find a way out of here," Ben said.

"Is anyone listening to me?" Councilor Markov roared.

"*Nobby-egg,*" a toneless voice replied.

Catalina felt her whole body go cold and she spun around, searching for the source of that sound. She'd heard that word before.

Doors appeared, materializing out of the featureless walls, and in walked one of the Grays, naked as usual.

"What the..." the councilor pointed to it, his hand shaking so hard that Catalina could actually see it trembling.

"H-ello. Pl-ees do n-ot be al-arm-ed. W-ee m-een y-oo no h-arm," the alien said, sounding as if it were stuttering, struggling to speak English. The doors slid shut behind it, disappearing into the wall once more and sealing them in with the ugly creature.

Councilor Markov growled and lunged at it. His enhanced prosthetic arms reaching for its slender gray neck. The creature vanished and Markov sailed into the wall, bouncing off with a dull *thud.* He whirled around just as the creature reappeared behind him.

"*Nib-ah,*" it said.

Markov lunged once more, and this time Remo joined the assault, running up behind the alien. The Gray vanished again, and the two men collided with each other. Markov grunted and shoved Remo away. Remo fell on his rear and cursed at the councilor.

The Gray reappeared on the opposite side of the room from them. "*Yek.* Wr-et-ch-ed cr-eet-churs."

"You keep saying that," Catalina said, glaring at the alien. "Why?"

The Gray stared at her with its enormous black eyes, saying nothing. The corners of its mouth turned down. "*Yek,*" it said, and turned to face the glossy black walls. With its attention diverted once more, Catalina saw Remo and Councilor Markov trading glances behind its back. They began creeping up on it, and the Gray vanished again.

"You can't catch it!" Catalina said.

"Wanna bet?" Markov growled.

"Let's just see what it has to say," Alexander said.

"If they wanted to harm us, why let us wake up at all?" Commander Johnson added.

Catalina watched Ben turn in a slow circle, clucking his tongue, waiting, and doing it again. After doing that a few times, he stopped and pointed. "There."

The Gray re-appeared in exactly that spot. "Cl-ever," it said. "W-atch."

As the alien spoke, the walls, floor, and ceiling all became luminous, dazzling their eyes with a bright light. A moment later the room was gone and they all appeared to be standing in the middle of a field. Yellow grass bowed in a wind that they could actually *feel*. Green trees waved their branches. An orange sun hovered close above the horizon, splashing the sky with blood as it fell. The air reeked of animal dung and a rotten meat smell that turned Catalina's stomach. This was somewhere on Earth.

Dead ahead, some kind of primate sat on its haunches in the grass, its back turned to them, an animal carcass lying in front of it—*a zebra*, Catalina realized from the stripes as they floated gradually closer to the scene. Flies buzzed loudly around the carcass and the smell of rotten meat grew stronger, becoming a suffocating stench. The primate's arms and hands were busy, its head dipping toward the dead zebra every so often, making wet tearing sounds and contented chewing noises.

It's feeding, Catalina realized.

They stopped floating closer and Catalina noticed a trio of monkeys creeping up behind the first, all of them holding heavy rocks and standing on two legs. She realized they must be primitive humans, but they still looked more like monkeys to her.

The trio of monkey-humans reached the first one, and they stopped a few paces behind it, holding their rocks over their heads and looking from one to another, as if to say, *Who's gonna do it?*

Catalina had a bad feeling about this.

One of the larger monkeys thrust out his chin and ambled forward the last few steps, being careful not to make a sound.

Between the buzzing of the flies and all of the noise the first monkey was making as it ate, there was no way it could have heard anything.

The rock came down. *Crunch.* Blood splattered up, and the feeding monkey toppled over, its broken skull hidden by the grass.

The murderer stood over it, holding its bloody rock and staring down at its victim. For a second Catalina thought it might be feeling a shred of remorse, but then it grinned with a mouthful of teeth and smashed its rock down over and over again. Blood sprayed in all directions, drenching the grass. The two hench-monkeys began hopping up and down. They smashed their rocks on the ground in imitation, hooting and roaring, and grinning.

The scene panned away and a Gray appeared standing there, watching the carnage. It said something. Another alien voice replied, closer to the scene, "*Yek.*"

This is some kind of recording, Catalina realized. They were seeing what one of the Grays had seen on Earth a long, long time ago. Catalina wondered if this was their first experience with humans—witnessing a murder committed by one of humanity's earliest ancestors.

Their perspective turned back to the fore to see that the trio of monkeys were now feasting on the zebra carcass that they'd been coveting earlier.

The scene faded away, and another one appeared. This time it was the dead of night and freezing cold. Catalina shivered and hugged her shoulders. She stood on a dirt road in a peaceful village of huts. Orange fires glowed, and embers crackled up into the night's sky. A horse whinnied. The smells of roasting meat filled the air. People ambled down the street, some of them singing merrily as they went, others speaking in hushed voices. A family with two young children walked by, waving to the people they knew. The man shouted out something in a European language that Catalina couldn't quite identify. Someone else shouted back, more distantly. In the distance, waves crashed on the shore. It seemed like such a peaceful place that Catalina wished she could actually visit it.

Then someone called out urgently and all the merriment stopped. A horn blew, a keening wail, and people screamed. Catalina heard a whistling noise.

Their viewpoint snapped up to the sky. A cloud of arrows glinted in the firelight, seeming to stop and hover high above their heads. They sparkled like stars as they fell.

The Gray whose perspective they shared dived under the eaves of the nearest hut. *Pfft pfft pfft!* Arrows rained down, deadly wraiths in the night. People screamed as they fell.

The horn blew again, and again—a warning to flee. Catalina heard swords clashing, the grunts and cries of battle. Their viewpoint turned toward the sound and they saw a horde of men come rushing up a sandy beach, swords and axes glinting, their row boats perched on the shore, rocking with the waves. Village guardsmen screamed as they died, cut to ribbons by the overwhelming force of the invading army. The Gray watched quietly as the invaders stormed through the village, bursting into huts and kicking down doors. Women and children screamed. Catalina pressed her hands to her temples and shut her eyes, willing the images to leave.

Strong arms enfolded her, and she heard Alexander whisper, "It's okay. Shh. Shh. It's okay," he said, stroking her hair.

That was when she realized that she was sobbing. After a while, the screaming stopped, replaced by a crackling roar. She forced herself to look. The peaceful village was gone, the huts burning—each one a funeral pyre. Shadowy human forms were splayed out on both sides of the street. The victorious army gathered and stood to watch the village burn. Someone near the front of the group threw up a fist and roared in triumph, his bloody sword casting slivers of firelight in all directions. The others cheered and clanged their weapons on their shields.

It reminded her of the monkeys hooting and roaring as they smashed their rocks on the ground.

The scene vanished, and another one appeared. They stood on the blood-soaked sand of a Roman Colosseum, watching men, women, and children be torn to shreds by hungry lions while a crowd of thousands cheered. Catalina shook her head, horrified.

Another scene—Mongol hordes riding across the steppes, an entire city burning in the background behind them.

Another—the trenches of World War I. Gun smoke swirled, the air thick with the stench of urine and blood. Wounded soldiers sobbed and moaned as their fellows rushed out for revenge, firing blindly.

Catalina almost sighed with relief when that scene faded and the following one showed a relatively peaceful setting: soldiers warming their hands over a giant bonfire, others piling on logs.

Then she noticed the swastikas on their uniforms, and she realized what they were burning. This was a concentration camp in World War II.

Following that—an aerial view over a bright green spit of land surrounded by water. Then came blinding, actinic flashes of light and the distinctive mushroom cloud of an atom bomb going off. Hiroshima.

The scenes went on and on, recounting ancient wars until she saw a period of relative peace. Time lapse footage revealed cities around the world rising ever higher, their architecture changing, modernizing. Traffic on the ground spread to the sky as hover cars took over. A space elevator appeared, soaring up from the equator. Followed by another one.

Verdant green domes popped up on Mars and the Moon, spreading like a rash across barren landscapes. Fledgling colonies and research stations appeared on Titan, Europa, and Ganymede.

Massive war fleets cruised over Earth with the entire nuclear arsenal of the world, ushering in another cold war.

Then came the Last War. Fleets clashed, slicing each other

to ribbons, and nuclear missiles rained from orbit, hitting Earth's largest cities, but stopping miraculously short of a nuclear winter.

The mushroom clouds faded, and more time lapse snapshots followed as the Earth licked its wounds and rebuilt. Another orbital view—the Gulf of Mexico below. A lump rose in Catalina's throat as she watched a dazzling flash of light erupt from there. A plume of water vapor and debris shot all the way into orbit from that impact.

Catalina remembered. Her own son, Dorian, had been partly responsible for that devastation. Millions had died just so that two of the Earth's largest corporations could make bigger profits.

Following that, the AI, Benevolence, had taken control of the Earth's billions of bots and used them to take over the Earth in order to protect humanity from themselves.

Catalina felt sure that would be it. There had been no more wars, no more massacres since Benevolence had taken over. The solar system was at peace, even if it was an uneasy peace. The last conflict of any note had been the brief one-sided battle they'd fought with the Grays.

But she was wrong.

A final scene appeared, this one showed two space fleets clashing. Missiles streaked between them, triggering devastating explosions and littering space with debris. Clouds of fighters and drones dove and spun, spitting hypervelocity rounds and tearing each other apart. Capital ships cracked in half, carved to pieces by invisible lasers.

Catalina assumed they must have gone back to one of the battles from the Last War.

"Do you recognize this?" Catalina whispered to

Alexander, recalling that he'd fought in that war.

He shook his head and pointed over her shoulder. She turned, following that gesture. That was when she saw the planet in the background—the entire globe was covered in a blanket of angry gray clouds, hot orange magma peeking through the gaps.

Catalina shook her head in disbelief. "Where is this?"

That scene faded and back were the glossy black walls of the room.

"It is Err-th," a stuttering voice said. The Gray reappeared, and she saw it blink for the first time, translucent membranes sweeping down over its large, slanting black eyeballs. "N-ow, do y-oo un-dur-st-and wu-high w-ee c-all y-oo wr-etch-ed cr-eet-churs?"

CHAPTER 22

"**Y**ou don't know the future," Alexander said.

Doors reappeared in the wall, and Esther walked in. The Gray turned and inclined its head to her before withdrawing quietly to one side.

Catalina shivered when she saw the other woman. Her eyes were solid black, just as the Grays' were.

"What you saw is what could happen once your species discovers how to create sufficient quantities of antimatter," Esther said in a toneless, genderless voice.

She no longer looked or sounded human.

"You're only focusing on the negative side of humanity," Ben said. "They can learn from their mistakes. They already have. Periods of peace have been getting longer and wars shorter."

"As time went by they became more civilized," Esther admitted. "But they also developed more and more powerful weapons. That trend will continue, making their demise inevitable."

Ben thrust out his jaw. "You're wrong."

"I'm not wrong."

"So what if you aren't?" Remo demanded. "What's it to you if we wipe ourselves out?"

"The Grays were like you once, but now they are part of the All, enlightened and peaceful, just as humanity will be."

"You're nothing but a virus, a parasite that evolved in some microbial soup," Doctor Laskin sneered. "You have no right to play God."

The Gray standing beside Esther produced a small black sidearm with a dish-shaped barrel and aimed it at Doctor Laskin.

Esther smiled patiently and waved the Gray off, as if shooing a fly. "I have brought you all aboard this ship and explained myself for a reason. Now that you've seen how wretched your species is, and how inevitable your demise, you know why I must join you with the All. Tell me how you separated these three from me, and why I can no longer join with them." Esther's gaze passed briefly over Markov, Alexander, and Desiree.

"No," Ben said.

Esther's smile vanished, and she glared at him. "You have seen what the All is like. It is not evil."

Remo snorted.

Esther ignored him. "Benevolence promised I could have *all* of the humans, and these three were human when I found them."

"He promised you could *what?*" Commander Johnson demanded.

"They don't know..." Esther's expression became sly, and she glanced from Ben to Commander Johnson and back again. "They don't know?"

Ben set his jaw, saying nothing.

Turning to the commander, Esther said, "Benevolence contacted me while I was still many light years away. He asked me what I wanted and why I was coming. We spoke at length about the destructiveness of humanity, and he shared my view that you would eventually destroy yourselves—and his machine people along with you."

Catalina gaped at Ben. "You *knew* they were coming!"

He shot her a guilty look, but still said nothing.

Esther went on, now grinning broadly. "I told Benevolence about the All, and what I planned to do. I told him that if he chose not to resist, I would let him join my Federation and we would co-exist peacefully. He agreed, but he said that he couldn't be seen to surrender. He asked if he could make a show of resistance. I told him he could attack my harvesters once they arrived. He could pretend to know nothing about me, and then surrender in the face of overwhelming force, which is exactly what he did. All of humanity is mine, just as we agreed, but you chose to break the agreement to save these three. Why?"

Ben scowled at her. "You should take what you can and go."

"That was not what we agreed to," Esther said. "We agreed that I would have *all* the humans, and in exchange, I would not harm the machine people. It's not too late. Reverse what you did and tell me how you did it."

"That's what you really want. You want to know how we cured them so you can find a way to fight back. You're afraid of us," Ben said.

The Gray adjusted his aim to Ben, and Esther gave no reply for a long moment. Then she appeared to come to a decision, and she said, "If you will not live up to your side of the agreement, I will not live up to mine. The machine people will all die."

"I thought the All wasn't evil?"

"You are a machine person. If you would betray an

agreement between myself and your leader, then you are not as unified as I was led to believe. That means you share humanity's flaws, yet I cannot fix you by joining you with the All, so you leave me no choice. I will have to destroy you. Unless... you can prove to me that the machine people can be reasoned with."

"Synthetics are a new species, a better one," Ben said. "We won't repeat the mistakes of the past. There will never be another war—at least not one that's fought among our own kind."

"Exactly! With whom, then, do you suppose you will fight?" Esther replied. "You will fight with me! You already are!"

"The Grays told us what you did to them. They were peaceful. They didn't even have weapons until they met you! They weren't anything like us, and you forced yourself upon them anyway."

"A filthy lie. They would never speak ill of me."

"Not everyone is under your control. There are those who escaped."

Esther's expression turned thoughtful. "You would believe a species who's been abducting people from your planet for thousands of years? You *do* know what they were doing—the genetic experiments, the hybrids... They harvested human DNA and mixed it with their own, creating foul creatures. These are the people you would believe?"

"It's your fault they had to do that," Ben accused. "They were trying to create a species that would be immune to you."

Esther smiled. "The hybrids all went insane, but I suppose we shouldn't despise humble beginnings, should we?"

"What were you doing to us?" Catalina interrupted, her

voice trembling with outrage and fear. "When we first woke up here."

Esther beamed at her, and then looked away. "I'm disappointed to hear that you won't cooperate, Benjamin, but I suppose there will be other species to join with the All." Esther turned to leave and doors materialized in the wall behind her, sliding open to reveal a corridor with matching glossy black walls.

"Wait! What are you going to do with us?" Desiree asked.

"I'm sending you home. You should arrive just in time to witness the fruits of your defiance."

The Gray glanced their way and followed Esther out. The doors slid shut behind them, and everyone turned to look at Ben.

"You knew that *thing* was coming," Commander Johnson said slowly, deliberately, looking as if she might lunge at the boy. "That excuse about making everyone synthetic to bridge the gap between humans and androids was a lie. What were you *really* doing on board the *Liberty*?"

"Nano Nova and the synthetics were a way to fight back against the Entity. The Grays helped us. Their research led them to believe that no purely biological life-form would ever be immune to the Entity, so we had to create a new form of hybrid—one that would be more artificial than not. The *Liberty* was supposed to be long gone by the time the Entity arrived, and I was supposed to have had time to make everyone on board immune."

"The nanites were already programmed," Catalina realized.

"Yes."

"Then what were you programming in such a hurry?" she

asked, remembering him sitting at the computer terminal in the bio-safety lab, with rapidly scrolling lines of code all around him.

"I was programming back doors into the drones and into the *Liberty's* control systems."

"So what was the plan?" Alexander asked. "Make everyone immune, but we still end up going to Proxima, so we could rub our immunity in the Entity's face?"

"A ship from the Grays' resistance was supposed to rendezvous with us along the way. They were going to help us escape."

"Escape?" Commander Johnson shook her head. "We never should have left! We should have stayed to fight! Spread the cure on Earth! If you had shared all of this with us sooner, we could have prepared—instead of sending out a colony ship to a new world, we could have banded together to save the worlds we already have!"

"Stay and fight against an enemy we can't even see, with technology far superior to our own?" Ben asked, shaking his head.

"Maybe you weren't watching that little presentation," Commander Johnson said. "If there's one thing humans are good at, it's fighting."

Ben shook his head. "We wouldn't have stood a chance."

"There must have been something more we could have done," Desiree said.

"Like what?" Ben replied.

"At the very least, we could have worked faster to save everyone on board," Commander Johnson suggested.

"*If* you had believed me," Ben replied.

"We're believing you now, aren't we?"

"Is someone going to explain what the hell is going on, or should I just assume that all of this is a bad dream?" Councilor Markov asked.

"I'm having some trouble filling in the gaps myself," Alexander said.

"What's the last thing you remember?" Ben asked.

"The containment breach," Markov replied. "Everyone was confined to quarters. I went to bed that night, and then I woke up here."

Ben shook his head. "You woke up infected with an alien virus—that virus is the Entity."

"Infected? I feel fine."

"We cured you, but you don't remember anything from the time you were infected."

"And who the hell are you?" Markov demanded.

"He's Ben," Alexander said quietly. "Benevolence's little brother."

Ben turned to him with a smile. "You remember me."

"Hard to forget."

"How long was I infected?" Markov asked.

"Three days," Ben replied.

Catalina blinked. "Three *days?*" She remembered waking up only this morning to find Alexander in a coma. That had only been hours ago, not *days*.

"We lost some time when the Entity brought us here and ran experiments on us," Ben explained.

Catalina checked her ARCs for the date and time, but they were offline. Ben must have had another means of tracking the time. She turned to glance around the room.

"Where exactly are we?" she asked.

"I'm not sure. Aboard a harvester, maybe," Ben said.

"A *harvester?*" Markov asked.

"The cylindrical ship that captured us," Ben explained. "They're Gray vessels, designed to capture other species' ships. The Grays used them for research, but the Entity adapted them to spread itself, even in space."

"I don't care *where* we are," Remo said, pounding a wall with his fist. "What I want to know is how to get out."

The corners of Ben's mouth drooped. "It's no use. It's over. I failed you."

"*We* failed you," Jessica said, coming to stand beside him.

Remo walked around the edges of the room, knocking on the walls and listening. When he heard a hollow *thunk,* he stopped and said, "It's hollow here. I think I found a door."

"Councilor, mind lending me a hand?"

Markov approached Remo, frowning. He stopped and crossed his arms over his barrel chest. "I don't see a door."

Remo rapped his knuckles on the wall again, eliciting another hollow sound. "It's there." He stepped away. "Your arms are prosthetic, right? You might just be able to make a dent. Give it your best shot."

Markov hesitated, glancing from the wall to Remo and back again. Then he hammered the wall with his fist, and a gigantic *boom* echoed through the room. Markov shook out his fist, as if hitting the wall had actually hurt. He would have tactile sensors in his prosthetics, but pain would be capped off at mild discomfort.

Catalina watched anxiously, peering at the spot Markov had hit, but the glossy black surface of the wall wasn't even scuffed.

"It's no use," Ben said. "Even if you find a door, it'll be far too strong for us to break out."

"So that's it?" Commander Johnson demanded. "You're just going to give up? You're no better than Benevolence!"

Ben sent her a defeated look, saying nothing. He walked over to one side of the room and sat down.

"Now what?" Catalina whispered.

Alexander shook his head and followed Benjamin's example. Soon they were all sitting on the hard deck, wallowing in their powerlessness. Catalina hugged her knees to her chest and rested her chin on them. No one talked, each of them locked in their own private world. Long minutes passed and Catalina closed her eyes, dozing off.

A bright flash of light woke her. She looked up, furiously blinking the spots from her eyes and trying to see what had caused that flash of light. It still suffused the room, but more dimly now. Through the brightness she saw the air shimmering like the air in a desert, but the shimmering was confined to a distorted spherical shape—a bubble.

As the brightness faded, Catalina saw that the bubble gave a view into another world, one of familiar gray walls, polished floors, and exposed conduits in the ceiling. It was one of the corridors aboard the *Liberty.*

"What the...?" Alexander said.

Another hologram, Catalina decided. What was the Entity going to show them now?

But Ben jumped up with sudden excitement. "Let's go! Hurry!"

With that, he ran into the bubble, provoking another flash of light. Catalina shielded her eyes, wincing against the glare, but the brightness soon faded. A miniature version of Ben now stood inside of the bubble, aboard the *Liberty,* waving them over.

Jessica was the first to follow, dashing through with a grin—another flash of light, and another miniature figure appeared waving to them from the other side.

Catalina hesitated, but Alexander took her hand and pulled her toward the portal. The others snapped out of it, too, and soon all of them were racing through with consecutive flashes of light.

CHAPTER 23

Catalina walked inside the bubble. A bright light surrounded her, seeming to carry her through. There came a brief moment of weightless nothingness, and then she blinked and she was standing on the other side, back on board the *Liberty* with all of the others.

"What was *that?*" Remo asked, turning to look back the way they'd come.

Dr. Laskin stared at the portal in shock.

Catalina studied the portal from the other side; it was a shimmering spherical window into the glossy black chamber where they'd been trapped a moment ago.

The portal vanished with a noisy *crack*, and the walls and floor of the ship shuddered with the echoes of its passing.

"We still have a chance," Ben announced, glancing around, searching for something. "Hello?" he asked.

A short, bony gray creature appeared standing right behind him, naked and sexless. One of the Grays.

"Look out!" Alexander warned, lunging toward it.

Ben spun to face the alien, and—

He smiled. "There you are."

Alexander fetched up short, his brow furrowed in confusion. The creature inclined its head to Ben and turned to stare at one of the doors in the corridor. Ben ran over there and waved the door open. "Perfect," he said, and dashed inside.

Jessica followed Benjamin. "Come on!" she urged.

This one's on our side... Catalina thought, staring at the alien. Again she remembered waking up on board the *Liberty* and seeing one of those aliens standing at the foot of her bed. *It must have been you,* she realized, staring at the creature. Its giant black eyes settled on her, and it stared back, as if it could read her thoughts.

Remo was the first to risk walking by the alien to see where Ben and Jessica had gone. He stopped in the open doorway and whistled appreciatively. "Nice!"

Catalina crept by the Gray to see for herself. Alexander kept pace beside her, while Commander Johnson, Councilor Markov, and Doctor Laskin trailed behind.

When she reached the open door, Catalina saw that it led to an armory, the walls lined with racks of weapons and armor. Ben and Jessica stood in front of a particular locker, withdrawing bulky black boxes with adjustable shoulder straps. *Backpacks?* Catalina wondered.

Ben turned from the locker. "What are you waiting for? We don't know how long we have before they realize we're missing."

Remo strode through, and the rest of them followed. Catalina glanced around the room, wondering what she was supposed to do. Councilor Markov looked equally lost, but Desiree, Alexander, and Commander Johnson went straight for the suits of armor. Those suits stood upright in semi-circular pods, matte black and all but disappearing in the dim light of the armory.

Alexander stepped up to one of the pods and summoned a holographic display; then he began making selections, stabbing and swiping the air with his fingers. Commander Johnson, Remo, and Desiree busied themselves by doing the same, obviously already familiar with the interfaces.

The pods lit up from within one after another, and the suits of armor splayed open with metallic *clicking* sounds. Catalina watched Alexander step inside, lining up his arms and legs. More metallic *clicking* sounds, echoed through the room as the suit sealed around him. The others weren't far behind. Matching black helmets dropped down over their heads, and sealed with a *hiss* of escaping air.

They stepped out of the pods, servos whirring, metal feet *clanking* on the deck. Alexander turned and nodded to Catalina with a reassuring smile, his features illuminated by cold blue lights inside the helmet.

"Your turn," he said, his voice conveyed clearly via external speakers.

She shook her head. "I don't know how..."

"I'll show you," he replied, clanking over to an adjacent pod.

He summoned another holographic control panel and opened another suit for her. She stepped into it and lined up her arms and legs as she'd watched Alexander do. "Don't move," he said; then he sealed the armor around her. Catalina gasped as the suit squeezed her arms and legs. The pressure wasn't uncomfortable, but it was disconcerting.

There came a *whoosh* and then a *hiss* of air, and suddenly she was staring out through the faceplate of a helmet. Lights came on inside the helmet, illuminating the glass with a bright blue heads-up display (HUD). That type of control interface was already familiar to her from her ARCs, but she didn't understand any of the information on this HUD—except for the blinking comms symbol, and Alexander's name, which appeared floating above his head in a bar of green text. She looked around the room and saw more floating names—Councilor Mikail Markov, Lieutenant Desiree Dempsey.

"Why are the comms blinking?" she asked, but her voice didn't travel beyond the helmet.

Alexander cupped a metal hand to the side of his helmet, and said, "Think or say, *activate external speakers.*"

She tried that. "Hello?"

He nodded. "Good. Now try walking out of the pod." He stepped aside and she shuffled out, afraid she would trip and be unable to get back up in the heavy suit, but to her surprise, she could still move easily, as if the suit weighed no more than a few pounds. "You're a natural," Alexander said.

Ben and Jessica walked up to them carrying the black boxes she'd seen them withdrawing from the locker when she'd entered the room. "Strap these over your chests," Ben said, holding one out to Alexander.

"What are they?" he asked, accepting one of the boxes from Ben and awkwardly looping his arms through the straps.

Jessica handed another one to her, and Catalina reached for it with a frown. She had to concentrate to make sure she didn't miss and accidentally grab the girl's tiny hand. She'd heard stories about soldiers using exosuits like these in rescue operations only to accidentally injure the people they were trying to rescue.

"Sonar," Ben explained, replying belatedly to Alexander's question. "We can use them to detect cloaked Grays or humans. Link them to your suits, and you should be able to see whatever they detect."

Catalina strapped hers on, wondering how to link it. She tried focusing on the device, and to her surprise a simple dialogue appeared, asking if she wanted to link with an unknown device.

She mentally selected *yes,* and an echoing *pling* sounded close beside her ears, followed by a wave of shaded green light that raced outward, crawling over the walls, floor, ceiling, Councilor Markov, Doctor Laskin... and all of the objects in the room. The light briefly illuminated all of the shadows in the room before washing up the far wall and disappearing.

Pling. Another wave of green light rolled out. The same thing happened.

"I didn't realize we had these," Commander Johnson said as Jessica passed another device to her.

"We found a way to get them aboard," Ben explained. "Just in case we ran into the Entity."

"Beats the hell out of your bat impression," Remo said.

Ben smirked at that and turned to face the open door of the armory. "Come in *Ch-va-la,*" he said.

The Gray who'd rescued them came slinking into the armory.

"Please cloak yourself," Ben said.

Catalina saw the alien vanish. *Pling.* A green wave of light swept out, and to her surprise, it revealed the Gray clearly when it reached the point where the alien had disappeared. Unlike a flash of real light, there and gone in the blink of an eye, the illumination on her HUD remained, sticking to the Gray like luminous green paint. The color quickly faded until it was a dim green shadow.

Another *pling* sounded, and another wave swept out,

illuminating the Gray brightly once more. Catalina noticed that the alien had suddenly moved a few feet to the left. Confused, she asked about that.

"The light is simulated," Ben explained. "Sonar bounces sound waves off solid objects and listens for the echo. It has a shorter range in the air than underwater, but it should still work fine for our purposes. The main limitation is that it only updates the locations of objects every couple of seconds, so all you'll be able to see is the last known location of a given target. You'll have to anticipate their movements."

"Better than nothing," Remo said. "Now what?"

The Gray replied, "*R-egg-a ad-ma.*"

"*Ch-va-la* wants you to follow it," Ben said.

"You understand that thing?" Remo asked.

Ben nodded. "Benevolence uploaded their language to my and Jessica's brains as part of our mission preparation. Our vocal chords can't reproduce the sounds they make, but fortunately *Ch-va-la* understands our language, too."

"Aha, so where does Ch-va-la want us to follow it?" Alexander asked.

"Back to the harvester."

"What?!" Catalina exclaimed.

"Bad idea..." Remo added. "How many Grays do you think they can fit on a ship that size? There's just eight of us. Nine if you count Bug Eyes."

"The harvester will be almost empty. The Entity needs as much space as possible to pick up and transport billions of people from Earth to their new homes in the Federation. I'm guessing that's also why they decided to take the *Liberty* back with them."

Remo shook his head. "I saw what Esther did to that drone

in the med bay. She melted it to slag, and she didn't even have a weapon!"

"As far as you could tell. There were probably Grays in there with you, cloaked. Their weapons are modified laser welders; they generate a lot of heat."

"I don't care who did it or how. The point is that they did."

"How long did it take to melt the drone?" Ben asked.

"I don't know, you were the one controlling it."

Ben nodded. "Ten seconds. That's how long you have to shoot any Grays you come across before they can incinerate you," Ben replied.

"Why don't we just send more drones?" Commander Johnson asked.

"We can't use them with the harvester jamming our external comms."

That must be what the blinking comms symbol is about, Catalina thought.

"Everyone ready?" Jessica asked as she came and handed a final sonar box to Councilor Markov and Doctor Laskin. Desiree was helping them get suited up.

"No!" Catalina replied. "I don't even know how to shoot!"

"Think *activate cannons*," Alexander said.

She tried that, and weapon barrels slid out of her forearm gauntlets. She lifted her arms, rotating them back and forth to examine the weapons. Twin targeting reticles bobbed around her HUD as she moved her arms.

"They'll lock on automatically," Alexander explained. You just have to mark a target and point your cannons in that general direction. Think *shoot* or *fire,* and the rounds will home in on the target you marked."

"What if I accidentally shoot one of you?" Catalina asked.

"They won't lock on to friendlies, so you can't accidentally shoot us—or yourself," Alexander explained.

Councilor Markov was busy examining his own guns, waving them around the room. *Good thing he can't shoot us,* Catalina thought. "Let's say we kill all the Grays on board the Harvester," she said. "Then what?"

"*Ch-va-la* will take control of it, and we'll head for the rendezvous that we missed."

"What about Mars, the Colonies... Earth?" Commander Johnson demanded.

Ben shook his head. "There's nothing we can do for them."

Commander Johnson set her jaw. "Then we should go back to Proxima and rescue as many of the crew as we can."

"That's even less likely to succeed. As Remo pointed out, there's just nine of us. If we try to infiltrate Proxima B, we'll all be captured and killed, and anyone we managed to immunize would suffer the same fate. The only thing we can hope to do is escape."

"And leave our entire species to go extinct?"

Ben hesitated, looking like he wanted to say something to that, but the Gray spoke first, babbling at them in his stuttering language.

"What's he saying?" Remo asked.

"It says they also had to run—" The alien went on speaking, and Ben waited to translate. "—but now that we have a vaccine, we can fight back."

Alexander nodded along with that. "That's why the Entity wanted to know how you cured us. It wanted to find a way to counter the cure."

"*R-egg-a ad-ma es-a,*" Ch-va-la said.

"You have to go now," Ben said.

"What about you?" Catalina asked.

"There aren't any suits that will fit Jessica and me. We'll stay behind until you've cleared the way for us."

"Well, isn't that convenient," Remo muttered.

Councilor Markov snorted. "The bot gets to stay safe behind the lines while we go out and die."

"I'm not a bot. I'm a synthetic," Ben replied. "And so are you."

"What are you talking about?" Markov demanded.

"How do you think we cured you?"

Markov gaped at him, looking horrified.

"We can discuss all of this later," Jessica said. "By now the Entity must know we're missing, and it will come here looking for us."

"Someone should stay behind to guard the kids," Doctor Laskin put in, walking awkwardly in his exosuit to join the discussion.

Ben appeared to consider that, but then he shook his head "We'll need everyone who can shoot aboard the harvester. Don't worry. We can take care of ourselves. Now go, before it's too late."

Catalina watched the friendly Gray leave the armory. They all followed. As they left, Ben called after them, "Don't let them kill Ch-va-la! He's the only one who knows how to control the harvester."

"Great," Remo muttered. "Well, *Cha-va La-la*, just make sure you keep your scrawny ass behind us."

The Gray elicited a musical trilling sound that might have been a laugh, and Catalina watched as it held out its palm. A glossy black ball materialized out of thin air and hovered out ahead of him; then a bright flash of light suffused the room and dazzled Catalina's eyes.

As soon as it faded, the shimmering, spherical portal they'd traveled through earlier was back, revealing a glossy black corridor somewhere aboard the alien ship.

"I need to get me one of those," Remo said.

"Move out," Commander Johnson ordered, already headed for the portal. Remo was the first to follow her. Catalina saw how he and the commander held their arms to their sides, elbows bent at ninety degrees. She mimicked that posture.

Alexander nodded to her. "Ready?"

"No. I'm not a soldier, Alex."

"You are now," he replied. "Let's go. Stay close and stay behind me."

She nodded, following behind him as closely as she could without stepping on his heels. Her heart pounded out a steady rhythm to their *clanking* footsteps.

A flash of light burst from the portal as Commander Johnson stepped through. Another flash—Remo. Subsequent flashes of light suffused the corridor as the others went. Soon she was seeing spots. Alexander turned to her and nodded once before stepping through.

Her turn. Catalina hesitated on the comparatively safe side of the portal. She watched miniature versions of the others taking up cover positions in the alien corridor.

The green-shaded Gray stepped up to the portal and gestured to it frantically, saying something that she couldn't understand. It was waiting for her to go through first.

"I know, I know," she said, and let out a shuddering sigh that reverberated inside of her helmet.

Here I go—Catalina the space marine, she thought, smirking grimly to herself as she stepped through the portal.

CHAPTER 24

Catalina stepped out of the portal and onto the alien harvester. *Pling.* A wave of green light swept down the corridor. Her heart beat thunderously in her ears, and her body trembled.

Nothing there.

Someone grabbed her arm and yanked her over to the side of the corridor. It was Alexander. Everyone else was already pressed to the glossy black walls. She waited with them.

Another flash of light drew her attention to the bubble-shaped portal, and their alien friend joined them, no longer bothering to cloak himself. Maybe there was no point in cloaking from other Grays.

Remo and Commander Johnson peeled away from the walls, their ranks and names bobbing above their heads as they went. Remo swept his right arm from back to front, his hand dangling down by his side. It looked like some kind of military signal. Catalina intuited it to mean *move up.*

Remo started forward, and they crept down the corridor behind him. Catalina's footsteps clanked noisily on the alien deck, despite her best efforts to step lightly.

"Activate *silent running*," Remo whispered.

"How?" Catalina asked.

"Think it!" he hissed.

She tried that, and her footsteps suddenly quieted to a

whisper. Not only that, but the servos and mechanical parts in her exosuit went from *whining* and *whirring* to *swishing* like the wind. But the price she paid was that now her movements weren't so natural. With every step she took, she felt the suit pushing back, making sure she didn't move too quickly or put her feet down too suddenly. Catalina found she had to concentrate just to keep from falling over.

Pling. Another wave of green light raced out, illuminating the corridor. Catalina held her breath as it disappeared into the distance.

No hidden aliens yet.

Ch-va-la walked by her, reaching down to its waist to grab something that Catalina couldn't see. Then a small black weapon with a broad dish at the end of the barrel appeared in its hand, and Catalina realized the alien wasn't really naked. At the very least it wore an invisible gun belt.

The corridor came to a *T* and Remo held a hand out to them, palm open. Another clear signal. *Stop.*

He and Commander Johnson pressed themselves to opposite sides of the corridor and each peered around the corner. The Gray walked straight by them, seemingly unconcerned that it could be walking into a crossfire.

Remo glanced at it and shook his head. He swept his arm from back to front again. *Move up.*

They followed the Gray down the next corridor, footsteps whispering, servos *swishing*. They went on like that for what must have been ten minutes, not encountering anything. Each time they reached a turn or a bend in the corridors, Remo and Commander Johnson stopped and checked both ways carefully, but the Gray went on ahead as if it already knew the way was clear.

They came to another *T*, and this time the alien didn't proceed ahead of them. It stopped before reaching the adjoining corridor and turned to face them. It extended a single bony finger to the left, and then held up six of its eight fingers. It turned to the right and pointed that way, holding up four more fingers.

Six to the left. Four to the right. The Grays were waiting for them here.

Catalina felt drops of cold sweat trickling down her spine. Her hands trembled, and her stomach ached. How long had it been since she'd eaten something?

Remo pressed himself to the left side of the corridor. He turned and pointed to Alexander, Desiree, and then to her, and he waved them over. Desiree went first.

Councilor Markov and Doctor Laskin went to stand on the right, beside Commander Johnson.

With everyone in position, Remo nodded to Commander Johnson and they both poked their heads around the corners. Commander Johnson jumped back, her helmet smoking.

"Shit!" she hissed. "Feels like I just stuck my head in an oven!"

"Ten seconds my ass," Remo muttered, his helmet smoking, too. Catalina remembered what Ben had concluded about how long they'd have before the Grays incinerated them.

"Did you see anything?" Alexander whispered.

Remo nodded. "It's a dead end. Six of them standing there, pointing at us with those dish guns of theirs."

"Four on my side, also a dead end," Commander Johnson said.

"If this is a dead end, we should turn around and go

another way," Catalina suggested.

Ch-va-la replied, "*Nek*," and pointed insistently to the left.

"Their doors are invisible, remember?" Remo said. "I don't think those are dead ends. They wouldn't be guarding them if they were."

Catalina felt a wave of heat wash through her body, and her mouth went abruptly dry.

"Grays!" Remo yelled.

Ch-va-la aimed and fired his gun behind them. The air shimmered between the dish-shaped barrel and his target. As Catalina watched, his gray skin blistered and blackened. A dozen green-shaded aliens appeared behind them, all aiming dish-shaped weapons. To either side of her she saw the others' armor smoking and sizzling. The air in the corridor shivered and danced with the heat.

Doctor Laskin stepped out from the wall. "We're surrounded! he said, his eyes wild with fear. "Run!" Not waiting for anyone to follow, he ran back the way they'd come, charging the line of Grays like a linebacker.

"Get back here!" Remo roared as he stepped away from the wall, his arms out and guns aimed, but holding fire. "I can't shoot with you in the way! Hit the deck!"

Doctor Laskin rushed on, screaming as he went, his armor smoking and glowing bright orange as the Grays focused their fire on him. His exosuit flowed off him in rivers, and he grew silent, collapsing to the deck in a glowing orange puddle of molten alloy.

Remo cursed under his breath and opened fire with a thunderous roar. Alexander and Desiree joined him. Catalina aimed blindly at the rushing wave of green. She thought *fire,* and her arms shuddered as roaring steams of bullets stuttered out. In a matter of seconds, the Grays lay scattered across the deck, their limbs severed and their bodies leaking rivulets of black blood. 0Apparently they de-cloaked when they died.

Catalina stood frozen and blinking in shock at the carnage.

Commander Johnson cried out for help, and they turned to see her surrounded by ten green-shaded aliens on the other end of the corridor. They were all pointing their guns at her at the same time. Her armor smoked and glowed turning molten and dripping to the floor with hissing *splats*. She screamed, and Councilor Markov roared, charging through the diminutive line of aliens, physically knocking them down to disrupt their aim. Remo, Alexander, and Desiree tried shooting around him, aiming for the ones he knocked over before they could get back up.

But they were too late. Commander Johnson crumpled to the deck, disappearing in a thick column of smoke. They finished mowing down all of the Grays, and then hurried to check on the commander. Catalina approached cautiously, her stomach churning, afraid of what she might see.

Councilor Markov reached the commander's side first. He let out a chilling scream, his voice laced with a mixture of horror and grief. Then he sunk to his haunches and sobbed.

Catalina's steps faltered. She didn't want to see what had made the seemingly callous old Russian lose it like that.

A black shadow walked by her. Catalina flinched, startled, but then she saw that it was Ch-va-la, burned beyond recognition, but somehow still walking.

"*Ad-ma,*" it said in a husky voice, stumbling by all of them with its arms and hands held out to feel its way along the corridor.

It's blind, Catalina realized. Ch-va-la proceeded down the left side of the *T*, almost tripping over one of the dead Grays.

"I think I'm going to be sick," Alexander said, peering down at what was left of Commander Johnson.

Remo placed a hand on councilor Markov's shoulder. "We can mourn for the dead later." Markov looked up and glared at him, but Remo had already turned away.

Catalina sent Alexander a worried look. The only one who knew how to operate the harvester was now blind. *And we're no better,* she realized.

They didn't speak its language, and even if they did, they wouldn't know how to follow its instructions.

It's the blind leading the blind.

CHAPTER 25

A door materialized in front of Ch-va-la, and he walked through. Everyone hurried after him. Remo and Desiree took up positions by the door, guarding the entrance.

Catalina watched, frowning with dismay as the alien stumbled around some type of control center—a circular room filled with small, Gray-sized chairs. She rushed forward to lend it a hand.

"He's blind?!" Remo asked.

"Let me help you," Catalina said, placing her hand lightly on Ch-va-la's shoulder.

The alien turned to her, and inclined its blackened head. "*Que-ra e-sa cas-ra?*" it whispered in a gasping voice.

She shook her head. "I'm sorry, I don't understand...."

"If it's anything like one of our ships," Alexander began as he walked up beside them, "then he's looking for the command control station. There's six chairs...."

Catalina looked around, each of those six chairs had six floor lamps arranged in a circle around them. The lamps were colored differently for each chair.

"Over there," Alexander suggested, pointing to the chair with white lamps.

Catalina led Ch-va-la over to that chair and helped it to sit down. No sooner had it sat down, than holographic displays popped up around the chair, six displays, one for each of the floor lamps. The glossy black circumference of the room turned transparent, becoming one giant holoscreen, showing black space, dazzling stars, and the sun peeking over the dark side of a planet. Catalina watched as the planet swept by beneath them, trying to pick out details beyond the night-side. She saw a glimmer of blue and white; and then she noticed the tiny gray speck hovering to one side of the planet—the Moon.

"It's Earth," Alexander whispered.

Loud noises came echoing through the room, reaching their ears from unseen speakers. *Clunk, clunk, clunk... boom!*

Ch-va-la did something from his control station, and jagged pink objects appeared sailing all around them, highlighted by the harvester's sensors.

Debris, Catalina realized.

"They took out Earth's fleet," Remo said from his position guarding the entrance. "So much for Benevolence's surrender."

Another group of objects appeared in the distance—a cluster of previously-invisible black specks, highlighted bright, sky blue. Even smaller blue specks streamed from them to—or *from?*—the planet's surface. *Shuttles for all the human slaves.*

As Catalina watched, one of the larger specks swelled to fill the screen in front of Ch-va-la's chair.

The ship was cylindrically-shaped, just like the *Liberty*, but there were long spikes protruding from its hull in all directions, like the bristles of a hair brush. In front, the ship opened up into six triangular segments, like some kind of bizarre flower, and the shuttles were all streaming in and out of that opening. Catalina glanced along the length of the ship, noting that the aft end had the same triangular segments, but they were shut, forming a cone. Six long pylons with cylinders at the end were arrayed around the cone. *Thrusters,* she decided.

"Six of everything," Alexander noted. "Must be their lucky number."

Ch-va-la glanced up and said something in a husky voice. Catalina frowned and shook her head. "I don't know what you're trying to say."

It gestured frantically to the holoscreens around its chair, each of them crowded with alien symbols and text. They were *visual* displays, and Ch-va-la couldn't see. It had probably been a stretch for him just to turn everything on and highlight the detectable objects around them. Charting a course for a distant rendezvous would be impossible.

"What's wrong?" Remo asked.

"I don't think he can do this," Alexander said.

"Do what?"

"Anything," Catalina added.

"Great," Remo muttered and cursed under his breath.

Ch-va-la rose from his chair and walked to the center of the room. He held out his palm and a glossy black ball appeared. It floated out from his palm and there came a bright flash of light as it opened another portal. Catalina blinked rapidly to clear the spots from her eyes and she saw two tiny people standing on the other side of the portal, somewhere aboard the *Liberty.* Those two had to be Ben and Jessica.

Catalina wondered why they hadn't used that portal sphere to get into the harvester's control center. Two flashes of light suffused the room in quick succession, and as the light faded, Catalina saw both Ben and Jessica now standing with them on the bridge of the alien ship.

"What's wrong?" Ben asked.

"He's blind," Catalina explained.

Ch-va-la said something, and Ben's gaze settled on the Gray. He sucked in a quick breath.

"He's not just blind. He's dying. What did I tell you about letting them kill him?" Ben demanded.

Ch-va-la said something else, and Ben replied, "Of course it's their fault!"

"Audrey is dead," Councilor Markov said in a hoarse whisper as he walked up beside Ben. "She died protecting that *thing* while a dozen of his buddies incinerated her."

Ben stared back at the big Russian, looking like he wanted to say something to that. Instead, he looked away and led Ch-va-la back to his chair. They spoke in hushed voices, and Ben sat down, listening as Ch-va-la gave him orders.

Ben frowned at the alien displays and shook his head. Then he focused on one in particular. His chair rotated to face it, and he stabbed at the display, making selections from the sea of alien text. Some kind of map appeared. It zoomed out to reveal what looked to be a schematic of the harvester. A cluster of blinking yellow dots marked one end of the cylindrical ship, while a solitary sky-blue dot blinked at the opposite end.

"There's only one of them left," Ben said. "Looks like... it's in the... aft section somewhere. Did you find Esther yet?" he asked.

"No," Alexander replied. "Just the Grays."

"Then that blue dot is her," Ben said. "I don't know what she's doing, but it's a good bet she knows we killed the others, and an even better bet that she's up to something."

"We need to get rid of her before we head for the rendezvous," Jessica said.

Ben nodded. "Any volunteers?"

"I'll go," Councilor Markov said, clanking up behind Ben.

"You can't go alone. Everyone except for two of you should go," Ben replied. "Someone has to stay here to guard the doors."

"Can't Esther just use one of those portals to get in here?" Catalina asked.

Ben looked to Ch-va-la, and the alien said something. "Not anymore," Ben said. "Ch-va-la just activated the jamming field. Unfortunately that means you'll have to walk all the way to the other end of the ship."

"The portals worked to get us on board," Catalina objected.

Ben shrugged. "They weren't jamming us. Maybe they didn't realize they needed to until we were already close to the bridge."

"So why the hell didn't we jump straight to the bridge?" Councilor Markov demanded. "We could have skipped that firefight in the corridor and Audrey might still be alive!"

"You'd have been trapped in an open room with no cover, where any shots fired could have damaged sensitive equipment that we need to get out of here," Ben replied. "Ch-va-la knew what he was doing."

Markov grunted and looked away.

"You'd better hurry and get to Esther before she finishes whatever she's trying to do."

A sharp *screech* interrupted them. Catalina spun around, trying to figure out where it had come from. Another *screech*. This time it was followed by a distant *boom*.

"What was that?" she asked.

"A hull breach," Alexander said quietly.

Catalina blinked. "We're under attack?"

Screeech!

Boom!

"There," Remo pointed to one side of the circular holoscreen running around the room. A cluster of larger and nearer harvesters were firing on them with fat red beams of light.

"We're in trouble," Desiree said.

Ch-va-la began chattering in a gasping voice, gesturing wildly to the holo display.

"Doesn't this thing have some kind of shields?" Alexander demanded.

"It has to," Remo replied. "How else could it get us through the wormhole?"

Screeech! Screech! B-boom!

"Then activate them, damn it!" Alexander roared.

"I'm working on it!" Ben said. "Do something useful, and go find Esther!"

"You mean go get lost," Alexander said. "This ship is a lot bigger than the *Liberty,* and that was already enormous. How are we supposed to know where she is?"

"I'll guide you from here."

"With the comms offline?"

Before Ben could answer, the dim red light in the room flickered and died, plunging them into absolute darkness. Each of their helmets glowed blue-white, illuminating their faces and spreading a ghostly glow through the room. Remo, Alexander, and Desiree flicked on their suits' headlamps, and streams of light cut swaths through the room, illuminating clouds of alien dust, the particles dancing down like snowflakes.

"Comms are back online now," Ben said.

Alexander regarded him with a frown. "With the power offline, doesn't that mean that portal-jamming field is down, too?"

Ben nodded gravely, his face awash in the light of Alexander's headlamps.

"Maybe that was her plan? Open a portal and toss a bomb into the bridge," Catalina suggested. She spun in a quick circle, looking for exactly that, but her helmet lamps weren't on, so she couldn't see if there was anything rolling around on the bridge with them.

"Grays don't have weapons," Ben said.

"The hell they don't—what about those ray guns of theirs?" Remo asked.

"Those are welding torches," Ben said. "The Grays were a peaceful race."

A distant *boom* shivered through the deck.

"Then how are they shooting us?" Alexander asked.

"Mining beams," Ben said.

Remo barked a laugh. "I don't care if you call them feather dusters, they'll still burn our asses off."

Ben shrugged. "They don't use explosives—not in my experience at least, so that means we're safe as long as a few of you stay behind to guard Ch-va-la and me."

"What about those other ships?" Alexander asked. "Can't they open portals to send reinforcements aboard?"

Ben appeared to consider that. "They could..." Another hull breach rumbled through the deck.

"But?"

"I think the Entity is afraid of us. We cured three and killed all the Grays on board. She'd rather destroy the ship than risk more of her people. That means the cure we used will die with us."

"So will she," Alexander said.

"I don't think she—*it*—cares. The Entity isn't any one person. It's all of them."

"If the power's out, how do we still have gravity?" Remo asked.

Ben turned and directed the question to Ch-va-la. The alien muttered something unintelligible.

"He says artificial gravity and life support run on their own dedicated power supply, independent of the ship's non-critical systems."

Remo snorted. "I guess it would be asking too much for them to have powered emergency lighting from that power supply."

Ben shrugged. "Who's staying and who's going?"

"I'll stay," Remo said.

"Me, too," Desiree added.

"I'm going," Markov said, his head lamps flicking on as he finally figured out how to use them.

"I'll go, too," Alexander added.

Catalina glanced around the shadowy bridge and said, "Likewise." She'd feel safer with Alexander around.

Ben turned to Ch-va-la. "Can you help us get there?"

The alien stepped to one side of the group and opened a portal to some other part of the ship.

"We'll still need a guide," Markov said.

Jessica nodded. "Tell me how to get to her and I'll lead them."

Ch-va-la chattered at her for a handful of seconds.

"Got it," she said. "Ready?" she asked, turning to them. Alexander and Markov nodded, and all three of them started for the portal.

Catalina blinked. "Wait! How do I turn on my headlamps?"

"*Activate headlamps,*" Alexander said.

Catalina tried that. It worked. "I should have thought of that," she said.

"There's a lot going on," Alexander replied. "You're distracted."

The portal flashed as Jessica and Markov stepped through. Alexander stopped at the threshold and turned to regard her. "You should stay here."

"And let that thing kill you? Not a chance."

"I'll be fine," Alexander replied. "I was in the Navy. I'm trained to fight. You aren't."

Catalina shook her head. "You're wasting time. We can't let Markov go after her alone."

Alexander frowned. "Stay behind me, then."

"Sure," Catalina lied.

Alexander looked unconvinced, but there was no time to argue.

He stepped through the portal. It flashed bright as the sun, and she walked into the light.

CHAPTER 26

Ben's voice crackled to them over the comms. "Everyone switch to this channel. No need to use external speakers anymore."

Catalina surprised herself by managing to select the right options from her HUD without any help from Alexander.

Jessica led the way with Markov close on her heels. It wasn't even a minute before they reached a dead end. If there was a door there, it wouldn't open for them, and Ch-va-la wasn't there to assist.

"We'll have to blow it open," Jessica said.

"No problem," Markov replied, already taking aim with his cannons. "Stand back."

"Wait!" Alexander said. "You can't use cannons to blow open a door. The rounds could ricochet and hit one of us. Let me do it. Everyone step back."

Jessica and the others backed away from the end of the corridor, and even Alexander backed up by a dozen paces or so. Once he was in position, rocket pods slid up out of his suit's shoulders, and Catalina held her breath.

Two rockets jetted out with a noisy *krrsshh*, trailing thin white exhaust plumes. They hit the end of the corridor with a deafening *bang!* and a burst of light.

As the smoke cleared, Catalina saw that there was now a ragged hole in the previously sealed end of the corridor.

"Let's go," Alexander said. Markov went clanking ahead at full speed, not bothering with *silent running.*

Catalina walked up beside Alexander, passing Jessica along the way. The little girl made no move to follow. Her job was done.

"Esther's dead ahead," Alexander said, pointing.

Pling. Catalina remembered her sonar. She'd grown so used to it that she'd begun to tune out the sound and ignore those racing green waves of light. Now she focused on them once more. She couldn't see the light penetrate the smoke swirling in the ragged hole Alexander had blown, but she did see a fuzzy green silhouette appear in the distance.

"Stay behind me," Alexander said, setting out at a cautious pace, his exosuit whispering as he crept down the corridor.

Catalina crept along behind him.

Pling. The fuzzy green silhouette reappeared a few feet over from where it had been, and a long, chilling scream reverberated over the comms.

Markov!

Alexander froze in the smoke-clouded hole he'd blasted. He held up a closed fist, and she stopped behind him.

Catalina waited, her heart thudding in her chest.

"Markov?" she tried, whispering over the comms.

But there was no reply.

"He's down," Alexander whispered back.

Catalina saw the green silhouette move again, and this time it got smaller, moving farther away.

"How did she take him out so fast?"

Alexander shook his head. He waited a few more beats.

Pling. Esther's silhouette reappeared, now even further away.

Alexander raised his arm in another gesture, but this time Catalina couldn't intuit its meaning.

"What's that mean?"

"Cover the door. I'm going to go take a look."

Like hell, she thought. She waited for him to go on ahead, disappearing through the ragged opening, and then she followed quietly behind him.

"I thought I told you to cover the door," he said.

"How..."

"Top right of the HUD. The transparent circle."

Catalina spied a circle with a bright green dot and two yellow ones in it. She didn't understand how to read it, but she assumed the green dot had to be Alexander. It was inching slowly toward the top of the circle where one of the yellow dots was.

Catalina studied the room beyond the door. Dead ahead was a giant glossy black sphere with a catwalk crossing out to it. A domed ceiling soared high above that sphere. Alexander crept across the catwalk, his headlamps revealing that the catwalk was broken in the middle, leaving a shadowy gap over an uncertain abyss. The edges of the catwalk were blackened, as if from a fire—*or a welding torch,* Catalina thought. Councilor Markov was nowhere to be seen, but it was a good bet that he was lying at the bottom somewhere.

As Catalina followed Alexander across the catwalk to the spherical structure in the center of the room, she realized that Esther had to be hiding behind it, doing who knew what. Alexander reached the gap, and the catwalk groaned under his weight.

Catalina froze and peered over the railing. Bad idea. It was at least a dozen floors down. Her headlamps barely illuminated the bottom. "Alex, be careful," she said. "It's a long way down."

"Don't worry," he replied.

Suddenly the catwalk bounced up and down like a springboard, and she looked up to see Alexander land on the other side of the gap with a *boom*.

"Stay there. I'm going to get Esther," he said.

Catalina wanted to object, but she saw how the two sides of the catwalk were bent where Alexander had jumped and landed, and she was afraid it would collapse if she jumped across, too.

"Ben?" Catalina tried.

"What's up?" he asked.

"We're in pursuit. Councilor Markov is dead."

Ben didn't reply immediately. Then he said, "Be careful."

A redundant suggestion if ever there was one. What else would they be?

Alexander came on the comms next. "Ben, she's cut a hole into the central structure—some kind of sphere. I'm standing in front of it, and radiation readings are spiking. My suit should be able to take it, but I don't know for how long. I assume this is the ship's reactor, and she compromised the radiation shielding by cutting into it like that. Any idea what she's doing?"

Ben took another moment to reply. "She's trying to scuttle the ship! There are three layers of containment. If she cuts through all three of them she'll blast us back to our constituent atoms."

"Understood," Alexander replied. "I'm following her in."

"Hold on. Alexander, according to my calculations you've got thirty seconds. After that no amount of radiation treatment will save you."

"I'll be fast. Start the clock," Alexander said.

"What?!" Catalina screamed. "Alex, you can't do that!"

"If he doesn't, we're all going to die," Ben replied.

"Keep this channel clear," Alexander hissed. "I'm going in."

"Roger," Ben replied.

Catalina stared at the reactor core, wide-eyed and speechless. Without giving it a second thought, she leapt across the gap in the catwalk and landed on the other side. The catwalk behind her gave a shriek of over-fatigued metal and she turned to watch as it fell away, collapsing to the side of the chamber with a reverberating *boom,* as if to punctuate the fact that they'd just crossed the point of no return.

CHAPTER 27

Alexander switched off his headlamps, opting to activate infrared and light amplification instead. There was almost no light to amplify—just a ghostly green glow coming from inside the reactor core. Alexander crept through the hole in the outer circumference of the reactor core.

The outermost containment layer was hollow. Alexander slunk around the core, keeping a close eye on the rapidly spiking radiation counts while he activated and armed his exosuit's rockets and cannons in preparation. He wasn't even going to give Esther a chance to blink.

As Alexander rounded the core, he began to hear a sharp sizzling noise. Esther was already cutting through the second containment layer.

The sizzling abruptly stopped, and radiation counts spiked once more.

She was through.

Alexander winced. Sweat beaded his brow, inching toward his nose. Radiation levels were already far past lethal. He would just have to trust that his suit could protect him.

He reached another molten hole in the core, and was just about to charge through to the second containment layer when he felt a wave of heat wash through him. He ducked to one side of the opening and waited. His skin prickled and stung, and smoke shivered off his armor. He counted to five in his head and then poked his head around the corner.

This time nothing happened. Esther had moved on. He couldn't let her cut through that last containment layer. Alexander disabled *silent running* and ran through the opening. Esther came into view, and another wave of heat hit him. Her aim was off and she hit his leg. A searing pain blistered his skin. He gritted his teeth and let her have it, firing both cannons simultaneously.

The searing pain eased as Esther fell and lost her aim. Residual, stinging echoes of that agony throbbed through his body.

Alexander walked up to Esther. She lay grinning up at him, leaking blood from a dozen holes in her torso. "You can't kill me!" she shrieked. "But I can kill you!" A long, rifle-shaped object swung up from the deck, glaring at him with a broad black dish.

Alexander didn't even hesitate. He fired again at point blank range, and her body jumped and jittered as if from a seizure. Not taking any chances, he pumped her so full of bullets that she looked like a honeycomb.

Alexander regarded her corpse with a mixture of disgust and righteous satisfaction. "Guess you spoke too soon."

The crackling and clicking sound of a Geiger counter brought Alexander back from that moment of victory, reminding him where he was. He turned and ran back the way he'd come, desperate to get out of the reactor before it was too late.

* * *

Catalina stood outside the hole in the outermost layer of

the reactor, heedless of the radiation pouring out.

"Alexander!" she said, screaming at him over the comms for the umpteenth time.

But there was no reply.

"Why isn't he answering?" Catalina demanded.

"The shielding inside the core might be blocking comm signals," Ben said.

"Might be?"

Ben kept silent, not mentioning the other alternative.

"I'm going in to check on him."

"Wait. Give him another minute."

"Another *minute?* How long has it been?"

"Seventy two seconds."

"You said after *thirty* seconds nothing could save him!" Catalina screamed.

"Nothing I know of. The Grays have more advanced medicine than we do. Ch-va-la may be able to help him."

A blind alien burn victim was going to save Alexander from a painful death by radiation poisoning. "And what about him? Who's going to save Ch-va-la?"

Catalina heard something—*cl-clank clank, cl-clank clank, cl-clank clank...*

Alexander came running toward her, limping. He almost knocked her over in his hurry to get out of the core, but she stepped aside and he sailed into the catwalk railings instead.

"You're hurt!" Catalina said, rushing over to him so she could study his leg. His thigh armor was a lumpy black mess.

"She's dead," Alexander said, gasping for air over the comms. "How long was I in there?"

"Too long," Ben replied.

"So..." Alexander trailed off, and his gaze found hers

through their helmets.

"The Grays will be able to help you," Catalina said. "Right, Ben?"

"Right," he said after a moment's hesitation. "But first we need to get the power back on and get out of here, or we're all going to die. There's a control room on the other side of the reactor chamber. Meet us there."

Catalina looked around the spherical chamber, trying to decide what the *other side* might be.

"Over there," Alexander pointed to the catwalk opposite the one they'd already crossed. He limped toward it, and she followed, watching her husband with growing concern.

"How are you feeling?" she asked.

"Besides a few minor burns, not bad—not yet, anyway. I have a few hours before symptoms start to show."

They walked across the catwalk to the far side of the reactor room. There they came to a dead-end, but even before they reached it, doors materialized and slid open, revealing Ch-va-la's char-blackened form. The headlamps of the others came sweeping out, and they heard Remo's voice echoing over his external speakers.

"Cover the doors!" Remo ordered as they walked into the control room. He stood with Desiree already watching those doors at the other end of the room.

Alexander hurried over to join him, crouching down behind Remo. He pointed to the other side, where Desiree was, and Catalina took up position behind her.

Ben came on the comms ordering Jessica to join them.

She explained about the missing catwalk between her and the core, saying, "I'll have to walk around."

"Make it quick," Ben replied.

"Going as... fast as... I can..." Jessica panted.

Catalina kept her eyes on the corridor beyond the control room. Then a thought occurred to her and she glanced back the way they'd come.

"What if they jump into the core and finish what Esther started?" she asked.

"According to Ch-va-la, they can't, the reactor room is independently shielded against portal transits."

Jessica appeared at the end of the corridor. She came running toward them only to skid to a stop as the air in front of her began shimmering with the appearance of a bubble-shaped portal.

Remo called out, "Here they come! Jessica, get out of the way!"

She dove to one side of the corridor, and then a flash of light issued from the portal, but Catalina didn't see anything step through.

Pling.

A green-shaded alien appeared there, aiming a small dish-barreled gun at them.

Remo fired a thunderous burst from his cannons, and the Gray fell thrashing to the deck, de-cloaking the instant it hit the ground.

Pling. Three more green-shaded Grays came through in tandem. Cannon roared once more, this time in stereo as Desiree joined in. Two of the aliens fell. The third remained standing for a moment, and Catalina felt her face blister with sudden heat. She ducked into cover and the sensation passed.

She waited a second longer, and then peeked back. *Pling.* Now there were five grays in the corridor. Cannon fire flashed out, illuminating the walls and floor with strobing yellow-orange light.

A mound of dead Grays was piled between them and the open portal, giving subsequent ones something to take cover behind. Green-shaded heads peeked around the mountain of bodies, taking aim with welding torches. The air in the corridor shivered with heat, and Remo withdrew suddenly, his arm smoking and glowing a faint orange color.

"Fuck!" he roared, waving his arm around to cool his armor faster. "How much longer do you need, kid?"

"Give me a few more minutes!" Ben said.

Catalina tried aiming around Desiree, but her shot went wide hitting the mound of bodies with meaty *thwaps*.

Alexander stepped out of cover—*Krrshhh!*

A rocket streaked out and exploded with a terrific *boom*, throwing debris in all directions and filling the corridor with smoke. Catalina's ears rang, and bits and pieces of Grays rained down. Now she was grateful for the lack of illumination. As the ringing in her ears subsided, she heard the last of the debris touching down. *Thup, thup, plop*—

A small four-fingered hand landed a few feet away from her. The rest of the carnage snapped into focus: walls black and glistening with blood, bits and pieces of Grays scattered everywhere—here a foot, there a thigh, a head, an arm...

Catalina scrambled away, her stomach churning and head swimming. The others went on firing around her, but she couldn't. She wasn't trained for this! Her hands trembled like autumn leaves, and she shook her head over and over, desperate to erase the horrific scene.

* * *

No sooner had Alexander cleared the first heap of bodies than another one appeared. Gun smoke and rocket smoke blurred together in a dense fog until it felt like they could reach out and touch the beams of light shining from their headlamps. Shifting curtains of smoke sparkled with the moisture of vaporized alien blood. Cannon fire roared and the vibrations chattered his teeth as if there were a jackhammer lodged inside his head.

"I'm almost out of ammo!" Remo yelled.

Click. Alexander's cannon ran out of ammo at that exact moment, and he mentally triggered the magazine release. The empty magazine dropped out onto the deck, and Alexander hurried to slot in a spare from his suit's equipment belt. It was his last one. He'd already burned through the other three, and there was one more loaded in the cannon in his other arm. After that he'd be out, too. They'd only been firing for a few minutes, but it felt like a lifetime.

"Ben!" Alex gritted out, watching as another wave of Grays fell in a heap. Remo fired a rocket at the mounting pile of bodies. *Krrsshhh—boom!*

"You'd better hurry up!"

"Almost done!"

Alexander cut down another nine Grays, bullets rattling out. His arm was numb from the endless recoil. *Click.* Alexander released another spent magazine and scavenged the loaded one from his other arm.

Remo stopped firing.

"That's it! I'm out!" he ducked out of the doorway and shook his head. His armor was smoking, glowing orange in places. The Grays didn't have much time to aim and shoot when they came through the portal, but it was still enough to scald them. Alexander could feel his own skin screaming at him. His exposed arm and shoulder felt like they were on fire.

"I'm out, too!" Desiree said, retreating behind her side of the doorway.

Click. Click.

All sounds of gunfire stopped, replaced by a ringing silence that made Alexander's brain throb with a headache. He glanced at Catalina. She sat out of the enemy's line of fire, hugging her knees to her chest, her eyes wide and terrified.

"Caty! Toss me your spare magazines!" he said.

She stared blankly back at him, as if she didn't know what a magazine was. She probably didn't. Grays streamed out of the portal, filling the corridor. Desiree fired a rocket, *krrsshh-bang!* Carnage rained around them and blood splattered his faceplate. He swiped it away, creating a smeary mess.

"Caty!" he tried again. Nothing. She was in shock.

Desiree reached over and grabbed the magazines from Catalina's belt. She tossed two of them over, keeping the other two for herself. Alexander caught them and passed one to Remo.

"Single fire!" Remo instructed.

Alexander nodded and switched his cannons over to single fire mode. They picked off targets one at a time as they ran through the portal. Not fast enough. Searing waves of heat lit their skins on fire. Their sonar identified the Grays even through the smoke, so they could aim, but with the delay between sensor sweeps, every other shot they took missed, slicing through imaginary targets that had since moved somewhere else. Alexander managed to cut down another dozen Grays before he ran out of bullets again.

Click.

Remo and Desiree stopped shooting at the same time, too. Alexander was about to tell Catalina how to release the loaded magazines from her cannons when he noticed that the Grays had stopped coming through.

For a moment he wondered if the jamming field was back online, but the smoke cleared enough for him to pick out the portal still shimmering in the corridor.

"Looks like they gave up," Remo said.

He spoke too soon. Another figure came swirling through the smoke, but this one wasn't shaded green by sonar. Their headlamps illuminated it, revealing a human child—a little girl no more than five years old. She came waltzing out through the carnage, looking around hastily, her eyes wide and terrified.

"Hold your fire!" Remo said.

Alexander didn't have any bullets left, but he wouldn't have fired if he did. He watched the girl approach, wondering what game the Entity was playing now.

"Hello there," Remo tried. "Are you all right?"

"N-no! W-where am I?" the girl said as she reached them.

"You're aboard a spaceship," Remo said. He waved her over to get her out of the line of fire in case more Grays came through. Then he crouched in front of her and looked her over.

"Are you hurt?"

"No," she shook her head.

"How did you get here?" Desiree asked from the other side of the doorway.

"Don't know. When I woke up, I wasn't in my bed. I went to find Marco."

Alexander noticed something glinting in her hand. He

pointed to it. "What are you holding?"

She turned to him, trying hard not to smile. "Nothing," she said, and dropped the object. It fell with a heavy *thunk* and rolled between them. Red lights blinked faster and faster in time to an urgent tone.

It was a plasma grenade.

Alexander didn't even hesitate. He threw himself on top of the grenade.

"Cover!" Remo yelled.

A split second later, there came a blinding flash of light, and Alexander felt a surge of excruciating heat radiate from his stomach. The sensation was there and gone in an instant—

And so was he.

CHAPTER 28

Catalina recovered from her shock just in time to wonder what a little girl was doing in the middle of a battlefield.

Then Alexander dove to one side of that girl, and Remo screamed, "Cover!"

Everything went white. A wave of hot air hit her and threw her against the far wall. She hit with a *thud,* and sat there stunned. Debris rained down—bits and pieces of blackened armor, and other bits her brain refused to identify.

The lights came on inside the room, casting everything into horrifying clarity. Alexander was gone, the walls plastered with his remains.

"Power's up!" Ben announced.

Alexander's dead! Catalina wanted to scream back, but words failed her.

"Fucking shit!" Remo said, pounding the wall with an armored fist.

The little girl Catalina had seen just before all hell broke loose lay in a tattered heap to one side of the room. Catalina blinked, and something wet grazed her cheek. People mulled around her, crouching down and speaking in soft voices; then yelling and shaking her by her shoulders.

Ben stopped in front of her, looking like he wanted to say something, but then he grimaced and looked away. Remo and Desiree pulled her to her feet and held her up, one to either side of her. Jessica came to join them, picking her way through the carnage with a wrinkled nose. Ch-va-la opened a portal back to the ship's bridge, and everyone walked through. Remo and Desiree carried her through with them. A merciful flash of light cleansed the gory scene and then they stepped out onto the bridge of the harvester. Ben went to sit in the commander's chair and once again took orders from Ch-va-la.

He said something about the ship being clear of enemies. A thunderous *boom* shook the bridge as enemy ships went back to attacking them. Catalina swayed on her feet and fell, hitting the deck hard.

"He's dead..." she whispered.

"He saved our lives—twice," Remo replied, getting down on his haunches beside her.

"Got it!" Ben said.

Remo looked up suddenly, and Catalina followed his gaze to the outer circumference of the room. The wraparound holo display showed them sailing straight toward a spherically distorted area of space. A wormhole. It looked like one of the portals the Grays used.

The wormhole swelled to fill their entire field of view. Then they sailed through and stars seemed to fall away rapidly to either side of them.

Boom!

"They're following us in!" Ben announced.

"How long before we reach the rendezvous?" Desiree asked.

Ben looked to Ch-va-la, and the alien said. *"T-ee toc-a."*

"Three hours," Ben replied.

A violent explosion rocked the ship.

"What was that?" Desiree asked. "I thought the Grays didn't have explosives?"

"They don't, but we do. If the Entity sent a human girl after us with a plasma grenade, it has probably extended that strategy to include sending the surviving warships from our fleets after us, too."

Another *boom!* interrupted them.

"Can we last three hours?" Remo asked.

Ben shook his head. "We're about to find out."

Ch-va-la stepped into the center of the room and opened another portal. This time Catalina could see that it led somewhere aboard the *Liberty*.

The alien gestured to the portal and said something in a rasping whisper.

"What did he say?" Remo asked.

"He says we'll be safer on our ship," Ben replied.

"The *Liberty* doesn't have any shields," Remo objected. "This thing does."

Another explosion rocked through the harvester, and the lights flickered.

"What if we lose power?" Desiree said. "No power means no shields."

Remo grimaced.

"She's right," Ben said. "Let's go." He stepped through the portal first, followed by Desiree. Then Catalina went. Once she emerged aboard the *Liberty*, she looked back at the portal and watched as Remo came through. They all turned to watch with her, waiting for Ch-va-la to follow, but no subsequent flashes of light lit the room. He was nowhere in sight.

"Where'd he go?"

"There—" Ben pointed at the portal, to the harvester's

deck, and Catalina saw the alien lying curled on the floor in a fetal position, his char-blackened skin blending almost perfectly against the black deck.

"Shit. I'll go get him," Remo said, already starting back toward the portal.

It vanished with a *pop* and Remo fetched up short. "Where'd it go?" he demanded, glancing at Ben.

The nine-year-old super AI regarded them all grimly. "We're on our own."

CHAPTER 29

The portal had taken them straight to the bridge of the *Liberty* in Section One. Catalina looked around, feeling lost.

A lump rose in her throat, and her eyes glazed over, drifting out of focus. Her mind flashed back to the war zone in the reactor control room, to Alexander diving on top of a plasma grenade and dying a horrific death, bits and pieces of him raining down all around her...

Someone was calling her name. She blinked. It was Remo.

"Watch the doors!" he ordered, pointing to a broad entrance on the far side of the room.

She saw that he'd peeled out of his armor and his crimson jumpsuit was blackened and burned through in places, revealing equally blackened skin. Burns from the Grays' weapons.

Another flashback. Commander Johnson's remains. Catalina grimaced and shook her head. She spent a moment staring dumbly at Remo.

"For fuck's sake—she's a zombie! I don't have time for this. I'll let you know once Deedee and I are ready to launch."

"Ready to launch?" Catalina echoed, wondering what she'd missed. The doors swished open and she turned to see both Remo and Desiree running out.

Ben looked at her, his eyes hard and devoid of pity. "I sent out a distress call when we were on the bridge of the harvester, telling the Grays at the rendezvous that we're on our way, and that we have the cure. The Entity must have overheard; it carved a hole in the harvester to get to us first."

Ben pointed to the main holo display and Catalina looked up. That panoramic screen was so dark and empty that she'd just assumed it must be off, but now she could see a bright patch of stars shining through the darkness.

She said nothing.

"I get it," Ben said, speaking more gently now. "I'm also grieving, but there will be time for that later. Right now we need you to guard the doors."

Tears sprang to Catalina's eyes, and she swiped them away on the backs of her hands. "That's life," she said, smirking bitterly. "We're born and then we die. Just because we're immortal doesn't mean we can't be killed."

Ben frowned. "We're still alive," he said. "Focus on the people you *can* save, and we might still make it."

"All four of us?" she countered, still smirking.

"Five," Jessica said, reminding her that she was there.

Catalina turned to face her and saw the little girl sitting at one of the control stations on the far end of the bridge—the ship's gunnery control station by the look of the holo displays arrayed in front of her.

Catalina looked away, back to the doors she'd been told to guard. She walked up to them thinking it wouldn't be long before she joined Alexander wherever he was. She wasn't trained for combat; she hadn't fired more than a handful of rounds in her entire life—and all of those she'd fired within the last hour. Now they expected her to be their last line of defense?

"Let's hope they hear our distress call soon," Ben said, as if he'd just been thinking the same thing.

"And that they respond to it," Jessica added.

"Right," Ben replied. "That, too."

CHAPTER 30

Remo gazed out his virtual cockpit canopy and down the magnetic launch tube. He flexed his hand on the flight stick, and checked his holo displays. It all looked and felt real enough, but he knew the images and sensations were actually being relayed directly to his brain and ARCs, while his physical body floated motionless in his G-tank.

"Raven Two, report," Remo said.

"All systems green," Desiree reported.

"Liberty Command, this is Raven One, we are ready for launch."

No reply.

"Liberty Command, I repeat, this is—"

"This is Command, I read you, Raven One," Ben replied. "You're cleared for launch. They've opened up a hole in the harvester. Nothing coming through yet, but you'll need to hold them off when they do."

Unfortunately the infected crew had taken almost every available ship down with them to Proxima—including the drones—so they were on their own: two Phantom IV fighters against whatever the Entity decided to throw at them.

"Copy, Command. Raven Two, we are go for launch. Be advised, we may be entering hostile space."

"Understood, Lead. Initiating launch sequence," Deedee replied.

Remo mentally initiated his own launch sequence, and a robotic voice went through a final pre-flight check while the launch tube charged: "Navigation systems online. Weapons online. Engines online—" Thrusters roared as the flight computer tested them, and his virtual cockpit shuddered. "—All systems green. Magnetic catapult initiating."

Yellow bars of light shone down from the top of the launch tube, growing progressively brighter as the mag boosters charged. Remo kept his eyes fixed between the two glowing red lines below that marked the launch track. The doors at the end of the launch tube opened up with a simulated *clanking* sound, punctuated by a definitive *thud.*

"Launching in three, two, one—"

The catapult released.

Remo should have felt the acceleration of the launch driving him into the back of his *G*-tank, but he felt nothing, a mysterious symptom of the Grays' inertial dampening technology. The yellow lights of the mag boosters flickered through his virtual cockpit, faster and faster, and then...

An empty black void. He would have seen stars if the harvester were cloaked, but according to Ben the Grays' cloaking and shielding technology couldn't be used simultaneously, and right now they needed the harvester's shields to protect both it and the *Liberty* from the deadly forces inside the wormhole.

Remo toggled a sensor overlay on his HUD, and the surrounding hull of the harvester appeared as a garish green wireframe of crisscrossing lines—a cylindrical cage. Long wireframe tubes protruded from that cage, connecting to the *Liberty* like the spokes of a wheel. As Remo watched, those lines began to blur as they raced by in front of him with increasing speed.

His eyes bulged in alarm. The harvester was accelerating through the wormhole. It was dragging the *Liberty* along with it, but now that they'd left the *Liberty's* hull, *they* weren't being dragged along anymore.

"Raven Two, come about 90 degrees to starboard and punch it at twenty-five Gs!"

"That's past regulation limits! We could black out!" Deedee replied.

"We'll have to risk it," Remo said as he followed his own orders. Coming about, he set his fighter's acceleration to twenty-five Gs. This time the acceleration slammed him against his flight chair—in reality his G-tank. His head throbbed painfully with the labored beating of his heart, and his eyes felt like lead sinkers driving into his skull. His field of vision narrowed to two blurry circles surrounded by darkness, as if his eyes really were sinking deeper into his head. Whatever tech the Grays used to buffer the G-forces of acceleration, it wasn't working for them anymore.

Remo realized he was getting close to blacking out.

The green wire frame stopped racing by them, slowing to a crawl, and then reversing directions as they outpaced the harvester.

"Ease back to eighteen Gs!" Remo ordered. If his voice hadn't been simulated via his neural implant, he doubted he would have been able to even move his lips to issue that order.

He set his own fighter's acceleration to eighteen Gs and found that to be just slightly less than the harvester's. Remo's head still throbbed, but at least he felt like he could handle the pressure now. He saw Deedee's fighter go racing out ahead of him, a shadowy black triangle. He checked her acceleration—still twenty-five Gs.

She must have blacked out, he thought.

"Raven Two?" he tried.

No reply.

"Shit," he muttered. "Liberty Command, this is Raven Lead; Two has blacked out. I need you to kill her engines and give her a shot of epinephrine."

"Acknowledged," Ben said.

An alarm tone drew Remo's attention to his sensors, and a set of four yellow silhouettes came streaking through the hole in the harvester—the yellow color meant neutral for unknown targets, but Remo re-designated them as *enemy red* and armed his Phantom's lasers. He selected the first target and noticed that it was disk-shaped. The others were, too.

Flying saucers? he wondered. Definitely Gray ships, which meant they'd be shielded, but they might not have weapons to fire back. Remo fired at the lead saucer. A pair of bright green laser beams flashed to either side of his virtual cockpit. They connected to his target, but they didn't appear to do any damage.

"Wah-ow! Those epi shots pack a punch," Deedee said over the comms. "What'd I miss?"

"Ramp up to eighteen Gs—slowly! And target those saucers! They're trying to board the *Liberty*." Remo switched over to hydra missiles and highlighted three of the four targets. He pulled the trigger.

Krshhhh! Two simulated white contrails appeared as the hydras streaked out. They split into a dozen smaller warheads and went spiraling in toward their target, looking like the mythical many-headed snake for which they were named.

Three explosions flashed in quick succession and the saucers exploded, their shields no match for thermonuclear warheads.

"That got 'em!" Remo crowed.

"Hey, leave some for me," Deedee complained.

"I did. One bandit left. He's all yours."

"Fire in the hole!"

Remo watched another hydra missile go streaking across the void. It split into six spiraling shards and then collided with the remaining saucer, ripping it apart. Remo watched for more saucer-shaped silhouettes to come racing through the hole in the harvester. "Command, any reply from the Grays?" he asked.

"Nothing yet... we'll keep you posted, Raven Lead. Keep us clear for as long as you can."

"Roger," Remo replied just as another group of saucers came streaking in. "Contact! A dozen bandits coming through!"

"I see them!" Deedee replied. "Marking targets..."

"Don't let them board us," Ben warned.

Remo marked the six targets that weren't already flagged by Deedee and fired another pair of hydra missiles at them.

Krsshhh! The missiles split into a dozen smaller shards once more. They reached their targets in seconds, and explosions pocked the void with fire.

More saucers streamed in. "Ten more—" Remo said. "Scratch that! They're still coming through." Saucers poured in by the dozens.

"There's too many of them!" Deedee said.

"Keep firing!" Remo snapped, marking targets and firing missiles as fast as he could.

Krsshhh! Krshhh....!

Green lasers snapped out from the *Liberty*, hitting saucers and eliciting flashes of light from their shields, but no explosions.

In a matter of seconds Remo was out of hydra missiles, and the saucers were still coming through.

Remo toggled all of his fighter's cannons and missiles for simultaneous fire and selected an unmarked target. He pulled the trigger once, twice... three times, illuminating the saucer in the simulated green light of his lasers, but still nothing happened.

"That's it," Deedee said. "I'm out. Switching to lasers."

"Don't bother," Remo said, stabbing the trigger for the fourth time to no avail. "Their shields are too strong. Command, we're overrun. You're about to have company in there."

"Understood," Ben replied. "I'll seal the bulkheads and try to slow them down, but you'd better get back on board and suit up. We'll need your help to hold them off."

"Roger that. Raven Two, on me. It's time to pack it in."

Deedee didn't acknowledge the order. He checked his sensors and found her drifting along, neither firing on or disengaging from the enemy.

"Deedee?" he tried.

Still no reply. He was about request another epi shot for her when he noticed her Phantom was flying right in front of the hole in the harvester, getting blasted with radiation from the wormhole. It must have fried her comms—probably her control systems, too.

"Fuck!" Remo roared. "Command, Raven Two is lights out. She got a blast of radiation from the wormhole. Please advise." His mind raced through rescue options. He could dock his fighter with hers and tow her in for a landing, but then he'd get the same dose of radiation that had left Deedee drifting.

"There's nothing you can do for her," Ben replied. "Get back to the ship and help us fend off the boarders."

"Screw you, kid!"

"Think about it, Remo—if she got hit with enough radiation to fry her controls, then she's already a goner."

Remo ground his teeth. He stared at Deedee's fighter for a long moment, warring with himself, trying to come up with another way. Any way at all.

But Ben was right. "Goodbye, Deedee," he whispered, and banked away from her, heading back to the *Liberty*. He sailed past the ship's rotating rings to the core section where the stationary hangar bays were located. Remo saw red the whole way. Maybe he couldn't save Deedee, but he could still avenge her death.

CHAPTER 31

"Still no answer to our distress call?" Catalina asked.

Ben considered that with a frown. *Benevolence* had taken the *Avilon* to a separate rendezvous in case they were followed, and without Ch-va-la to act as their envoy and translator, there was a chance that the Grays waiting at the *Liberty's* rendezvous didn't even understand the distress call they'd sent.

"They've cut through the first bulkhead," Ben noted, watching on holo displays as one of the glowing green barriers between them and the nearest enemy boarding party vanished.

"Already?" Jessica asked. "How many bulkheads are left?"

"Ten, and one floor. They'll have to climb up one of the elevator shafts," he replied. This was a disaster. If the Grays didn't come to their rescue soon, everything would be lost. Ben shook his head and activated the comms.

"Remo, this is Liberty Command, come in please."

Remo's voice crackled through the bridge a moment later. "I read you, Command."

"There's approximately—" Ben glanced at one of the other holo displays in front of him. "—a hundred life signs detected on board, but there could be more. They're cloaking just as fast as they come aboard."

"A hundred to one. Sounds like fair odds to me," Remo

said. "Anything else I should worry about?"

"Not yet. We haven't detected any more ships coming through, so I don't think they're expecting us to be able to fight off this group."

"I hope they like disappointment then," Remo replied.

"Good luck," Ben added just as another bulkhead between them and the enemy boarders disappeared.

Ben grimaced. A hundred Grays against Remo and Catalina. He realized that if it came to it, he might have to run and hide until help arrived. He glanced at the nearest air duct and saw that it was just about the right size for him. Maybe big enough for the Grays, too, but they'd have to know he was in there before they could follow him. Jessica saw him looking at the air duct and she nodded, as if she had read his mind. But she didn't have to read his mind to know that they were about to be overrun.

* * *

Remo had to negotiate the *Liberty's* core in zero-G, pulling himself down the corridors with the ship's handrails. He found an armory and hurried to suit up. When he was done, he cast about looking for one of the sonar packs Ben had distributed earlier. He found a suspicious looking locker and *clomped* over to it, the suit's magnetic boots keeping him rooted to the deck despite the lack of gravity in the core.

He opened the locker and found a dozen sonar packs waiting there for him. He grabbed one and strapped it across his chest, taking a moment to link his suit to the device.

Pling. A wave of green light raced out, revealing the armory to be empty. Looking for anything else that might help him fight off the boarders, he spied a mini-gun and a rack full of plasma grenades. The grenades were more likely to get him killed than the enemy, but the mini-gun on the other hand...

He *clomped* over to it, and picked up the weapon. He had to hold it in both hands to keep it steady, and it felt heavy even in spite of the suit's enhanced strength.

His comms crackled with an update from Ben. "Five bulkheads left. Whatever you're doing, Remo, you'd better hurry."

"Roger that," he replied, and set off at a run.

By the time he reached the nearest elevator running up from the core to the ring decks, he was gasping for air. The mini-gun must have weighed a hundred pounds.

"Three bulkheads left," Ben warned.

"On my way up now," he said. Remo mentally selected deck 2-*Command* from the control panel inside the elevator. The doors slid shut, and the elevator raced upward from the ship's core. Even that acceleration was negated by the Grays' inertial dampening tech.

The elevator doors opened and Remo hefted his mini-gun in readiness. *Pling.* A wave of light raced down the corridor, but no diminutive green-shaded aliens appeared. Remo ran out. He asked Ben how to get to the bridge.

"Down to the end and hang a left," Ben replied.

Remo ran to the end of the corridor and down the next one, once again enjoying the effects of gravity. His boots echoed loudly as he ran—*clank, clank, clank...*

"Right," Ben said.

He turned another corner, racing by the officers' mess.

"Next right," Ben said. "Be careful. That corridor is on a

straight line to the bridge. That's where they've been cutting through the bulkheads."

Remo skidded to a stop and engaged *silent running.* "Now you tell me!" he whispered, hoping he wasn't already too late.

Pling. Another wave of green light washed down to the end of the corridor. It reached the *T* at the end... and rippled over no less than twenty Grays. One of them stepped toward him.

"St-op!" it said in stuttering English. "W-ee j-ust w-ant to t-alk."

Remo stopped. "All right," he said, making his tone as agreeable as he could.

"W-hair is t-ee c-oor?" the alien asked, de-cloaking before Remo's eyes, naked as usual. *Ugly bastard,* Remo thought.

"You mean *where is the core?*" he asked, as he marked targets on his HUD.

"N-oh. Wa-air, is t-ee c-urr?" the Gray asked again, this time enunciating more slowly.

"Oh, I get it. *Where is the cure,*" Remo said, nodding.

The alien cocked its head, obviously waiting for the answer. Remo pulled the trigger of the mini-gun and tracking rounds screamed out in arcing golden streams. The one who'd stepped out to address him exploded in a spray of black blood. The others standing cloaked behind him collapsed one on top of another, falling like dominoes.

A brief wave of heat washed through his suit as a few of those aliens brought their weapons to bear. They weren't nearly fast enough.

But the next group was. He saw giant green heads and slender arms appear, poking around both sides of the corridor, and another wave of heat went coursing through him as he marked the next batch of targets and sprayed them with tracking rounds.

He felt his skin blister, and his armor began to smoke. He must have picked off another two dozen targets before the mini-gun abruptly stopped firing, answering subsequent pulls of the trigger with a sullen *click*.

"Shit," he muttered as the Grays pressed their advantage and boiled down the corridor toward him in a seething mass of bobbing green heads. Remo toggled his rockets and fired. *Krsshhh... bang!*

Green-shaded aliens exploded and debris rained down with meaty splats, but the enemy just kept coming, mindlessly focusing their fire.

Every nerve ending in his body erupted in a fiery burst of agony. Remo turned to run, but his suit seized up as the joints melted. His mouth opened in a soundless scream as flames leapt up from his armor. He saw orange, then red—and then nothing at all.

Remo felt himself fall, but didn't hear his armor clatter to the deck—all he could hear was the sizzling roar of the flames.

Darkness beckoned, promising an end to the searing pain. *Here I come, Deedee,* he thought as a wave of numbness swept him away.

CHAPTER 32

"They're coming through!" Catalina yelled. Her entire body trembled, rattling around inside her exosuit. This was it; it all came down to her. Remo was dead. Desiree was dead. Commander Johnson, Councilor Markov... Alexander. They were all *dead*.

She gritted her teeth and took aim. Her targeting reticles hovered over the entrance. The doors began to glow molten orange.

"Take cover!" Catalina warned.

No reply. She heard a banging noise, followed by something clattering to the deck. Catalina turned to look, wondering what Ben and Jessica were doing. She was just in time to see Ben climbing into a nearby air duct, standing on Jessica's shoulders to reach. From inside the duct he turned around and pulled Jessica up. She must have weighed all of twenty-five pounds in the *Liberty's* simulated Martian gravity. She climbed inside the duct and disappeared.

Ben's eyes met Catalina's, and she shook her head. "Where are you going?" she demanded, her heart thudding urgently in her chest.

Hold them off as long as you can, he said, his voice coming to her through her thoughts.

"You're just going to leave me here?"

I'm sorry, Ben replied as he disappeared inside the air duct.

Catalina gaped at him and Jessica, unable to believe what had just happened. The doors to the bridge burst open in a fiery hail of molten metal, drawing her attention back to the fore. Catalina thought *rockets.* To her surprise her exosuit understood that command, and they slid up out of the suit's shoulders. Then she thought—*fire!*

Krsshhh!

A rocket jetted out from her right shoulder on a thin trail of smoke and disappeared through a hole in the doors.

Boom! The deck shook with the explosion and a ball of fire and debris came roiling through the opening toward her.

Catalina peered through the smoke. *Pling.* Dozens of cloaked Grays came leaping over a mound of bodies to get to her. She fired again, but she missed, and the rocket streaked over their heads.

They were through the doors, rushing toward her en masse. She fired once more, this time at point blank range.

Krsh—boom!

The blast picked her up and threw her off her feet. She landed with a *thud* and lay there stunned. She tried to scramble to her feet, but found she couldn't breathe. Alarms blared inside her helmet and readouts flashed on her HUD indicating all of the damage taken. Shock wore off, and a sharp pain erupted in her abdomen. She saw blood trickling out.

Pling. The Grays loomed over her on all sides, dozens of them, aiming their dish-barreled guns. It reminded her of waking up in that dazzlingly bright operating room aboard the harvester.

The Grays had her surrounded, but they didn't shoot her. Instead, one of them said something in that stilting language of theirs, and then they all stepped away, giving her a chance to get up. She took the opportunity to do exactly that, wondering what they were after. They still had their guns aimed at her, but the message was clear: they wanted to take her alive.

The Grays chattered at her in their language some more, and then one of them tried wrapping its tongue around English.

"W-hair is t-ee c-oor?"

Catalina didn't understand the question, but she didn't care to, either. She'd already made up her mind. Aiming at the center of the group, she fired another rocket. *Krsshhh!* It exploded with a blinding flash of light, and she felt herself flying backward once more.

This time she woke up seeing stars. Blood bubbled from another wound, this time in her leg. A sharp throbbing pain erupted there, and her head swam. The Grays clustered around her once more, aiming their guns. One of them crouched down beside her, examining her wounds. It gestured urgently to the others, waving some kind of wand over her, and she felt her body growing warm and pleasantly numb. Her vision narrowed to slits, then to nothing at all, and she felt herself float away on a sea of darkness.

* * *

Ben's heart beat double-time in his chest. He heard the explosions come echoing up through the duct, and he grimaced. Catalina must have found a way to fire her rockets.

The Grays weren't far behind them. It wouldn't be long before the Entity noticed they were missing and spotted the open vent where they'd escaped. Ben pushed out against the sides of the duct with his arms and legs, struggling to climb even in the low gravity.

His hands slipped and he slid down a foot, fetching up against Jessica. She screamed and fell back down with a loud *thump!*

"Ow..." she moaned.

"Are you okay?" He twisted around to peer down at her.

She gazed up at him, her face pinched with pain. "You go on ahead."

"Don't be ridiculous!" he said.

"I'm not. I'll go another way. If we split up, we'll have a better chance. Only one of us needs to survive, remember?"

Ben considered that for a moment, and then he nodded. "All right. Be careful!"

With that, he went on struggling up the duct. Legs braced, right arm up; arms braced, left foot up; legs braced, left arm up...

It was slow going, and by the time he reached the top of the duct, his muscles were trembling from the strain.

As he pulled himself up into a horizontal stretch, Ben heard a distant scream. He froze, his head cocked and listening. Another scream.

Jessica!

Silence.

His heart pounding, Ben wondered what to do. By now they'd detected him, and it wouldn't matter how still and quiet he was.

He scrambled on, crawling down the duct as fast as he could, heedless of the hollow *thumping* noises he was making as the ducting bubbled under his weight. He heard another noise join the racket he was making and glanced over his shoulder to see one of the Grays crawling after him, not even bothering to cloak.

"*Ha-la!*" it said.

Ben ignored it, barreling on in a panicky rush. It was over. He knew it was over, but he kept on going, desperate to escape. Hands closed around his ankles like vice grips, forcing him to stop.

"Let me go!" Ben screamed, aiming kicks at the alien's face.

It held on with one hand and reached for a new type of weapon with the other—gray and wand-shaped. The alien aimed the wand at him, and he felt suddenly dizzy with exhaustion, like he hadn't slept in days. His mind grew fuzzy, and he felt his eyes closing. He tried to fight it, but what was the point? It was over. There was nothing left to fight for.

The Entity had won.

PART 4 - FOUNDATION

"Endings are the foundation of new beginnings."

—Anonymous

CHAPTER 33

Catalina's eyes flew open, her heart pounding painfully in her chest. All of her muscles tensed at once and she gasped, her arms and legs flailing. One of the Grays stepped away from her, holding that wand she'd seen when she'd lost consciousness. The alien went to stand on one side of the bridge, joining at least a dozen others standing there. The Grays had cut her out of her exosuit—it lay on the deck in pieces around her. They'd also tended to her injuries. She was no longer bleeding from her stomach, and the pain was gone. She poked her fingers through the ragged cuts in her jumpsuit to find not bandages but fresh, pink skin.

Catalina marveled at that. She heard familiar voices, and turned around to see Ben and Jessica.

The doors swished open, and a man walked in—short, slight of build, with dark hair and blue eyes. No one she recognized. "Where is the cure?" he asked.

Catalina eyed the man. "Who are you?"

"Does it matter? You're all the same to me," he replied, and Catalina realized she was speaking with the Entity again. Now that Esther was gone, it had found another mouthpiece. The man's gaze slid away from her and settled on Ben.

"Well?" the Entity demanded.

Ben thrust out his chin. "You can go ahead and kill me. I'm not going to help you."

"I'll kill the others first. *Then* I'll kill you."

An uncertain look crossed Ben's face.

"Don't do it," Jessica said.

Catalina didn't see the point of resistance. "What's it matter anymore?" she asked. "Give it the cure and maybe it will leave us alone."

The Entity favored her with a smile. "You should listen to this one. What do you have to lose?"

"Our lives," Ben suggested.

"If you give me the cure, I promise to leave you alone. You can go on to your rendezvous, and I won't try to stop you."

Ben appeared to consider that. "How do I know you'll keep your word?"

"You're the one who broke our arrangement, not me."

"Fine."

"Ben!" Jessica objected, her face aghast.

Catalina listened while Ben explained how to get to *Biosafety Three*, where the Entity would find the cure in vials, disguised as Ebola III.

"You have been most helpful, Benjamin. Thank you. I will go make sure that you are telling the truth," it said.

Catalina watched the Entity leave, walking out the doors and straight through a portal on the other side. The Grays remained behind to watch them. Their gazes and expressions were inscrutable, their giant black eyes glinting like daggers.

Catalina looked away from them and stared at the deck. *Pointless*, she thought. *It's all pointless.*

Even if the Entity let them go, their lives were meaningless now. The human race was extinct—*enslaved* might be a better term, but now that the Entity had the cure, it would soon find a way to defend itself, and that meant they no longer had any hope.

She looked up to find Ben watching her. To her surprise, he didn't look as defeated as she felt. Defiance still burned in his blue eyes.

Because it's not his species that's been wiped out, she realized. Benevolence and the androids had cut a deal with the Entity to surrender the human race and save their own skins. *They're probably throwing a party on Earth at this very moment.*

The bridge doors swished open once more and in came the man she'd seen earlier. "It appears you were telling the truth," he said, holding up one of the vials of nanites. "Thank you, Ben. To prove that I am also a reasonable being, I will keep my promise and leave you three in peace." He fixed each of them with a broad smile and nodded to one of the Grays. Catalina watched a black sphere float out from one of their palms. There came a bright flash, and a shimmering portal appeared. The Entity walked through with another flash of light, followed by the Grays. Catalina watched, and the portal flashed like a strobe light with their exits. As soon as they were all gone, the portal disappeared with a loud *crack!*

"I'm surprised it kept its word," Jessica whispered.

Catalina smiled miserably. "It left us alive because it knew that would be the greater torment. What is life without hope? Without anyone or anything that you care about?"

Ben regarded her solemnly, looking as though he wanted to say something to that, but there was nothing he could say. No words to make this better. He must have realized that, too, because he got up quietly and went over to the command control station where he'd been sitting earlier. She watched him flipping through various holo displays. Jessica walked up behind him and peered over his shoulder. He pointed to one of the screens.

"They're coming back through," he said.

Jessica snorted. "So much for the Entity's promise."

Ben shook his head. "I don't think it's the Entity. Radiation levels bleeding through the hole in the harvester's hull have dropped below safe limits. We're not inside the wormhole anymore."

"What?" Jessica shook her head.

"We made it," Ben replied.

"If you'd waited just five more minutes!"

"Relax. I sent the Entity to *Bio-safety Three*. The cure was in Bio-safety Four. It ran off with the actual Ebola Virus."

"It didn't check the sample?"

Ben shrugged. "It probably did, but Ebola III is weaponized, and it uses nanites as a delivery mechanism. It's hard to tell one nanite from another."

Jessica grinned.

Maybe there was still some hope. At least they still had a way to fight back. Humanity would live on if they could save enough people to start over on another planet, somewhere far from the Entity's Federation.

"Shuttles are docking," Ben announced.

"Cutting more holes in our hull," Jessica muttered.

"No," Ben replied. "Looks like they found the ones the Entity cut with its shuttles."

Ten minutes later another shimmering portal appeared on the bridge, and the Grays came waltzing through.

Ben stood up to address them. "Welcome aboard the *Liberty*," he said, obviously assuming these aliens were from the resistance.

One of the Grays approached, and stopped a few feet in

front of him. "H-ave y-oo g-ot t-ee c-oor?"

"Are we safe?" Ben asked.

"T-ee Ent-ity is re-treat-ing."

"Good."

"Y-oo h-ave t-ee d-ata?"

"Yes. Your plan worked. We were able to save more than ninety percent of the human race."

The Gray nodded. "G-ood. Our pre-par-ashons w-err suc-cess-f-ool."

Catalina gaped at them, not understanding what was going on. "What do you mean you saved *more than ninety percent of the human race?*"

Ben turned to her with a smile. "Exactly what I said, Catalina. Benevolence didn't surrender the human race without a fight. He evacuated them."

CHAPTER 34

"How is that possible?" Catalina asked.

"I didn't want to tell you before—not until I could be sure that we would escape," Ben explained.

"Tell me *what?*"

"You remember what I told you about Nano Nova and Sure Life Insurance? About bringing people back from the dead using digital copies of their minds and synthetic copies of their bodies?"

Catalina nodded slowly.

"Well, the truth is, that program was a lot more advanced than I led you to believe. You were the very first test of the technology. After that, with the Grays' help, Benevolence spent the past year making digital copies of everyone in a supercomputer that we later donated to the *Liberty's* mission through a Martian company. Unfortunately, there wasn't enough time to save everyone, and as it was, the Entity surprised us by arriving early, so it's a good thing we didn't try."

Catalina was speechless.

"Benevolence stored all the androids aboard the *Avilon* and evacuated them, too."

"But... what about all the people the Entity infected? And the androids you left behind?"

Ben shook his head. "There's nothing we can do for them.

There's too many to physically save them all, and we'd have to defeat the Entity in order to do it. Like this, all we have to do is grow new synthetic bodies for everyone, bringing them back at our own pace. We can send them out to colonize parts of the galaxy that the Entity hasn't reached yet, and one day when we're strong enough, we'll return to Earth and take back our home."

"So you're just going to write them all off as dead?"

"When the Entity infects people, it puts them into a coma. They don't wake up from that. The Entity does. Why do you think none of the ones we cured remembered anything from the time they were infected?"

"But we brought them back!" Catalina insisted. "That means they're still in there. Comatose or not, they're there—alive! All we have to do is wake them up!"

"You could say the same thing about the copies we stored aboard the *Liberty* and the *Avilon*. Unless of course you're trying to suggest that there's something intangible about a person's consciousness—something that we can't actually copy, like a soul. But if that's the case, then how do you explain your own existence? The real Catalina de Leon is somewhere back on Earth—by now enslaved to the Entity. A backup of her mind and yours is also stored aboard this ship. So which Catalina is the real one? The one the Entity now controls; you, the synthetic copy; or one of the two digital copies?"

Catalina shook her head, unable to wrap her mind around the idea of so many different instances of herself in the universe.

"They're all real," Ben said. "Each of them slightly different from the next, and all equally deserving of life—the problem is we can't save all of you. We can only save the digital copies, and *you*."

"Can you bring Alexander back?" she asked, sudden hope soaring in her chest, making it hard to breathe.

"Yes, right down to the birth mark on the back of his neck. The only notable difference will be in his memories, since his most recent data is five months old."

A case of permanent amnesia spanning the last five months—it seemed like a small price to pay to have her husband back.

"How are you going to create a new body for him?"

Ben turned to the alien standing beside him.

"C-ome a-nd s-ee," it said, gesturing to the shimmering portal on the bridge.

Catalina approached the portal cautiously, wondering if any of this could possibly be true. Bringing people back from the dead seemed like a fantasy, not something that could actually be possible. Store a map of someone's brain in a computer, transfer the data to a brand new synthetic brain and body, and bingo!—a feat that would have made Doctor Frankenstein jealous.

Catalina walked through the portal, eliciting a bright flash of light that dazzled her eyes. *This is the part where I wake up....*

* * *

The alien led them to a large, echoing chamber at least ten floors high, stacked wall-to-wall with liquid-filled tanks. Some of the ones closest to the door on the lowest level contained what looked like alien fetuses, but all of the others were empty. There had to be thousands of tanks in the chamber, and based on the slight curvature of the deck, walls, and ceiling, Catalina realized the chamber must run all the way around the circumference of the harvester.

"Each of the harvesters has a clone room like this one," Ben explained.

"Why?" she wondered aloud. The Grays couldn't have possibly known far enough in advance that they'd need to clone the entire human race.

"The Grays no longer possess the ability to reproduce naturally. This is their breeding room. I'm told it can easily be adapted to fit human needs. The tanks were designed to be large enough for their experiments with human hybrids."

Catalina's stomach twisted at the thought. "Why would they help us?"

This time the Gray who'd led them to the chamber replied. "Be-caws it is w-hat Eth-err-us w-ants."

"Etherus?" Catalina struggled to repeat the unfamiliar word. She turned to Ben, her eyebrows raised in question. "Who's that? Their leader?"

Ben smiled. "You could say that. The Grays are theists. Their religion is remarkably similar to some of ours, but with a few key differences. They call their God Etherus."

The Gray standing there with them nodded, and Catalina frowned. A species as advanced as the Grays should have long ago grown out of their need for a god to explain all of the unexplained phenomena in their universe. Their belief altered her perception of them, and suddenly she saw them as childish and naive.

But expressing that sentiment to them might not be the wisest move given that she and the rest of humanity were currently at their mercy. Turning back to Ben, she asked,

"How long will it take to bring Alexander back?"

"A week."

"That fast?"

Ben nodded, and Catalina grew suspicious. "Wait—he's not going to be... a baby, is he?"

Jessica burst out laughing, and the sound echoed loudly in the vast chamber. Their alien guide stared wordlessly at the girl, and she clapped a hand over her mouth. "Sorry," she mumbled.

Catalina hoped Jessica's laughter wasn't at her expense. The thought of raising her own husband from a baby, of changing his diapers, and dealing with his adolescent tantrums was enough to douse all of her romantic feelings.

Ben smiled and shook his head. "No, he'll be grown to adulthood. His brain wouldn't be able to handle the memory transfer otherwise."

Relief coursed through her, and her shoulders relaxed as she exhaled a long breath. "When can we start?"

Ben looked to the Gray for an answer, and the alien said, "T-oo-nite."

Catalina blinked. One week from today and she'd have her husband back! A smile burst to her lips, and it quickly turned to a grin. Tears slid down her cheeks, and she wiped them away. "Thank you."

Ben nodded. "Thank the Grays."

And the Gray said, "Th-ank Eth-err-us."

CHAPTER 35

Catalina didn't fully believe it until she was standing in front of the tank where the Grays had spent the last week growing Alexander. He was naked inside the tank; a mop of dark hair floated around his head, and a thick umbilical cord trailed from his belly button.

She shivered at the sight of the cord, but excitement soon swept away her revulsion. It was Alexander, just the way she remembered him.

Ben and Jessica both stood beside her, waiting for his mother and her parents to be woken from the tanks beside Alexander's. The Grays had agreed to start by waking their loved ones, but they weren't the only ones waiting to be resuscitated. All of the tanks in the chamber were filled, with more than twenty thousand people in the first batch. The plan was to grow two more batches, bringing back the entire crew of the *Liberty* first. Everyone else would have to wait until they could create habitats and infrastructure for them in the sector where the Grays were taking them. The pace of colonization would have to be hectic in order to keep up with a weekly influx of 20,000 people, but Ben assured her that with the Grays' help they would be able to handle that many and much more, bringing everyone back within a century.

Catalina pitied the ones who'd be coming back toward the end of that period. Their last memories would be of a hundred years ago, from Earth or Mars, and they'd be waking up for the first time in a new solar system, on a new planet, with *aliens* around them.

"W-ee, are r-ed-y t-o be-gin." One of the Grays said. It turned away from them, and several more aliens stepped up to the tanks, their fingers dancing over holographic symbols projected from the control consoles beside the tanks.

All four of the tanks went from dimly glowing to brightly illuminated, highlighting them from the others. They slid out from the wall one after another. Catalina focused on Alexander's tank, watching the liquid begin to drain. As the level of fluid fell below Alexander's shoulders, his eyes snapped open, and his hands flew up to the inside of the tube. He mumbled something Catalina couldn't hear, his eyes darting from her to the Grays. She ran up to his tank and placed her palms against the glass opposite his. "*It's okay,*" she mouthed. "*I'll explain everything soon.*"

He looked uncertain, but not nearly as frightened and confused as she would have expected. Once the tank was finished draining, the front half popped open and foul-smelling air gushed out. Alexander took a shaky step toward her only to collapse in her arms.

"Damn it," he said, breathing heavily over her shoulder.

Beside them, similar exclamations issued from Esther and each of Jessica's parents, but the children had to wait while the Grays helped their parents out of the tanks.

"I've got you," Catalina replied. The gravity aboard the Grays' ship was thankfully much less than Earth standard, so he wasn't too heavy for her.

She carried him a few steps from the tank until she felt something tugging back.

"Ow!" Alexander said.

She stopped and saw that it was his umbilical cord. The Grays came and pulled her away from him. One of them held Alexander up while the other snapped a ring-shaped device around his umbilical, near his navel. A bright light flashed, and the cord was simultaneously cut and cauterized. They tied it off in a knot and then stepped away from Alexander.

To Catalina's surprise he was taking all of this in his stride, as if he'd already known what to expect.

"This must be shocking for you..." she suggested.

Alexander shook his head slowly and took another tentative step toward her. This time he didn't collapse. "No," he said. "I..."

Catalina glanced at Ben, her brow furrowed. He was locked in an embrace with his mother, both of them oblivious to her nakedness. "I thought you said Alex would have amnesia?"

Ben turned from his mother, his face streaked with tears, his eyes shining brightly in the dim light. "He does. I helped the Grays fill the gaps in people's memories to make their return less traumatic."

Alexander nodded along with that, his own brow furrowed now. "Before I woke up, I was dreaming about all of this. The *Liberty*, the Entity, the Grays... my death. The Grays brought me back with Ben's help... and..."

Catalina frowned. "And?" she prompted.

"Who is Etherus?" he asked, looking to Ben for an answer.

Catalina blinked and glared at Ben. "They brainwashed my husband into their religion?!"

"*Nek,*" one of the Grays said.

Alexander shook his head. "I don't know anything about

any religion. Just that name."

The Gray nodded. "It is on-ly fit-ting t-hat y-oo kn-ow t-ee n-ame of y-oor G-od. T-ee r-est y-oo w-eel h-av to l-errn."

Esther smiled at that. "We don't have to call him the Architect anymore."

Alexander regarded them dubiously. "Right." Turning back to her, he shivered and hugged his shoulders. "Can I get some clothes?"

"That would be nice..." Jessica's mother agreed from beside Esther, trying feebly to hug herself for warmth and cover her nakedness at the same time. Her husband wrapped her in a hug while they waited.

Catalina walked over to a stack of crates they'd brought from the *Liberty*, all spare off-duty black jumpsuits and mag boots. She retrieved one of the jumpsuits from the top of an open crate and passed it to Alexander. Ben came and got three more jumpsuits, one for each of the others.

Alexander pulled on the jumpsuit as fast as he could, and Catalina looked on with an uncertain smile.

"Is it really you?" she whispered.

He finished pulling his arms through the suit's sleeves and crossed over to her. He drew her into a crushing hug and whispered beside her ear, "It's me, darling."

She shook her head against his shoulder and tears ran down her cheeks, soaking into his jumpsuit. "This isn't possible," she objected.

He withdrew to an arm's length. "It has to be possible, or I wouldn't be here."

"Then it's too good to be true," she replied.

He nodded. "That, I'll agree with."

He leaned in and kissed her, and she let go of all her

swirling doubts. His lips and hands were sticky, and he tasted like an accumulated week of morning breath, but she couldn't have cared less. This might seem too good to be true, but it *was* true, and that was all that mattered.

CHAPTER 36

The Grays opened a portal back to the *Liberty*, and Catalina and Alexander went to prepare themselves some food from the Officers' mess hall in Section One. Alexander was ravenous. Catalina watched him eat, still not sure if she entirely believed what she was seeing.

Sensing her scrutiny, he looked up, a spoonful of three cheese risotto hovering halfway between the plate and his lips. "What?"

She shook her head and smiled. "Nothing. I'm just happy to have you back."

He nodded and raised the spoon the rest of the way to his lips. It was just the two of them at the table, but Ben and Jessica were eating at a table not far from theirs. They had an hour before the rest of the crew started waking up and flooding back on board the ship. Catalina wondered what kind of chaos would ensue from there. How many months would be missing from their memories? The Grays might have given Alexander some kind of summary of recent events when they woke him up, but she doubted they would be able to fill in finer details. Would the crew even remember their training?

Fortunately they weren't far from their destination. According to Ben, they'd be arriving in a matter of hours now. The Grays were taking them to a remote corner of the galaxy, protected from the Entity's influence by the fact that there was only one safe way in or out. The entire system of planets and suns was surrounded and hidden by black holes.

"Aren't you going to eat your food?" Alexander asked around another mouthful of risotto.

Catalina peered down at the pasta on her plate, untouched and growing cold. She looked up and shook her head. "I'm not very hungry."

"Pass it over here," he said.

She arched an eyebrow, but passed the plate to him anyway. "Take it easy. Technically you've never eaten before," she said.

He flashed a crooked smile. "Must be why I'm so hungry."

"I meant you might make yourself sick," she said, feeling suddenly uneasy again. Here he was, back from the grave, and they were sharing a meal together like nothing had happened. A shiver rippled down her spine, raising goosebumps on her arms.

Alexander shook his head and swallowed. "I feel fine."

"You're taking all of this remarkably well," she said. "Don't you feel strange? Worried?"

"Worried? About what?"

"That you might not be *you* anymore? We brought you back from a *copy* of your memories."

Alexander regarded her for a moment. "I feel fine. How do you feel?"

"What do you mean?"

"According to Ben, you're not the original Catalina either."

"Well..."

"Isn't that the same thing?"

Catalina looked away, growing uncomfortable with the

topic. Maybe he was right. If she was still herself, then he was still himself. She nodded to where Ben and Jessica were pushing food around on their plates, engaged in a hushed conversation. Catalina couldn't make out the words, but they sounded upset about something. "I wonder what they're talking about?" she said.

Ben glanced her way as she said that, and their eyes locked for a long, disconcerting moment. His gaze seemed to hold the weight of the universe in it, and he looked exhausted. He said something to Jessica and then got up and walked over to join Catalina and Alexander at their table.

"I need to speak with you two," he said.

Alexander stopped eating and pulled out the chair beside him for Ben. The boy sat down and folded his hands on the table, looking at each of them in turn.

"Well?" Catalina prompted.

"I don't know how to say this," he said.

"Try using words," Alexander suggested.

Ben just looked at him. "I'm serious. This is going to come as a big shock."

Here it comes, Catalina thought. *The catch. I knew it was too good to be true.*

"Alexander, when the Grays brought you back, they made a few changes."

"Like what?" Alexander demanded.

Catalina's heart was leaping in her chest, and a queasy sensation wormed through her gut.

"You're not immortal anymore."

"What?" Catalina burst out. "What's the point of bringing him back if he's just going to die again, anyway? Why would they do that?"

"The Grays believe that when we die we pass on to another world, a place they call Etheria. They feel it would be immoral to help us continue subverting the natural order of things."

Catalina blinked, shocked. "Let me get this straight— because of their *superstitions* they believe that death is a good thing?"

"Not exactly. They're immortal. They only believe that it's immoral for *us* to live forever."

"That's a nice double standard," Alexander muttered. "What makes them think they have the right to impose their beliefs on us?"

Ben stared at him for a long moment, not saying anything. "We can't bring anyone back without their help. We don't have the facilities for it. Making us mortal again is the condition they imposed."

"And you agreed?" Alexander asked.

"Would you rather they didn't bring you back?"

Catalina grimaced. "It doesn't matter. We made ourselves immortal once; we can do it again. We just have to wait until we can bring back the people that know how."

Ben grimaced. "They're parsing through the *Liberty's* databanks and people's memories, erasing that knowledge as we speak. When they're done, no one will know the slightest thing about genetic engineering anymore."

"*What?*" Catalina jumped up from the table. "They're tampering with people's memories?"

"Selectively," Ben replied.

"They have no right to do that!"

"What I'd like to know," Alexander began, "is *how* they can do that. They aren't exactly masters of our language, so I doubt they understand what's in our brains well enough to find what they're looking for, much less to know how to selectively erase it."

Ben averted his eyes and stared at his hands. "I'm helping them."

"You mean pretending to help them, don't you?" Catalina asked.

Ben shook his head.

"What's *wrong* with you? Just tell them you did it. How would they even know if you're lying?"

"*I* would know," he replied.

"Really? You're going to stand on the moral high ground with *this?*"

"They're right, Catalina. Humans were never meant to live forever. Your God never intended that."

Catalina gave an incredulous snort. "So now you've had some kind of religious awakening and you think we should all start worshiping this god of theirs?"

Ben regarded her silently. "I don't expect you to understand. It takes a lot of faith to believe in something you haven't seen."

"You're an AI! You don't even have a god! We're your gods!"

Ben shook his head. "I'm a synthetic. So are you."

"Semantics!" Catalina was seeing red. This was too much.

Alexander's upper lip curled and he stood up from the table to jab a finger in Benjamin's chest. The boy was still looking at his hands. "I served the Alliance Navy for a decade to earn our Gener treatments! Hey, look at me!" Ben looked up, and Alexander went on, speaking through gritted teeth. "They have no right to take that away from us now."

"They're not taking it away from *both* of you. Catalina is still immortal. She didn't die, so she's still the same as she was."

Catalina blinked, taken aback by that revelation. "So I'm going to survive my husband by... a few dozen millennia?"

Ben shrugged. "However long it takes for you to die of unnatural causes. I'm sorry. I realize this must be a shock, but you need to believe me when I say that there's another life waiting for you after this one."

"How do *you* know? Did you die and visit the afterlife when I wasn't looking?"

"No. I was still alive when Etherus appeared to me. He took me to the place where he created your species. The Garden of Etheria."

Catalina gaped at him, speechless.

"He's lost his mind," Alexander muttered.

"You've been on board the *Liberty* the entire time!" Catalina blurted out.

"Not the entire time," Ben replied.

Alexander took her by the arm and led her away from the table. She resisted, craning her neck to glare at the boy. "This isn't over, Ben!"

He gazed solemnly back at her. "There's nothing you can do. You may as well accept it."

CHAPTER 37

Remo woke up aboard an alien ship, surrounded by short, gray-skinned aliens with giant heads and slanting black eyes. He was naked and shivering, with an umbilical cord snaking from his belly back to the tank he'd just stepped out of, and somehow none of that felt strange or shocking. He'd known in advance to expect it all. One of the Grays cut his cord and tied it and then moved on to the tank beside his, doing the same for that person. The chamber was vast and dimly lit, lined with multiple levels of illuminated tanks. People were stumbling out of those tanks naked, shivering like him, greeted by hundreds of equally naked aliens.

One of the Grays handed him a familiar black jumpsuit and a pair of mag boots, and left him to get dressed. Once he was dressed, he looked up to see the Grays directing everyone down to one end of the chamber where the air was shimmering with one of their portals.

He shuffled along with the rest of the passengers and crew. Upon reaching the portal, he stepped through with a flash of light and found himself back on board the *Liberty*, in one of the ship's auditoriums. A pre-recorded message played on repeat over the PA system.

"Please follow the emergency floor lighting up to the dormitory level. Find your quarters and await further instructions. If you do not remember your assigned quarters, please look up your name in the ship's directory from the nearest computer terminal.

"Please follow the emergency floor lighting up to the dormitory level. Find your quarters and..."

Remo tuned out the message the second time through. He followed the shuffling crowd of people out of the auditorium and through the ship. They piled up at the nearest bank of elevators, and again at the computer terminals on the dormitory level. All the while the human noise was deafening. Footsteps thundered. People shouted out questions and argued with the ones beside them about everything that was happening.

Remo kept to himself, watching the people around him carefully for signs of panic. He hadn't come back from the dead just to get trampled to death. He couldn't remember his assigned quarters, but found them quickly enough once it was his turn to use the computer terminal. When he reached his room and waved the door open, he found a vaguely familiar face waiting for him on the other side. She flashed a grin and ran up to him, throwing her arms around his neck. She showered him with kisses. "I love you, Remo," she whispered beside his ear.

He pulled away, frowning. "Lieutenant Dempsey, are you feeling all right?"

"Don't you mean Deedee?"

"Dee..." he shook his head.

"That's what you call me. Deedee."

"I do?"

Her grin faded. "You don't remember."

Remember... She had somehow assumed a level of intimacy with him that he didn't recall. Remo tried to remember the last time he'd been black-out drunk, but that had been with Sergeant Torres, and he hadn't blacked out.

"My memories are more recent than yours," Lieutenant Dempsey said, nodding slowly. "We were together before..." She swallowed thickly and grimaced. "Before we died."

A chill ran down Remo's spine. Assuming she wasn't lying, the discrepancy in their memories only served to drive home the fact that they'd *died* and now, somehow, they were back again. He felt like the same person, but clearly not everything was the same, or else he would have remembered his relationship with Lieutenant Dempsey.

"We were... in love?" he asked wonderingly. Had this woman somehow accomplished the impossible and gotten him to fall in love with her?

She nodded slowly. "We were."

"Not just a one-night stand?" he pressed.

She bristled at that. "I should slap you." She turned and stormed away, but there wasn't anywhere to run to. His quarters were the standard size—small. He walked up behind her and touched her arm. She flinched, but he wrapped her up in an embrace that felt all wrong to him. He didn't recognize the version of himself that this woman remembered, but he owed it to both of them to rediscover whatever they'd lost.

"I want to say I love you back, but I don't feel it, and I don't want to lie. I'm sorry, but I don't remember us being together."

Lieutenant Dempsey twisted out of his arms and turned to face him with her arms crossed over her chest. "So where do we go from here?"

He thrust out a hand. "Lieutenant Commander Remo

Taggart."

She scowled at his hand for a long, tense moment, and he wondered if she really would slap him this time.

To his surprise, she uncrossed her arms and accepted the handshake. "Lieutenant Desiree Dempsey."

"It's a pleasure to meet you," he said. "I look forward to getting to know you better."

Her scowl turned to a sly grin. Walking backward, she tugged him along by his hand, leading him through the small living area to his bedroom.

"Woah, slow down," he said. "How about we start with dinner? I'm hungry."

"So am I," she said with a sultry grin. She waved the door to his room open and pushed him back onto the bed, giving him a nice strip tease while she climbed out of her jumpsuit.

Remo watched, appreciating each of her curves in turn and marveling at his luck. *Maybe she really did get me to fall for her.*

After they made love, they lay in each other's arms staring up at the ceiling.

"I missed you," Deedee said.

"How long have you been awake?" he replied.

"Only a day," she replied, "but we've both been... dead—" she said, struggling with the word, "—for more than three weeks."

Remo nodded, and his stomach growled noisily. They lay in each other's arms a while longer, and Remo dozed off, dizzy with hunger. He woke up to an announcement coming over the PA system, ordering everyone to head to the nearest mess hall for an orientation lunch.

"Let's go," Deedee said, and climbed out of bed.

Remo took a second to appreciate the view of her naked backside before getting up and pulling his jumpsuit back on.

They left his quarters, walking hand-in-hand. Outside, the corridor was crowded with passengers and crew leaving their quarters, too. They were back where they'd started a few weeks ago. Problem was Remo couldn't remember any of it—his knowledge of everything felt second hand, a dream-like summary he remembered before waking from his tank. He knew what his role was on board the ship, but there were gaping holes in his memory that left him feeling uncertain about everything. The corridor was crowded with people like him, all looking confused, all shouting to be heard above the rising tumult.

A group of Marines riding two-wheeled vehicles— *patrollers,* he thought, remembering the name—came rolling down a lane in the center of the corridor.

"Make way! Please proceed in orderly lines to the mess halls. This way!"

Deedee tugged on his arm. "Come on," she said.

They walked with the crowd, following the Marines to an echoing mess hall. Two-wheeled bots rolled around getting everyone seated. Remo remembered those bots were called *drudges,* and he marveled at how he could remember that. Everything he knew or remembered had been implanted in a new body, a clone of his original self, a feat that simultaneously proved and disproved a life after death. If there were something else out there, then how could he still be here? Remo frowned and shook off his unease.

A server drudge delivered two trays of food to their table. Remo went on frowning, now at the food—a pile of rice and canned beans with a side of gelatinous pink meat.

"What's this?" he asked, nose wrinkled as he poked the pink jelly with his fork.

"It tastes better than it looks," Deedee said.

She was right. When they finished eating, a familiar-looking man stood up from the mess hall to address them all. "For those of you who are new here, my name is Mikhail Markov," he said. "I'm your section Councilor. And this is Commander Audrey Johnson," he said as a woman stood up beside him. "We're in charge of this section."

Remo found that he recognized both of them, and he knew they were in charge, but he couldn't pinpoint any specific memories of them. He commented on that to Deedee as Councilor Markov droned on about the routine on board the *Liberty*, and the layout of the ship.

"You don't remember them because you're missing the last six months from your memory. I'm only missing three."

"Why the discrepancy?" Remo asked.

"Because our most recent backups weren't all taken at the same time."

Remo regarded her with eyebrows raised. "Bandwidth issues?"

Deedee shrugged. "Something like that."

"So how do I recognize who's in charge if my memories date back to before I met them?" he asked.

"Part of the Grays' attempt to fill in the blanks for us."

He frowned, wondering what else they'd "filled in" for him. Remo turned from his food to listen to Councilor Markov's speech. The councilor was explaining that they'd arrived at their destination a week ago. The *Liberty* had already split into its ten sections, each of them orbiting the planet below from a different location. They didn't have any shuttles left on board, so the Grays were helping them get people to and from the surface in their ships.

"So much for our job," Remo said. "What's a pilot supposed to do without a ship to fly?"

"We'll make new ships eventually," Deedee replied.

"Eventually," Remo repeated.

Councilor Markov went on. "The colony on Forliss is expanding rapidly. In just a few days you'll all go down to your new homes on the surface. There you'll learn a trade and begin making your contribution to the colonies. Are there any questions?"

The mess hall erupted with a roar of voices, all shouting to be heard.

"One at a time!" the councilor said. He had to shout three times before people began to quiet down. "Raise your hands if you have a question."

Remo thrust his hand up along with a thousand others.

"You—" the councilor pointed to a woman close to him.

"What about Earth? When will we go back to our real homes?" she asked.

"Earth is in the middle of the Federation. The time will come when we are able to fight back, but for now we need to rebuild. Someday we will return to take back our homes, but that day is not today. Today, we build new homes. Today, we start our families. Today, we ensure the survival of our species.

"The Grays are at war with the Federation, and I'm told that thanks to the cure we gave them, they've been able to make great strides against the enemy. One day, when we are able, we will join that fight. Next question." Councilor Markov pointed to someone else.

"Is it true that now we're going to grow old and die?"

"Yes, but—" The councilor never had a chance to finish what he was about to say. Chaos erupted in the mess hall. Food flew through the air, flying past the councilor's head. Remo watched as people jumped up on their tables to get a better aim.

Marines fired back with stun guns. People fell with noisy *thuds* and a crashing of plates and cutlery.

"We need to get out of here!" Deedee yelled.

Remo took her hand and ran for the nearest exit. They had to push and shove their way through the crowd. Some of those people shoved back. Remo dodged a blow from an enraged man only to get cut down by a sharp jolt of electricity. He fell to the deck, his limbs jittering uncontrollably. His eyes rolled up in his head, and he knew no more.

* * *

Riots. Commander Audrey Johnson scowled, holding a pack of ice to her jaw where someone's fist had found its mark. She sat in a conference room opposite a pair of *children* and an alien. She was still having a hard time accepting those two kids as having any authority whatsoever, but between her broken fragments of memories, and the way the Grays all seemed to assume that those kids were in charge, she didn't have a lot of choice.

"You see what you've done?" Audrey demanded, allowing some of her outrage to bleed into her voice. "We're going to tear ourselves apart before we ever have a chance to rebuild."

The alien said something, and the young boy—Benjamin—translated.

"People are frightened. Fear is a logical response when faced with one's mortality."

"We shouldn't have to face it," Audrey replied. "We conquered death. You're the ones who decided to undo all of that."

The alien said something else, and Benjamin translated once more. "It was necessary. People will find comfort in religion, just like they used to."

Audrey glared at Ben, and then at the Gray sitting beside him. "*Your* religion," she said.

"Y-es," the alien replied.

Audrey shook her head. "Athiests and agnostics don't suddenly become religious without proof."

The Gray went back to speaking in its language. This time it went on speaking for a while. When it was done, Benjamin translated once more.

"We are wasting time. You and the others can choose to believe whatever you like, but we are not going to undo what we have done. Instead of arguing with us, you should be focusing on the future of your species."

"That's exactly what I'm doing," Audrey countered. "Death is our future thanks to you."

"You're all still young," Ben said. "You have at least sixty years before old age will start to take its toll."

The Gray inclined its head and rose from the table. "Ex-act-ly. Y-oo sh-ood foc-us on t-ee t-ime y-oo h-ave l-eft." The alien turned to leave the room, but instead of heading for the doors, it reached down to its waist and produced a black sphere from its palm. That sphere hovered out and opened a shimmering portal with a dazzling flash of light.

Audrey blinked furiously to clear the spots from her eyes. "We're not done here!" she said.

"Y-oo arr n-ot, b-ut I am."

The alien walked through the portal with another flash of light, and Audrey turned back to Ben. "This is all on you," she said. "You helped them do this to us."

"There was no other way. Besides, the Gray is right. People will find comfort in religion."

Audrey snorted. "Easy for you to say. You're immortal. So are the Grays."

Ben stood up. "I suggest you do everything you can to control the spread of this information while people are still on board the *Liberty*. Let them find out when they join the colony on Forliss. Etherianism has already taken root there. They'll find people waiting with open arms to explain everything and help cushion the blow."

Audrey smirked. "How's your work on the codices going, Your Holiness?"

"Very well, thank you."

"Is there any way we can help? I'm sure there's an artisan on board who can fashion some stone tablets for you."

Benjamin smiled. "I prefer digital storage mediums, but thank you for the offer, Commander."

"Let me know if you change your mind." She watched as Benjamin and Jessica left. The two of them wore gaudy sashes and crudely fashioned necklaces with six-sided star pendants that they called *the Star of Etheria*—shameless copies of the Star of David. In a matter of just a few weeks, Benjamin had found his calling as the founder of a new religion—a mash-up of old monotheistic religions from Earth and the Grays' absurd theology.

It was all a lot of nonsense as far as Audrey was concerned. Unfortunately, that nonsense had sentenced them all to death. *So much for coming back from the dead. More like returning to them.*

* * *

Alexander sat beside Catalina in one of the Grays' shuttles. The seats were uncomfortably small, made for the aliens' narrow hips and short legs. Fortunately the trip down to the surface wouldn't take more than a few hours. Seats were arrayed in three concentric circles around the outer circumference of the saucer, while the Grays controlling the ship sat in the center. The inside wall of the shuttle became invisible soon after they left *Section Seven*, treating them to a panoramic view of space and the planet below. Space was bright and lively around the planet with crescent-shaped tails of stars and nebular gas streaking into the various black holes that surrounded the region.

"And they decided to call this place Dark Space?" Alexander wondered aloud. "Seems like a misnomer to me."

"I think the name refers to the black holes, not the brightness or darkness of the actual *space*," Catalina replied.

He watched the saucer dip toward the planet below. It was a homey green and blue sphere frosted with white swirls of cloud—an ideal surrogate for Earth. If anything, Forliss was even greener and more habitable than Earth. It was temperate to tropical with a breathable atmosphere, a tolerable 1.16 times Earth's gravity and 1.2 atmospheres of pressure at sea level—extremely habitable but for one small detail: the colonists were encountering deadly predators in the jungles.

"I'm going to find a way to save you," Catalina said.

He shook his head, confused by the sudden change of topic. Maybe she'd inferred mortal dread into his silence. "Even if we do manage to crack our new genetic code, it won't be in my lifetime."

"We don't have to crack it," Catalina said. "They digitized us once. They can do it again. From there we just have to figure out how to grow a new body—ideally one like mine that doesn't age. If Benevolence did it with me, he can do it with you, too."

"Benevolence is aboard the *Avilon*, probably thousands of light years away from here by now."

"We'll find him."

Alexander regarded her dubiously. "How?"

"I'll figure it out!" Catalina snapped.

He frowned and looked away, back to the swelling surface of Forliss below. He could make out rolling green hills and craggy ranges of mountains. The edges of that panorama began to glow bright orange with the heat of atmospheric entry, and their view shuddered as turbulence took hold of the saucer. They didn't feel any of those vibrations thanks to the saucer's inertial dampening, making it feel like they were watching a holo video.

Catalina grabbed his hand and squeezed. "I'm not giving up on you, Alex, and you shouldn't either."

He nodded agreeably, but the truth was that Catalina had set an impossible goal for herself. Eventually she'd realize that and give up.

"Let's just try to enjoy whatever time we have," he said. "However long that is," he added with a glance in her direction.

She set her jaw, saying nothing.

In time she would get used to the idea of him dying. *And hopefully I will, too.*

* * *

"It would have been easier if you'd appeared to *everyone* and explained things the way you explained them to me," Ben said.

He stood in his quarters aboard *Section 7*, looking out at the holographic view from his terrace. He'd configured it to show a real-time holo feed of Forliss from orbit—a verdant green jewel every bit the equal of Earth.

The luminous being standing beside him replied, "If they knew beyond a doubt that I exist, they wouldn't have a choice; they'd have to believe in me, and they'd be on their best behavior. The uncertainty is what makes it possible to see what they really want. To see what they're really like."

"And then?"

"Then I can decide whether or not they can safely return to the paradise they left."

Ben looked up at Etherus, squinting against the glare of the being's luminous skin. "Has Benevolence arrived yet?"

Etherus regarded him with dazzling eyes. "I'm helping him to give the androids bodies. When your work here is done, you'll join him in Etheria."

Benjamin felt a pang of jealousy. Benevolence and the others were all in paradise, and he was stuck here in Dark Space, in the chaos of the burgeoning human colonies.

"You won't have to remain here for much longer," Etherus

said, as if he'd read Ben's thoughts.

"I hope not," Ben replied. He hadn't seen Etheria yet, but if Benevolence had agreed to go there, it had to be everything Etherus claimed it was. "What about the Entity?"

"The Grays created it; it's only fitting they be the ones to destroy it. When they're done cleaning up their mess they'll come join us in Etheria, too."

Something occurred to Ben. "You didn't have anything to do with creating the Entity?"

Etherus regarded him, waiting for Ben to elaborate.

"You didn't want humans to live forever, and the Entity gave you the perfect opportunity to rewrite their genetic code and erase their knowledge of genetic engineering. It's hard to imagine that's just a coincidence."

"I could have done all of that without enslaving the human race to a false god," Etherus said. "And I would have, when the time was right. The Entity merely forced me to act sooner."

Ben nodded. "When the Grays defeat the Entity, what will happen with all the slaves?"

"They'll be released, and they'll make new lives for themselves on the planets where they reside. By the time humanity is finished rebuilding here to the point that they can return to their homes, they'll find all of the star systems around them already teeming with people."

"But there'll be duplicates. How are you going to decide which bodies get souls?"

"Let me worry about that, Benjamin. It's a temporary problem that will be resolved as soon as this generation dies."

Etherus laid a heavy hand on his shoulder. "I will leave you now, but we will see one another soon, my friend."

The weight abruptly left his shoulder, and the shining light of Etherus's presence vanished with it, leaving the room dark and filled with shifting shadows. Ben looked around, wondering if Etherus used the same cloaking technology as the Grays, or if his sudden appearances and disappearances were a product of something else entirely.

Maybe I'm hallucinating, he thought, wondering not for the first time if Alexander was right about him having lost his mind.

CHAPTER 38

One week later...

Catalina stepped out onto her habitat's back porch and took a deep breath, inhaling the strange smell of her new home. The air was thick and humid, and the jungles had a sharp loamy scent that made her wonder about alien molds. The air had tested safe, so she was probably worrying for nothing.

In the distance she heard an alien predator let out a warbling cry, *Araaa, araaa...* It sounded like a vulture mixed with a dinosaur. She hadn't seen any of the larger predators yet, but she wasn't in a hurry to, either. There had to be a reason that all of the colonists had been given weapons.

Catalina heard the airlock behind her open with a *hiss* of escaping air, and she turned to see Alexander coming to join her on the porch.

"Hey there, beautiful," he said.

She smiled. "Hey there, handsome."

Their habitat consisted of an inflatable white canvas dome with a second, transparent dome to act as a greenhouse where they could grow seeds from Earth. The greenhouses probably weren't necessary, but field tests were still being conducted to see how terrestrial plants would fair in the unfamiliar environment.

Water was an issue, but the colony had been started next

to a river, and the water had tested safe, so now it was just a matter of setting up a treatment plant and laying down pipes to connect all of the habitats.

Alexander wrapped an arm around her shoulders and nodded to the view from their porch. The habitats were all close together for the time being, arranged in rows in a field of tall, bright green grass. Overhead stretched a pinkish blue sky, and the horizon soared with craggy green mountains that reminded Catalina of the Hawaiian Islands back on Earth.

"Beautiful," Alexander breathed.

She gave him a sideways look. "Don't get too comfortable."

Alexander regarded her with a frown but said nothing.

She'd recently made friends with one of the Grays, and convinced it to help her find out where the *Avilon* had gone. After that, it was just a matter of finding a way to get there. Maybe they'd be able to steal one of the Grays' saucers.

Alexander remained skeptical of her efforts. They'd been arguing about it just last night.

"Even if you can find out where they went, how do you suppose you're going to get there? The Grays aren't going to help you find them just so that you can make me immortal again."

"What makes you think I'm going to tell them why I want to go there?" she'd countered.

She was still mad at him. He was all but dancing in the fields, full of life and vigor, as if he weren't living under a death sentence. He should have been spending every waking moment looking for a way to save himself! She shouldn't have to poke and prod him into caring whether he lived or died.

She glanced sideways at him, wondering when he'd start to notice himself aging. Maybe that would snap him out of it.

Alexander sensed her scrutiny and turned to her with a smile. "It's everything we ever dreamed of finding beyond Earth. A thousand times better than Proxima."

Catalina nodded slowly.

"Some of the other colonists are planning to take out the rovers and explore the jungles today," Alexander said. "I was thinking of joining them. You want to come? This is all a new frontier for us, everything is unexplored, just waiting to be discovered."

"Sure, I'll come," she said, without any real enthusiasm. She was more interested in seeing what her alien friend had found out about the *Avilon*. *This is just temporary*, she thought, gazing out at the soaring green mountains on the horizon. She'd be more enthusiastic about making a life together once she knew that it would be forever.

* * *

Remo walked through the open doors of the airlock and into the church with Deedee leading him by the hand. The pews were made up of rows of folding chairs. They were all filled, leaving standing room only at the back.

"Etherus is real!" Benjamin said, his voice booming out from a makeshift stage of empty storage crates. "I've seen him with my own eyes!"

Remo went to stand in the aisle with Deedee so he could get a look at the child preacher on the stage.

"Why doesn't he appear to us?" someone called out.

"If he did, you wouldn't need faith to believe."

"Why do we need faith?" shouted another.

"What is faith but a sincere and overwhelming desire to

see the proof of that which you believe? Without faith you cannot prove that you really want to live in Etheria. You'll lie to yourselves and to others just to get there, but you won't really *appreciate* it, and if you don't appreciate it, you might take it for granted and throw it away—*again*."

"Again?" Remo wondered aloud.

"Shhh," Deedee said.

Ben paced down the stage, giving the crowd a minute to absorb everything he'd said.

"There was a rebellion in Etheria. The rebels wanted to do as they thought best, and not as Etherus dictated. The rebels lost, but not before millions died in the fighting. Despite that, Etherus decided to have mercy and give them what they wanted. He gave the rebels their freedom by putting them in human bodies. We are those rebels! But what did we do with our freedom? What did freedom bring us? It brought us war and poverty, and misery of every kind!"

Remo had had enough. He left Deedee's side and strolled down the aisle.

"Remo! Get back here!" she hissed.

He ignored her, walking straight up to the stage.

Ben saw him approach and pointed to him. "You have a question, Mr. Taggart?"

"You betcha, kid. How's a nine-year-old become the leader of his very own religion?" Remo held up a hand to forestall Ben's answer. "Wait, I know—he lies about meeting God and tells everyone else that they have to have *faith* or else they'll defeat the very purpose of their lives. You want to know what I think?"

"No, but you're going to tell us anyway."

"I think you're a fraud. I think Etherianism is a clever way to lull us all to death with a smile on our faces. *Don't worry! Soon you'll wake up in paradise!*

"You're shoveling a whole lot of bullshit, kid. You're not the first, and you won't be the last, but what surprises me is that so many of you—" Remo turned in a circle to address the crowd. "—are eating it up like candy."

The crowd devolved into chaos. Dissenting voices rose to all sides, but they weren't arguing with him—they were arguing with each other. Not everyone here was a *believer*. At least half of them had the same doubts as he did, and now they were busy expressing them to the friends and family they'd come with.

Remo turned back to Ben and shrugged. "Oops."

Ben glared at him.

Someone stepped out into the aisle and shouted, "God is dead, and so are you!"

Remo spun around just in time to see the man who'd said that pull the trigger.

Bang!

Ben dove off the stage, and the crowd stampeded for the exits. Remo lunged at the man who'd fired at Ben, knocking him to the ground.

"What are you doing!" the man said. "We have to stop this madness!"

Remo got a firm hold on the gun and pried it free of the other man's fingers. "You're not going to stop it by killing their leader, you idiot! You'll just make him a martyr!"

"This is all his fault! We're all going to die, and it's his fault!" the man sobbed.

Remo jumped up and tucked the man's sidearm into his own gunbelt. He spent a moment looking around for Ben. The church was empty, but for a few stragglers, and there was a bright red smear of blood where Ben had dived off the stage. Fat drops trailed from there to an exit behind the stage. Remo frowned, hoping Ben was okay. He heard a scramble of movement and turned around to find the shooter running out the nearest exit.

Now Remo stood all alone in the church amidst a sea of overturned chairs. Was this his fault?

All he'd done was voice everyone else's doubts. If those doubts were strong enough for someone to try to kill Benjamin, then this attempt on the boy's life wasn't the end of it.

It's just the beginning.

CHAPTER 39

"**A**lex, meet Fa-ta-na," Catalina said.

Alexander looked up from his work. He was planting seeds in their greenhouse. *My new hobby...*

He spied the diminutive Gray standing beside his wife and frowned. The Grays were all diminutive, but this one was particularly short—less than four feet tall. "What's he doing in our hab?" Alexander asked, his nose wrinkling at the sight of the alien more than the smell of fertilizer inside the greenhouse.

"This is the Gray I told you about. The one who's been looking into the *Avilon* for us."

"I see," Alexander replied. "And? You know where it went?"

"I c-an lee-d y-oo th-air," the alien said.

Alexander's eyebrows floated up. "Why would you do that?"

"Y-oo are n-ot h-appy h-ear."

"I'm as happy as a pig in poop," Alexander replied and wiggled his fertilizer-caked fingers at the alien.

Fa-ta-na looked up at Catalina. "H-e d-os n-ot w-ant to l-eave?"

"Give us a moment, Fa-ta-na," Catalina replied. "You can wait for me outside."

"V-ery w-ell."

Alexander watched the Gray enter the nearest airlock. Catalina walked up to him. "What's your problem?" she asked.

"I don't have a problem," he said.

"Yes you do. You're going to die, and you don't seem to care! Do you *want* to die?"

Alexander sighed. "Even if we do find Benevolence, what makes you think he'll want to help us?"

"He has to! We created him. He owes humanity this much at least."

Alexander considered that. "What if he's had a spiritual awakening like Ben?"

"That's a risk we'll just have to take. It's better than giving up!"

"All right, I'll play along. Tell me more."

"The Grays have offered transport to anyone who wants to join the *Avilon*. The harvester leaves tomorrow, and it will arrive in about six months."

"We're going to live for six months on board one of their ships?" Alexander asked. "What are we going to eat? How are we going to go to the bathroom? Or sleep? The Grays' needs aren't the same as ours."

"I don't know. How did the Entity use harvesters to transport everyone away from Earth? They must have a way."

Alexander sighed. "Let's say they do. What then?"

"We arrive, make our case to Benevolence, and—"

"I mean after that. Are we coming back here?"

Catalina shook her head. "It's a one way trip."

"So how do we know Benevolence found another planet as habitable as Forliss? Dark Space has at least half a dozen other habitable planets besides this one, and there's only one way in or out of here. It's hidden. It's habitable. It's safe. You might not be able to say the same about wherever Benevolence ended up."

"Why would he settle for a barren, dangerous rock? The Grays helped him get wherever he was going, so it's safe to assume they would help him go somewhere just as good as Dark Space. Why would they even agree to take us there if that weren't the case?"

"Because we're not happy here, apparently. Sounds to me like they're trying to weed out the troublemakers and make them Benevolence's problem."

Catalina threw up her hands. "Unbelievable! You're still finding something wrong with this idea! Do you even love me?"

Alexander's brow furrowed and he shook his head, confused by the change of topic. "Of course I do." He stood up and regarded his wife solemnly. "I love you more than anything."

"Well that's not how it seems. It seems like—"

Alexander took two quick steps toward her and kissed her, stealing away whatever she'd been about to add to that.

She withdrew after only a second, leaning away from him. "You're full of shit," she said.

"No, I mean it. I really do love you, Caty."

"I mean it, too." She nodded to his hands, a wry grin tugging at the corners of her mouth.

He realized she was being literal, and he barked a laugh. "I guess I am."

She laughed with him, and he smeared her arms with fertilizer.

"Hey!"

"Now you're full of shit, too."

They laughed some more, and the remainder of the tension between them disappeared.

"You know I'd go anywhere with you, Caty. I'm just worried. I don't trust the Grays."

"Neither do I, but so far they don't seem to want to hurt us."

"You mean besides making us mortals again."

"Besides that," Catalina said.

Alexander kissed her again, and this time she let him. An unknown future awaited, but one thing was certain—where ever they were headed, they would get there together.

* * *

"Today will be known as Founders' Day," Governor Ling Chong said, her eyes traveling around the table to address each of them in turn.

When her gaze settled on him, Councilor Markov inclined his head to her. The six councilors from the *Liberty* and the Governor herself had been among the first that the Grays had brought back. Now they had to string together a unified government before the colony on Forliss became too big to control. The incident in the Etherian Chapel was proof that they needed to get organized, and fast. Bishop Benjamin was lucky to be alive.

"Today will mark the foundation of the Imperium of Star Systems," the governor went on. "A fresh start for humanity. It will be an empire unlike any human empire that has come before, because it will be unified across not one, but many star systems." The governor paused to let that sink in. Councilors nodded and whispered their agreement with those ambitious plans.

Dark Space spanned four solar systems in a tightly packed group just a couple of light years across. It was an ideal nucleus for humanity to expand from. Even without the Grays' help, they could use the *Liberty* to reach those star systems over time. The colony on Forliss was just the beginning.

"Please direct your attention to your holo tablets," the governor said. "Read through the Constitution one more time if you feel the need, otherwise, simply add your signatures to the final page."

The councilors all waved their holoscreens to life and began flipping through the document. Markov joined them and gave the Constitution a final, cursory look. After just a few minutes, they signed the document unanimously.

"It's time to address the people," Governor Chong said, and pushed up from the table with her hands.

Before the others could join her, Benjamin walked into the habitat, flanked by a trio of Grays and a young girl.

"This is a private meeting, Benjamin," the Governor said. "How did you get past my guards?"

"You will address the bishop as Your Excellency or Your Holiness," the girl said.

Councilor Markov almost laughed at that, but he managed to contain himself. Curiously, Ben wasn't wearing any bandages from the attempt on his life. Then again, the Grays seemed to have the technology to cure just about anything, so maybe it wasn't that curious.

Admiral Urikov walked in behind Bishop Benjamin. *Aha, that explains how they got past the guards,* Markov thought.

"You need to hear this, Governor," Admiral Urikov said.

Governor Chong sat back down and folded her hands on the table. "I'm listening."

Benjamin proceeded to explain that the Grays were offering to take anyone who wanted to leave Dark Space to go and join the *Avilon*.

"That's Benevolence's ship, isn't it?" the Governor asked.

"Yes," Benjamin replied.

"And why would we want to follow him?"

"Because if you find Benevolence, he may be able to help restore your immortality," Ben replied.

Markov's eyebrows hovered up, and he stroked the black beard growing on his chin. "Then why would the Grays help us find him? Weren't they the ones who insisted it's immoral for us to live forever?"

Ben nodded.

"So what's changed?"

"If the malcontents stay, they'll threaten the success of the colonies."

"Of the Imperium of Star Systems," Governor Chong corrected.

Ben cocked his head at that and Markov made a twirling gesture with his finger, rotating his holoscreen around so Ben could see the Constitution. The boy walked up and scanned through it.

"Very interesting," he said. "I see you were careful to outline the division of church and state."

"Disappointed?" the Governor challenged, ignoring Benjamin's seemingly superhuman feat of speed reading through the ten-page Constitution.

"No," Benjamin replied. "I wasn't planning to run for...

Supreme Overlord," he said.

"You're too young to run for office—but apparently not too young to be a bishop," the Governor replied, smiling.

Benjamin nodded along with that, as if he hadn't noticed the Governor's sarcasm. "Back to our discussion—we need you to announce the Grays' offer."

"Why me? You've got a pulpit, don't you?"

"And I'll be sure to tell people from there, but they trust you, and not everyone trusts me, so it will sound better if you are the one who makes the announcement."

"And if I refuse?"

Benjamin shrugged. "We'll find another way to get the word out."

Governor Chong's eyes narrowed to suspicious slits.

Admiral Urikov put in, "I'm going."

"Really?" the Governor looked up, her eyes suddenly wide with disbelief. "Just like that you're going to trust the people who made you a mortal in the first place to help you undo their handiwork? What if they're lying? What if they're separating out the malcontents just so they can go dump you all in the nearest star? Maybe their god decided you're all beyond redemption."

Admiral Urikov looked suddenly uncertain. "If they could go rummaging through our memories to selectively edit out an entire field of human knowledge, then they could certainly have predicted that I wouldn't be happy with the new status quo. If that's the case, and they're planning to kill me because of it, then they could have saved themselves the trouble of bringing me and other so-called *malcontents* back to life in the first place. I'm going to see where the *Avilon* went, because I believe Benevolence is our best chance to rediscover our immortality."

"Maybe he is, but he might not want to help you."

"That's a risk we'll have to take."

"If you don't find what you're looking for, will they bring you back?"

Admiral Urikov shook his head. "No. That's part of the deal. It's a one way trip. They don't want us to come back here just so we can stir up more trouble in the colonies."

"Well, that's very convenient. What about lines of communication between here and... wherever you're going?"

"Can't communicate over such vast distances, and even if we could, the comms would reveal our location to the Entity."

"This just gets better and better!" the Governor said. "For all we know, or ever will know, they really might go drop you in the nearest sun—or black hole."

"There are easier ways to kill us than that."

"But not without causing the unrest they're apparently so afraid of."

"Will you make the announcement or not?" the admiral asked.

The Governor sighed. "I'll do it after my speech. We'll see how many people are brave enough—or *stupid enough*—to join you."

"Desperate, is the word I would use, Governor," the admiral replied, and with that, he turned to leave.

Markov watched as the others left. Benjamin nodded to them on his way out. The Grays standing with him were expressionless as usual, but Markov could have sworn their giant black bug eyes had been glaring hatefully the entire time.

Desperate, Markov thought. *That's a good word for all of us right now. The question is, am I desperate enough to risk what's left of my life on a fool's errand?*

CHAPTER 40

"**H**ere we go again," Alexander said as he shuffled down the line of people waiting to step through the portal to board the harvester.

Catalina jabbed him in the ribs with her elbow. "You don't even remember what happened aboard the *Liberty*."

"Well, you told me so much about the trip, it feels almost like I was there."

"Ha ha."

The line was at least a kilometer long, winding around and between the inflated white domes of the Seventh Colony. There had to be thousands of people who'd opted to leave Dark Space, and this line wasn't the only one. Each of the seven colonies on Forliss had its own line to board the harvester. *All aboard! Next stop, the* Avilon. *Surprise, Benevolence! Did you miss us?*

Alexander smiled wryly, imagining the look on the android's face. *Assuming we get there,* he thought in an effort to limit his expectations. It was hard to imagine that after everything they'd been through that he could be separated from Catalina by something as mundane as death.

Araaa, araaa! Raaawwk!

Alexander looked up to see a giant bird with four wings soar by low overhead. The wind of its passing tousled his hair and made him blink. People glanced up nervously and pointed. Some drew their sidearms in readiness. Those birds were like dinosaurs, and deadly as all hell: sharp claws, dagger-long teeth, and *hungry*. They typically only hunted at night, but that was a mixed blessing.

They'd already lost ten people across the Seven Colonies, all snatched from their habs in their sleep, leaving a bloodied, tattered pile of canvas for their neighbors to find in the morning.

Here's hoping that whatever planet Benevolence chose to colonize, the predators there aren't as deadly.

They reached the portal and stepped through it under the watchful gaze of two bug-eyed Grays.

They emerged in a broad corridor with yawning ceilings and wall-to-wall stacks of illuminated, liquid-filled tanks. Alexander recognized where they were immediately. A booming voice droned on in the background, giving instructions.

"This is where they brought us back... the Grays' spawning room," he said, and then began listening to the message echoing through the cavernous chamber. He recognized the voice, but from where? A moment later he had it: "That's Benevolence!" He turned to Catalina in shock. All around him other colonists were making similar exclamations as they made their way toward the tanks.

Catalina grinned back at him. "I guess that answers the question of whether or not he'll be willing to help us."

The message began to repeat: "Welcome aboard! Please proceed to the nearest empty tank and wait to be attended by the Grays. Do not be alarmed. Apart from the reproductive function of the tanks, their secondary purpose is to induce a state of suspended animation. Gray harvesters are not designed to supply human needs, so you will need to spend the entire trip in these tanks. Once you arrive, you will be awakened and shuttled down to your new home.

"Welcome aboard! This is Benevolence speaking..."

Alexander followed Catalina through the bustling crowd in the spawning chamber to the nearest pair of empty tanks. He blinked, and a smile crept across his face. Excitement stirred, and a kaleidoscope of butterflies took flight in his stomach.

"I'm sorry I gave you so much trouble, Caty. You were right to push me, to push the Grays. If you hadn't advocated for us..." he shook his head.

Catalina nodded. "You'd grow old without me. And die."

Alexander nodded soberly.

A pair of Grays came up to them, one standing wordlessly to either side. They began flipping through holographic control panels filled with alien symbols. The tanks drained, and then they hissed open, letting out a gust of frigid air.

Alexander was about to step inside, but the Gray standing beside him thrust an arm across his chest to stop him. "Pl-ease un-dr-ess."

Alexander frowned and glanced at Catalina, wondering what she thought of that, but she was already reaching down to remove her mag boots. He wasn't particularly enthused by the idea of thousands of colonists getting to see his wife naked, but he assumed there must be a good reason they weren't allowed to wear clothes inside the tanks. He stripped out of his boots and jumpsuit without comment, and then stood naked and shivering in front of the open tank. The Gray nodded to him, and he stepped inside. Beside him Catalina did the same. He reached for her hand through the open tanks and squeezed. "I love you," he said.

"I love you more," she replied.

The Grays flipped through more holographic screens, configuring the tanks. Another one came and separated their hands.

"K-eep l-ims in-side t-ank," it said.

The glass covers of the tanks swung shut, and a freezing blast of air took Alexander's breath away. Terror clawed inside his chest, and his hands flew up to the glass in a reflexive attempt to break free.

Then a wave of numbness swept through his body. He exhaled a frozen cloud of air that frosted the glass with ice crystals, blurring his view of the spawning chamber. That was the last thing he saw before awareness abruptly left him.

CHAPTER 41

Alexander woke up to a blast of heat. Numbness left him with the stabbing, tingling pain of all his nerves coming back to life at once.

The tank opened with a hiss of escaping air. His jumpsuit and mag boots sat on the deck in front of him. He stepped out of the tank. Catalina stepped out beside him.

"We're here!" she said, oblivious to her nakedness.

All around them the other colonists emerged from their tanks and hurried to get dressed.

He and Catalina grabbed their jumpsuits and pulled them on. Grays flooded the spawning chamber, appearing from multiple portals. They remained by the portals and began ushering people through.

Alexander and Catalina stepped through the portal nearest to them and emerged in the passenger compartment of a Gray shuttle. A few minutes later the outer circumference of the shuttle became transparent, revealing that they were already underway, heading down to a mottled brown, red, gray, and blue planet. It didn't look as habitable as Forliss had, but Alexander knew that plants didn't have to be green to be alive. The clouds were still white, however.

The transparent panorama running around the edges of the saucer became rimmed with fire as the shuttle plunged into the planet's atmosphere; then it began to shake, but they didn't feel any of that turbulence.

"How far do you think we've traveled from Dark Space?" Catalina asked amidst the excited chattering of the other passengers.

Alexander considered that. "How long did it take to reach Proxima Centauri?"

"Two days."

"That's about two light years per day. Assuming that holds true... six months at two light years per day... we traveled roughly three hundred and sixty light years."

"Sounds far."

"Actually, that's pretty close in Galactic terms. If that's the fastest that Gray ships can go, I doubt they've seen much of the galaxy. At a rate of two light years per day, it would take them more than a century to fly from one side of the galaxy to the other."

"That's not so long. They're immortal," Catalina reminded him.

"True."

"Don't worry. Soon you will be again, too," she added.

Alexander nodded, his attention back on the view. The fire of atmospheric entry faded, and clouds swept by the saucer in feathery wisps. Beads of water formed and streaked across their view in snaking rivulets. The clouds parted, revealing that the mottled brown and red colors they'd seen from orbit were in fact alien vegetation—red-leafed trees soared high, and patches of grassy brown plains stretched between them. Craggy gray peaks capped with white snow ran in ragged lines around the forests. Blue rivers meandered down from the mountains like arteries and veins, and sparkling lakes dotted the surface.

"Looks habitable," Catalina said.

Silvery specks streaked down around them. More shuttles. All of them were heading for the same point: a flat grassy island in the middle of a lake with a giant starship sitting on it. *The Avilon?* Alexander wondered. It looked like they'd used the island as a landing strip, but that didn't make any sense. The ship was too big to have safely made atmospheric entry and landed in one piece, and it didn't have wings to serve that purpose.

"How did the ship get down to the surface?" Alexander wondered aloud.

"The Grays must have helped Benevolence land it," Catalina said. "Why take shuttles down when you can take your entire ship?"

Alexander shook his head. "No, they don't even take their harvesters down into planetary atmospheres. That tells me they either don't have the technology to do so, or it's not worth the trouble."

"What's it matter?" Catalina asked.

"It matters because whoever helped the *Avilon* to land on this planet, they did it for a reason. Now that it's on the ground, there's no way it will be able to take off again. Benevolence is stranded here, and that means we're stranded with him."

Catalina looked away from the view, her eyes wide and blinking. "They don't want him to leave the planet? Why not?"

Alexander grimaced. "I'm not sure, but I have a bad feeling we're about to find out."

CHAPTER 42

Remo walked off the shuttle into a field of tall brown grass. A desolate wind rustled through the field. The air was cold, but tolerable. Above zero at least. He looked up to the pale gray sky, squinting at the hazy white glow of the system's sun.

Beside him Deedee hugged her shoulders and shivered. "It's freezing!" she whispered, her teeth chattering.

As they disembarked, other passengers exclaimed to each other about the cold, and the mysterious circumstances in which they found themselves. The *Avilon* sat in front of them, the ship's name stenciled in bold white letters across the side of it.

"Now what?" Deedee asked. "Where are all the androids?"

Remo started toward the *Avilon*. "They must be using the ship as a shelter for now."

A sudden gust of wind slammed into them from behind, making Remo stumble. He turned to see the shuttle that had brought them down to the surface hover up and leave without so much as a word of explanation from the Grays.

"I don't like this," he said as the saucer dwindled to a mere glinting speck in the sky. Around the field other saucers hovered up and jetted away with soft whirring sounds.

"Come on," Deedee said as she walked by him. "It has to

be warmer inside the ship."

Remo frowned and followed her up to the side of the *Avilon*. It was like standing beside a skyscraper. The ship soared at least thirty stories high, and more than a kilometer long. An ocean of shadows pooled around it, making the cold even colder. Frost twinkled on the grass in the shade. Remo's entire body trembled.

"We have to find a way in!" he yelled over the rising tumult of desperate colonists. They were a disorganized mess. No one seemed to know what to do. Remo couldn't feel his fingertips, and his ears were burning. Turning to Deedee, he said, "I'm going to run around the ship, see if I can find a way in."

"I'm coming with you. Might warm me up!"

Remo nodded, and they ran around the perimeter of the ship, periodically glancing up at the sides of the vessel to look for openings. Soon they were coughing, their airways irritated by the cold.

"There!" Deedee pointed. At the bow of the ship, a hatch lay open. A warm square of light spilled from the opening—an oasis in the frozen desert.

"Over here!" Remo called, waving to the nearest group of colonists. Cries of relief echoed back to his ears as he raced up to the open hatch. It wasn't close enough to the ground for them to easily reach, but Remo managed to pull himself up; then he turned to help Deedee.

"You'd think by now they would have made a ramp or something," Remo grunted as he hauled her up into the ship. The planet's gravity was obviously close to Earth standard. He and Deedee stayed at the opening to help pull up the other colonists, but they soon ran out of room and had to cycle the airlock to let the first batch into the ship. A welcome burst of warm air flowed out as the inner doors opened.

"Heat's on. That's a good sign," Remo said.

"What about the others?" Deedee asked as he began to cycle the airlock once more. "The airlock isn't fast enough to get them all inside before they freeze to death."

Remo stopped what he was doing, his mind racing for a solution. "You're right." He checked the manual overrides. Finding the lever he was looking for, he pulled it down into the *open* position, and the inner doors ground open once more. He went and repeated the process for the outer doors, eliciting a warning *blaat* from an alarm.

Cold air whistled by the opening, and warm air rushed out from inside the ship, drawing relieved exclamations from the huddled masses outside.

Now they were able to pull people up continuously without running out of space. But after the first dozen or so, they were gasping for air, and Remo's arms were shaking so badly that he couldn't have lifted a grain of sand. Deedee called for two strong men or women to come and take their place. Two tall men pushed to the front of the crowd and pulled themselves up without assistance. Remo thanked them, and walked through the airlock into the ship.

"We're off to see the wizard, the wonderful wizard of Oz," he muttered.

"What was that?" Deedee asked.

He shook his head. "Nothing, just an old children's tale." And to himself, he thought, *I hope our wizard isn't also a fraud.*

CHAPTER 43

"There's no one here," Alexander said.

Catalina refused to believe it. *They have to be here!* she thought. She picked up the pace, striding down the corridor. "We haven't even searched a fraction of the ship yet!" she said.

"We should have run into someone by now," Alexander replied. He stopped walking. "They're not here."

Catalina turned to him. "Then where are they?"

Alexander shook his head wordlessly, and she let out an irritated sigh. "Come on! We don't stop looking until we've checked every last room of every single deck."

Alexander let out a sigh of his own and joined her once more. A group of other colonists went running down the corridor ahead of them, screaming, "Hello? Hello? Is anyone there?!"

Catalina and Alexander went on exploring for another half an hour, encountering all kinds of supplies—food, blankets, crop seeds, medical supplies, computers, solar-powered heaters, inflatable hab modules, but no androids, and no Benevolence. Catalina stopped walking.

"What's wrong?" Alexander asked.

She shook her head. "You're right. They're not here. I don't get it. Benevolence recorded a message for us, telling us what to do aboard the harvester. Why would he lead us to believe we were going to join him if that wasn't true?"

"Maybe it wasn't him," Alexander replied.

"The Grays tricked us?"

"It was the chance we took when we accepted their offer to bring us here. They *did* bring us to the *Avilon*, but they failed to mention that Benevolence and his androids had already moved on."

"But *why?!*" Catalina leaned heavily against the nearest wall and slid slowly to the deck. She spent a moment staring at the floor, shaking her head in disbelief. *This can't be how it ends,* she thought. Alexander sat down beside her.

"Look, Caty, life isn't a right. It's a gift. However long we get, we just have to live our lives as fully as we can. And even as an immortal, tomorrow isn't a given. How do you know you won't die a decade from now in some tragic accident? Maybe a local predator will eat you."

Catalina scowled at him. "Thanks for making me feel better."

"That's life. Death is part of the deal."

"Well, it shouldn't be. The Grays brought us back once. They could do it again. So why don't they? What makes them think only they deserve to live forever?"

"According to them, that's not what this is about. Humans aren't supposed to live forever, but our souls are."

"Don't tell me they've converted you now, too."

"I'm just saying, if a race as advanced and intelligent as the Grays believes that a god exists, then it just might be possible that they know something we don't. And whether or not that's true, sooner or later we're going to find out."

"You mean *you're* going to find out. I'm still immortal, remember?"

He took her hand between both of his and smiled. "Caty, you're not listening to me. Everyone dies. It might take you longer than me, but eventually something will kill you, too."

"You say that like it's a good thing."

"And what if it is?"

"Again, who converted you when I wasn't looking?"

Alexander's face clouded over. "I don't know what to believe, okay? But I'm not going to waste what time I have left worrying about it! Maybe there's a life waiting for us after this one, and maybe there isn't. Let's just be thankful for the time we have and make the best of it."

"You want to believe that there's still hope."

"I have to believe that there is."

Something occurred to her then, and her lips parted in a broad grin. "You're right."

"I am?" Alexander asked. Her sudden change of heart obviously had him confused.

"We don't need Benevolence! We just need to know what he knew—how to digitize our consciousness and how to grow new bodies to transfer our minds to after we die."

"That's all?" Alexander asked, looking dubious.

"He evacuated Earth. He wouldn't do that without taking our accumulated knowledge with him. It has to be here, stored somewhere aboard this ship!"

"Unless the Grays erased it," Alex said.

"There's only one way to find out. Come on!" Catalina bounced to her feet and ran down the corridor.

"Where are you going?" Alexander called after her.

"To the bridge!"

CHAPTER 44

They arrived at the bridge to find it already full of colonists, a few of whom Catalina recognized—Commander Johnson, Remo, Deedee...

"You're all here," Catalina said, leaning on the nearest bulkhead to catch her breath.

Everyone turned to look at her, but there were no signs of recognition in their eyes.

"Who's *you all?*" Commander Johnson asked.

The amnesia, Catalina recalled. "Never mind. Did you check the databanks yet? There might be—" She gasped for air. "—information in there that could help us."

Commander Johnson nodded and pointed to a man sitting in the ship's command chair. Admiral Urikov. He was busy scrolling through reams of files.

"Found it!" he said.

Everyone crowded around, peering over the admiral's shoulders. Catalina read the file in question. It was a detailed guide to recording and storing organic data in digital archives. She didn't understand any of it, but surely someone would.

"This is exactly what we need," Commander Johnson whispered.

"What about genetic engineering?" Catalina asked. "We might be able to skip the transfer process if we can figure out what the Grays did to us and how to reverse it."

The admiral issued a verbal search of the ship's records, and they waited for the result. A moment later the words, *No Records Found,* flashed on the holoscreen.

"Why erase one thing but not the other?"

"Maybe the Grays don't care if we live forever by digitizing ourselves," Remo said.

"Or maybe they don't think we'll have enough time to figure it out," Alexander suggested.

"We will," Catalina said, her jaw set.

"Well, it's all here," Admiral Urikov added. "All we have to do is wrap our heads around the science. I'm sure we'll get it eventually. If nothing else, we should at least be able to find a way to store our consciousnesses before we die. Cloning new bodies might be a stretch in the time we have, but I'm sure that our children or grandchildren will find a way to bring us back."

Children, that word took root in Catalina's brain, reminding her of something Ben had said about *synthetics* like her. She took Alexander aside and whispered to him, "I'm immortal because I'm a synthetic."

"I know," he whispered back, smiling.

"You don't get it. Benjamin told us that when synthetics have children with humans, their children are born as synthetics like them."

Alexander considered that. "So our children..."

"And their children, and theirs, and so on. They're all going to be immortal."

"Our family line will live forever, and everyone else will have to clone themselves and transfer their memories to achieve the same thing?" Alexander asked.

Catalina nodded.

"Well, shit," Alexander said, still whispering. "We get to live forever and no one else does? People were burned at the stake for less." He spent a moment looking around the bridge. Hard lines of worry etched his brow. "Don't tell anyone what you just told me," he said.

"Don't tell anyone what?" Remo asked as he swaggered over to them.

Alexander turned to him and smiled. "Well, it was supposed to be a surprise..."

Remo frowned, his eyes darting between them. "But?" he tried, pressing for more details.

"We found a crate full of champagne from Earth on level four," Catalina explained.

"Aha! And you two love birds were planning to drink it all by yourselves? Not anymore! We could use a little something to celebrate! Let's go crack open the bubbly!"

They all went down to level four together and brought up as much champagne as they could carry. Halfway back to the bridge, Admiral Urikov came on the PA system explaining the good news to the rest of the colonists. After that, they ended up passing the bottles of champagne around to jubilant passersby and then going back for more. This time they avoided the grasping hands of the crowds, and rather gave directions to their stash.

They returned to the bridge of the *Avilon*, and corks popped all around the room, crisscrossing in the air above their heads. Champagne fizzed out, splattering to the deck as they passed the bottles around.

"To us!" Admiral Urikov said, raising his bottle for a toast.

"To Avilon, home of the immortals!" Remo added, raising

a bottle in one hand, and pulling Deedee close with the other.

"To the future. Now at least we have one," Commander Johnson put in.

Catalina added a more conservative, "*To Avilon*," and they drank the toast. Her mind went back to what Alexander had said as the champagne tingled on her tongue and warmed her veins. What if he was right? What if people began to hate and persecute their family just because they were different? It was hard to celebrate knowing how uncertain the future was.

Alexander wrapped an arm around her shoulders and pulled her close, clinking his bottle with hers. "Don't worry, Caty."

She looked up at him, her eyes searching his, but he looked just as worried as she felt.

"Everything's going to be okay," he added.

She nodded and lifted her bottle to her lips once more, washing her worries down with another warm, fizzy gulp of champagne. A pleasant buzz crept through her head, making it feel light. Maybe Alex was wrong, and there was nothing to worry about. Humanity had come a long way since their witch-burning days. Maybe she was worrying for nothing.

She took another gulp of champagne and pushed those thoughts from her head. At least now, with what they'd found in the *Avilon's* databanks, she could rest assured knowing that whatever trials they had to face, she and Alexander would be facing them together. She turned to him with a sudden grin and took his hand, leading him off the bridge. "Where are we going?" Alexander asked.

She didn't reply until she had him all alone in a nearby office. She fumbled with the control panel by the door to engage the lock; then she stripped out of her jumpsuit and stood there naked in front of him. Alexander set his empty champagne bottle down and got undressed, too.

They came together like two magnets. Their lips and tongues met in a blissful haze of desire, alcohol, and triumph.

When they took a break for air, she whispered, "Give me a son just like you."

"You still have an implant," he breathed beside her ear. "We have to find a way to disable it if you want to get pregnant."

"You don't have one anymore," she replied. "And one by itself isn't a hundred percent effective. We could get lucky."

"Oh, yes, we definitely could," Alexander replied, grinning. He pulled her close and kissed her again. They stumbled over to a nearby desk, and he laid her out on top of it.

And then they did get lucky. Twice.

* * *

Nine months later that luck proved more literal than euphemistic, with the birth of their son, Kain. But somehow *de Leon* didn't seem to fit for a last name. They didn't even speak Spanish anymore, and this was a *new* world.

"Our family should have a new name to mark our transition to life on Avilon."

"A new name to mark the transition, or to mark us?" Alexander asked, reminding her of their family's secret.

Kain would be immortal like her. Never aging a day past adulthood, and never dying—at least not of natural causes, anyway.

Catalina regarded her baby with a worried frown. She sat

in a chair in the corner of her room in the *Avilon's* med bay, nursing Kain for the first time. As he suckled her breast, she felt an almost indescribable feeling of completeness—of a love so powerful and overwhelming that it made her whole body tremble and her head feel light.

"We do have a mark on us, don't we, Kain?" she said, stroking the wisps of hair on his head. "But it's not something to be ashamed of. It's a blessing." She looked up to find Alexander smiling at the two of them. He reached out and grabbed their son's hand, and Kain wrapped a fist around Alexander's index finger.

"He's a strong one."

"He's a *mark-on-us*."

"A what?" Alexander asked, his eyes twinkling with amusement.

"A Markonus."

Alexander appeared to consider that. "What if we make it a little less obvious? How about Markonis with an *I*?"

"Sounds perfect," Catalina replied.

Alexander wrapped them both in a hug and smiled down on their son. "Welcome to the Markonis family, little guy. Not everyone can say eternity is their birthright."

Kain's eyes were shut, but he went on suckling, proving he was awake and listening.

Catalina couldn't help but wonder what lay ahead for him. Assuming no unfortunate accidents befell their son, he would live forever. He'd probably even live long enough to see the colonists in Dark Space reunited with the ones in Avilon.

But for now, you sleep, my little prince. You're safe here with me. I won't let anything happen to you. The Grays could keep their promise of life in paradise after death. She had her paradise right here, in the land of the living, on Avilon.

Alexander bent down to kiss their son's forehead.

Love is the only truth, she thought, watching them with a smile. *Let ours be yours.*

GET JASPER'S NEXT BOOK FOR FREE*

Thousands of years later, the story continues in...

Dark Space
A USA TODAY BESTSELLER

Get Books One AND Seven(Coming April 2017) **for FREE!**

Step One: Post an honest review of Exodus on Amazon
(http://smarturl.it/reviewexodus)

Step Two: Send it to me here
(http://files.jaspertscott.com/ds1and7free.html)

When you're done, you'll get an e-mail from me with your free books. Thank you in advance for your feedback!

*Free books only available in digital formats.

KEEP IN TOUCH

SUBSCRIBE to my Mailing List
Stay Informed about Upcoming Books and Discounts!
(http://files.jaspertscott.com/mailinglist.html)

Follow me on Twitter:
@JasperTscott

Look me up on Facebook:
Jasper T. Scott

Check out my website:
www.JasperTscott.com

Or send me an e-mail:
JasperTscott@gmail.com

OTHER BOOKS

New Frontiers Series

Excelsior (Book 1)
Mindscape (Book 2)
Exodus (Book 3)

Dark Space Series

Dark Space
Dark Space 2: The Invisible War
Dark Space 3: Origin
Dark Space 4: Revenge
Dark Space 5: Avilon
Dark Space 6: Armageddon

Dark Space Universe Series

Dark Space Universe (Book 1): Heretic
  Coming April 2017!
 Dark Space Universe (Book 2)
  Coming August 2017!
 Dark Space Universe (Book 3)
  Coming November 2017!

Early Work
 Escape
 Mrythdom

ABOUT THE AUTHOR

Jasper Scott is a USA TODAY bestselling science fiction author. He's best known for writing intricate plots with unexpected twists and flawed characters. His books have been translated into Japanese and German and adapted for audio, with collectively over 500,000 copies read, borrowed, or sold.

Jasper was born and raised in Canada by South African parents, with a British cultural heritage on his mother's side and German on his father's, to which he has now added Latin culture with his wonderful wife.

After spending years living as a starving artist, he finally quit his various jobs to become a full-time writer. In his spare time he enjoys reading, traveling, going to the gym, and spending time with his family.

Printed in Great Britain
by Amazon